PRAISE FOR THE DCI RYAN MYSTERIES

What newspapers say

"She keeps company with the best mystery writers" – *The Times*

"LJ Ross is the queen of Kindle" – *Sunday Telegraph*

"*Holy Island* is a blockbuster" – *Daily Express*

"A literary phenomenon" – *Evening Chronicle*

"A pacey, enthralling read" – *Independent*

What readers say

"I couldn't put it down. I think the full series will cause a divorce, but it will be worth it."

"I gave this book 5 stars because there's no option for 100."

"Thank you, LJ Ross, for the best two hours of my life."

"This book has more twists than a demented corkscrew."

"Another masterpiece in the series. The DCI Ryan mysteries are superb, with very realistic characters and wonderful plots. They are a joy to read!"

Also by LJ Ross

THE DCI RYAN MYSTERIES

1. *Holy Island*
2. *Sycamore Gap*
3. *Heavenfield*
4. *Angel*
5. *High Force*
6. *Cragside*
7. *Dark Skies*
8. *Seven Bridges*
9. *The Hermitage*
10. *Longstone*
11. *The Infirmary (Prequel)*
12. *The Moor*
13. *Penshaw*
14. *Borderlands*
15. *Ryan's Christmas*
16. *The Shrine*
17. *Cuthbert's Way*
18. *The Rock*
19. *Bamburgh*
20. *Lady's Well*
21. *Death Rocks*
22. *Poison Garden*
23. *Belsay*
24. *Berwick*

THE ALEXANDER GREGORY THRILLERS

1. *Impostor*
2. *Hysteria*
3. *Bedlam*
4. *Mania*
5. *Panic*
6. *Amnesia*
7. *Obsession*

THE SUMMER SUSPENSE MYSTERIES

1. *The Cove*
2. *The Creek*
3. *The Bay*
4. *The Haven*

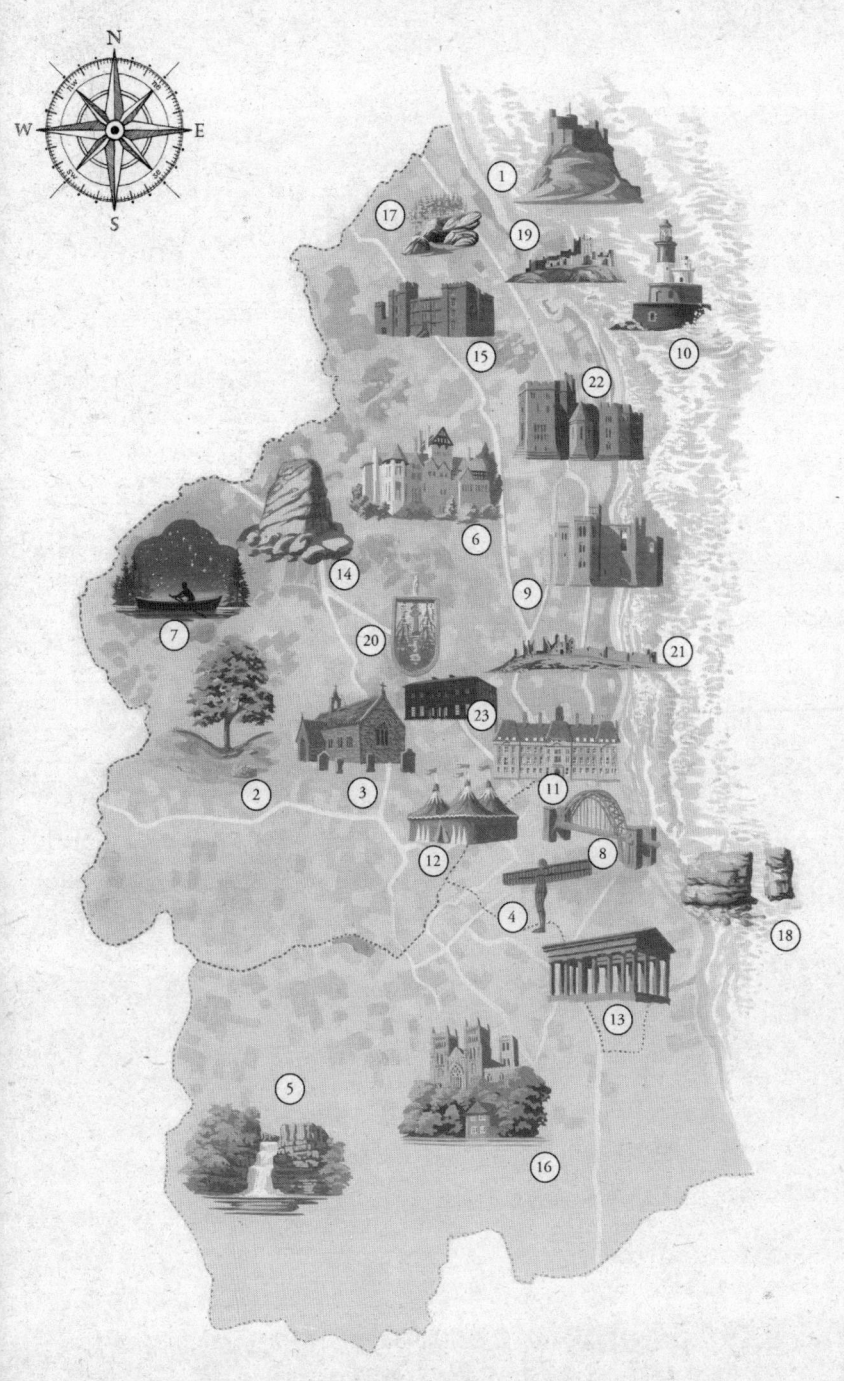

BAMBURGH

A DCI RYAN MYSTERY

BAMBURGH

A DCI RYAN MYSTERY

LJ ROSS

PENGUIN BOOKS

PENGUIN BOOKS

UK | USA | Canada | Ireland | Australia
India | New Zealand | South Africa

Penguin Books is part of the Penguin Random House group of companies
whose addresses can be found at global.penguinrandomhouse.com

Penguin Random House UK,
One Embassy Gardens, 8 Viaduct Gardens, London SW11 7BW

penguin.co.uk

First published by LJ Ross 2022
Published in Penguin Books 2026
001

Copyright © LJ Ross, 2020
Extract from *Lady's Well* © LJ Ross, 2023
Cover artwork and map by Andrew Davidson
Cover layout by Stuart Bache

The moral right of the author has been asserted

Penguin Random House values and supports copyright. Copyright fuels creativity, encourages diverse voices, promotes freedom of expression and supports a vibrant culture. Thank you for purchasing an authorised edition of this book and for respecting intellectual property laws by not reproducing, scanning or distributing any part of it by any means without permission. You are supporting authors and enabling Penguin Random House to continue to publish books for everyone. No part of this book may be used or reproduced in any manner for the purpose of training artificial intelligence technologies or systems. In accordance with Article 4(3) of the DSM Directive 2019/790, Penguin Random House expressly reserves this work from the text and data mining exception.

Set in 11.35/15.5pt Minion Pro
Typeset by Riverside Publishing Solutions Limited

Printed and bound in Great Britain by Clays Ltd, Elcograf S.p.A.

The authorised representative in the EEA is Penguin Random House Ireland,
Morrison Chambers, 32 Nassau Street, Dublin D02 YH68

A CIP catalogue record for this book is available from the British Library

ISBN: 978-1-804-96033-2

Penguin Random House is committed to a sustainable future
for our business, our readers and our planet. This book is made
from Forest Stewardship Council® certified paper.

For Ethan and Ella

*"It is not in the stars to hold our destiny,
but in ourselves."*

—Cassius, from *Julius Caesar* by William Shakespeare

PROLOGUE

June, 2007

Newcastle upon Tyne

Gemma heard raucous laughter coming from the direction of her sister's bedroom.

She looked up from where she'd been studying a textbook covering advanced mathematics for A-Level students, mildly irritated. Technically, she wasn't due to start the course until the new term began in September, but she liked to be prepared.

Goody-Goody Gemma, her sister called her…amongst other things.

More laughter filtered across the hall and, if she'd been more confident, she'd have set aside her book and gone to find out what was so funny, but she knew Melanie wouldn't welcome the intrusion. It wasn't that she and her sister didn't love one another, they were just polar opposites—despite having been born only a minute apart, with identical features. Where she was quiet and studious, Mel was vivacious and worked just hard enough to get by without their parents having to cut off her allowance. Where she kept her hair long and wore minimal make-up, Mel had recently cut hers into a shorter style she knew their mother hated. Mel never lacked friends, or boyfriends, whereas she…

Gemma sighed.

Between sports practice, schoolwork and helping at the local animal shelter, there never seemed to be any time left for boys or make-up or…well, fun.

She heard the bedroom door open across the hall and, a moment later, hers swung open without so much as a cursory knock.

"I'm going out," Mel declared, leaning her slim body against the doorframe. "Mum and Dad aren't back until tomorrow, but I need to know you won't rat me out when they get home—okay?"

Gemma looked down at her book, to hide sudden tears.

"I've never told them about any of the other times, have I?"

Melanie heard the note in her sister's voice and felt a stab of guilt. It was true that Gem never squealed, but there was always the possibility her innate honesty would lead her to do the worst of all things when it came to dealing with their overbearing parents: tell the truth.

"Okay, cool," she said, in bored tones.

Gemma looked up again, and her eyes were drawn to Melanie's risqué attire, which consisted of a black miniskirt barely larger than a belt, fishnet tights with knee-high boots, and a red 'boob tube' style top that left her midriff bare to the summer winds. To complete the look, she'd applied a liberal layer of make-up and any number of bangles and rings that jangled every time she moved.

"Dad would never let you go out in that," she said, with the ghost of a smile.

Mel grinned.

"Why d'you think I'm wearing it?" she said, with a flick of her new fringe, and then cast her eyes over Gemma's simple jeans and t-shirt combo. "You should try getting your legs out, some time. They could probably use the vitamin D."

Gemma thought of the contents of her wardrobe and wondered whether she even owned a skirt or a pair of shorts that still fit. She should probably go shopping for some new clothes, but she wouldn't know where to start.

Her eyes slid over to where her sister still hovered in the doorway. "What is it?" she asked.

Mel shrugged. "I'm down to my last tenner," she admitted. "I need to borrow a few quid—I'll pay you back."

It wasn't the first time Gemma had subbed her sister's lifestyle; in fact, it was an almost weekly occurrence. Yet, this time, she hesitated.

"It isn't as if you need it," Mel pressed. "You never go out."

Gemma looked up sharply.

No, she thought. She didn't.

She came to a sudden decision. "I'll lend you the money," she said slowly. "But, this time, I'm coming with you."

Melanie laughed harshly. "You must be kidding. Goody-Goody Gemma underage drinking? Going clubbing? You'd be breaking the law, you know…"

There was a challenge in her voice, and Gemma heard it. "Don't call me that," she snapped. "I might not like the same things as you, but that doesn't mean I don't know how to have a good time. You aren't the only one who can wear a miniskirt—or maybe you're worried I'll look better in one?"

Melanie's eyes widened—not in offence, but in newfound respect.

"All right," she said. "You're on. What are you going to wear? You can't go out clubbing looking like that."

Gemma tipped up her chin. "I'm lending you beer money," she said. "You can lend me one of your skirts."

Melanie laughed, and folded her arms across her chest. "You won't like it," she decided.

"I'll be the judge of that," Gemma argued, and went off to raid her sister's wardrobe.

As it happened, Melanie was right.

Gemma didn't like the skirt.

More accurately, the dress, which was a skin-tight electric-blue sheath that clung to her body in all the right places. Paired with long, curled hair and heels she could scarcely walk in, let alone dance in, she felt like a Barbie doll—all stiff limbs and frozen features.

"It isn't too late to go back," Melanie told her, as they made their way from the train station towards the bright lights of the city centre. Her friends trailed behind them, already half-cut after a session drinking the cheap corner-shop booze they'd bought and consumed in her room.

"I'm fine," Gemma lied.

Some sense of common decency compelled Melanie to convey a simple truth. "You look…really good," she said.

Gemma shot her a surprised glance. "Thanks…so do you."

And Melanie did, in her own way. Not everybody could pull off charcoal eyeshadow without looking like they'd suffered a black eye.

"Where are we going, anyway?"

"The Boat," Mel replied.

Gemma gave her a blank look.

"It's a party boat called the Tuxedo Princess, moored on the Tyne," she explained, with a roll of her eyes. "Most people call it 'The Boat'. It has a revolving dance floor and a few different rooms playing all kinds of music, but mostly dance stuff or R 'n' B. Best of all, a tenner gets you inside with free drinks all night."

"A tenner?" Gemma queried. "That seems…cheap."

"Yeah! Great, isn't it?"

Gemma thought privately that there must be a catch somewhere…perhaps they watered down the drinks—which wouldn't be such a bad thing, in her case.

"The options are pretty limited," Melanie admitted. "A few of the bouncers at the other clubs know we're not eighteen, so they won't let us in."

"I thought everywhere had to check ID?"

Mel's smile held a touch of condescension.

"Yeah, maybe they're supposed to, but they don't," she said. "They're always a lot more lenient with the girls, anyway. All you have to do is spin some sob story about forgetting your provisional licence at home, and they wave you inside."

"What if they don't believe me?" Gemma wondered aloud, and could only hope they turned her away so that she could go home and rest her weary feet.

Fate was not kind to Gemma that night, nor any other night that followed.

The two overweight, pigeon-chested men who stood like sentries at either side of The Boat's entrance cast an appreciative glance over the young woman in the bright blue cocktail dress and evidently decided she would be a decorative asset to its interior, so didn't bother with trifling things like identity checks. The other young woman who, upon closer inspection, bore a strong resemblance to her fine-boned sister, was also granted admittance since she had a nice pair of legs too.

As for the rest of their cohort, they flashed a set of fake ID cards and avoided eye contact, which did the trick, no questions asked.

The small party made their way along the gangplank and onto the boat, which had probably seen better days as far as marine vessels went, but for a sixteen-year-old girl who'd never stepped inside a club before, it was a floating palace of colour and sound. The air was hot and carried a heavy scent of body odour and methane, offset by a layer of cigarette smoke. A nationwide smoking ban was due to come into effect but, until then, clubbers continued to puff on their little white sticks and shoved all thoughts of cancer or passive smoking out of their minds for a few short hours.

"What d'you think?" Mel asked, raising her voice to a shout, so that she could be heard above the thumping notes of Voodoo Child.

Gemma looked around at the gyrating bodies of men and women. "It's…loud," she decided.

Melanie slung an arm around her sister's shoulders, feeling a rare moment of kinship.

"Your ears'll be ringing in the morning!" She laughed, and then tugged her in the direction of the bar to claim their first 'free' drink.

Dancing in a circle with Melanie and her friends, laughing with them while sipping an over-sweet alcopop in a dubious, radioactive shade of bright green, Gemma felt she was part of a tribe for the first time in her young life. Finally, a barrier had been breached; a wall between her and Melanie had fallen away, and the two girls were almost giddy with delight.

Gemma couldn't have known she had only a few, precious hours left to enjoy it.

Melanie couldn't have known it, either; and, in the long years that followed, would berate herself for not telling her sister the words she longed to say above all else…

That she loved her.

CHAPTER 1

Spring, 2022—fifteen years later

Bamburgh Castle

"Howay, man, I look like a *reet knacka* in this!"

Detective Sergeant Frank Phillips threw his friend a pained glance, which was met with a similar expression of long sufferance. Detective Chief Inspector Maxwell Finley-Ryan could think of many things he'd rather be doing on a Saturday evening, but he'd promised his wife their attendance at the fancy dress ball, and he was a man of his word.

Besides which, if he was going to be subjected to several hours of costumery, he knew one single, unassailable fact…

He'd be taking Frank down with him.

"I distinctly remember you tellin' me there'd be live music," Phillips said, pointing an accusatory finger. "And a buffet. You definitely used the word, 'buffet.'"

He paused to pat his paunch which, though vastly diminished since its hey-day of chip butties and bottomless bacon stotties, remained in a limited capacity to provide an extra layer of warmth on chilly days.

"Speakin' of which, I'm narf clammin' for a bite to eat…"

Ryan pressed his advantage.

"Coming from someone who has more comedy ties than Krusty the Clown, what difference does it make to you?" he argued. "And there is a buffet—it starts in half an hour."

Phillips sniffed, and began counting the reasons on his fingers.

"For one thing, the last time we all dressed up like prize turkeys, the lights went out and some poor sod ended up dead," he pointed out, recalling their time spent at Cragside House. "If that isn't enough to make us think twice, the material on these trousers is narf itchy…"

He gave his arse a good scratch, to illustrate the point.

"I don't make the rules," Ryan said, with an elegant shrug. "I'm a slave to my Better Half—and so, I might add, are you."

Phillips opened his mouth to deny the charge, possibly to say something incredibly manly along the lines of standing one's ground, showing one's wife who was 'boss' and so on and so forth, but before he could formulate the words, he caught sight of a red-headed goddess standing across the room—one he happened to be married to—and the words evaporated on his tongue.

"Aye, well," he said, clearing his throat and lowering his hand for another surreptitious scratch. "Let's not let this happen too often, eh? Some of us have a reputation to uphold, y'nah."

Ryan raised a single black eyebrow. "If I didn't know any better, I'd say, he doth protesteth too much."

Phillips craned his neck, which was being strangled by a starched white collar.

"I'm just cheesed off that you get to be Sherlock Holmes," he said. "Why've I got to be Doctor bleedin' Watson?"

He scowled, which had the effect of twitching the ostentatious fake whiskers stuck to his upper lip.

"If the shoe fits," Ryan said, and raised a false pipe to his mouth, getting into character.

"If the hat fits, more like," Phillips shot back, nodding at the deerstalker adorning Ryan's crown. "You need a big one, with a heed the size o' yours…"

Ryan let out an appreciative rumble of laughter.

At that moment, his wife and aforementioned 'Better Half' approached them, balancing several drinks in her hands. Doctor Anna Taylor-Ryan wore a costume that was part-Game of Thrones and part-Wonder Woman, consisting of breast plate and short skirt, leather cuffs on her forearms and knee-high leather boots. The ensemble was completed by a large, plastic sword tucked into a leather belt around her waist. When Ryan had politely enquired which famous historical figure she was supposed to be, she'd told him, "Boudica, Warrior Queen of the Iceni people, of course"—as if it should have been obvious.

Whoever she was, he certainly wasn't complaining.

"Having fun?" she asked them.

Both men pasted broad smiles on their faces, nodded dumbly, and made effusive sounds of agreement.

She grinned at the pair of them.

"Only a couple of hours to go," she promised. "Just think, it's all in a good cause—and at least the venue is beautiful, isn't it?"

They couldn't argue with that. They stood in the King's Hall of Bamburgh Castle, a mighty fortress perched atop a crag of volcanic rock on the edge of the North Sea, whose original foundations dated back to the fifth century, when it was the capital of the old kingdom of Bernicia. It had passed through various hands over the years, before eventually being purchased by the Victorian industrialist, William Armstrong, whose dazzling wealth had enabled him to restore it to its former glory. It remained privately owned by a family trust, albeit various apartments and wings were open to public use and leasehold tenancy. For Ryan and his team of murder detectives, the castle would forever be associated with their former Detective Chief Superintendent, Arthur Gregson, whose fall from grace almost coincided with a literal fall from the castle's outer wall a few years earlier. Ryan and Anna's wedding on the green below the castle walls had gone some way to dispelling that memory, but the echo of past events still lingered, much like the ghosts who were rumoured to haunt the castle walls.

"I s'pose it'll do," Phillips joked, tipping his head up to look at the high, vaulted ceiling above his head and then down at the polished wood beneath his feet. "This floor's no good for dancin', mind. I'd slip and do myself a mischief."

"How you haven't put a hip out before now is beyond comprehension," Ryan muttered.

"Flexibility," Phillips said, with a wink for Anna. "If I've said it once, I've said it a thousand times: these hips don't lie."

"You could've fooled me, Frank Phillips."

Like an apparition, his wife and superior in the police hierarchy materialised behind him.

"Balls alive!" he exclaimed, nearly jumping out of his breeches. "Are you tryin' to give me a heart attack, woman?"

"If all those bacon stotties haven't done that by now, I doubt my sneaking up on you once in a while is going to have any effect," she quipped. "Anyway, what's this I hear about you having hips like Shakira? They sounded like a pair of creaky old gates when you got out of bed this morning."

"Just need a bit more oilin', that's what it is…" he said, and wriggled his moustache suggestively, to make her laugh.

Detective Inspector Denise MacKenzie, who, in a nod to her Irish heritage, was dressed as the famous warrior pirate Grace O'Malley—complete with fake parrot—accepted one of the glasses Anna offered and took a deep swig of the fruity red liquid.

"Thank God for that," she said, with feeling. "I can't remember the last time we had a child-free night out."

"Aye, it's been a while," Frank agreed, and made a mental note to remedy that. Their adopted daughter, Samantha, was not far off being old enough to be left on her own for a few hours…in fact, he was certain she was independent enough to have been left alone long before now, but he and Denise weren't ready to take any risks. If that made him 'overprotective', then so be it.

Better safe than sorry.

"We manage a night out when Sam's staying over at a friend's house, and we know a nice lass who comes round to babysit, now and then, but it's not the same as the old days when we could just gad about. Must be the same for you two, with the littleun?"

He addressed this question to Ryan and Anna, whose baby girl had celebrated her first birthday the previous summer.

"Ryan's parents come up to visit every few weeks," Anna said, with a smile. "When they do, they usually chase us out of the house—"

"And we put on a convincing show of protestation—while I rev up the car engine and Anna searches 'flights to Timbuktu,'" Ryan put in, with a smile.

The truth was, neither of them was ready to leave their daughter with a stranger. His job carried a degree of risk; there were nefarious personalities who'd love nothing more than to exact revenge for some collar or another, and the easiest way to do that would be to harm those he loved the most.

"Charles and Eve are visiting us at the moment," Anna continued, shaking her head at him. "I keep trying to convince them to move up north, but they're having none of it, so far."

"Dad will never leave Summersley," Ryan murmured.

The home where he'd been born was a rambling, Grade I listed mansion built of soft Devonshire sandstone, and came with hundreds of acres of land. If it wasn't enough that the estate had been passed down through generations, his late sister, Natalie, was buried in the family crypt and he knew that neither one of his parents would ever wish to be too far from her.

"Beautiful place," Phillips said politely, being the only one present aside from Anna who'd ever visited. "Mind you, it makes me think of one of those country piles where a bunch of strangers go for dinner all dressed up in their finery and one of them winds up dead, face-first in the turtle soup."

"Charming," Ryan intoned. "I'll be sure to pass on your regards to my mother…"

"No offence, lad, but, to the ordinary proletarian like me, your gaff looks like one of those places they visit on Most Haunted."

"Only if you cross the moor in those dark hours, when the powers of evil are exalted, my dear Watson," Ryan said.

"He's gone off his rocker," Phillips said to the others. "All that tweed has addled his brain. Well, they do say, these aristos are all inbred."

Ryan laughed. "That may be," he said. "But what's your excuse, funny man?"

Phillips raised his glass in a toast. "It's all the bad company I keep," he said. "You're all barmy, the lot of you, and it's catchin'."

"I'll drink to that," Anna chuckled, and clinked her glass with Denise. "To barminess."

"And crackpottery," MacKenzie added.

"And fruitcakery," Ryan put in. "Don't forget the fruitcakes."

"Good lad," Phillips approved. "If I've taught you nothing else, it's never to underestimate a fruitcake."

"I'm not sure that's the *precise* terminology used in the Police Handbook to refer to those suffering from mental illness."

This stern intrusion to their light-hearted merriment came from a man in his early forties who was dressed in authentic Victorian garb, complete with whiskers and sideburns to rival Phillips' best efforts. A tiny diamond pin held his silk cravat in place and glinted beneath the chandelier overhead.

Instantly, their smiles faded.

"Ah—?" Phillips began.

"Can we help you?" Ryan asked, in a deceptively mild tone.

Before he could reply, Chief Constable Morrison approached their small party dressed as a suffragette—presumably, Emmeline Pankhurst—and beamed at them all.

"I see you've already met—"

"No, not at all," Ryan continued, flicking his gaze back to the man who continued to regard them with disapproval. "Perhaps you'd do the honours."

"Well, I was planning to make the formal introductions on Monday but, since we're all here, it seems as good a time as any to present your new Detective Chief Superintendent," she said, with a bit of a flourish. "Andrew Forbes, meet the dream team: DCI Ryan, DS Phillips and DI MacKenzie."

Forbes turned to each of them with watery brown eyes, one of which sported a small, slashing red scar at its outer edge.

"I'm afraid I interrupted a…private moment," he said, and smiled suddenly. "Let's start again, shall we? I'm very pleased to meet you all. Naturally, your reputations precede you."

He paused to assess Anna, obviously trying to remember her name and rank.

"My wife, Doctor Taylor-Ryan," Ryan informed him. "It's often been said she'd make an excellent addition to our team, but she prefers her own work to ours."

"One could hardly blame her," Forbes said, affably. "If you aren't solving crimes, may I ask what it is that you do, Doctor Ryan? Are you a medical doctor?"

"I'm a historian," she said, distilling years of expert study into a single word. "This evening's ball is to raise funds for an archaeological dig that's due to begin on Monday, within the castle grounds. Although I'm not an archaeologist, I know the team and sometimes consult on projects like these."

"Good for you," he said, in a tone she imagined he used with toddlers and those slow of wit.

Anna reminded herself this was Ryan's new boss, and held her tongue.

"Hurt yourself, did you?"

Forbes turned to Phillips, who'd asked the question, and raised a hand to touch the healing wound near his eye. "War wound, I'm afraid. I stumbled into an attack-in-progress, while I was out jogging. I tried to intervene, but I got this for my trouble…"

He gave what he hoped was a self-deprecatory smile.

"Bloke ran off, and the woman didn't want to press charges, unfortunately."

"Bad luck," Ryan murmured. "Looks painful."

"My wife tells me I look more dangerous, now," Forbes joked. "Next thing, she'll have me wearing leather and driving a motorcycle."

They laughed politely, but couldn't imagine it.

Sensing an awkward lull in conversation, Morrison stepped into the breach. "Ah—no Jack and Mel, this evening?" she asked.

"They're around, somewhere," MacKenzie told her. "I think I heard them say they were going outside to watch the sunset."

"Oh, well, let's take a walk and see if we can find them," Morrison said, turning to her companion. "Shall we?"

Once they'd left, there was a second's pause before Phillips was the first to pipe up.

"I don't recall Jack or Mel saying anything about goin' to watch the sunset," he remarked.

MacKenzie shrugged. "Oh? Must be going deaf, in your old age. Either that or I wanted to give us all a few minutes' reprieve from Captain Buzzkill."

Anna almost choked on her wine. "He's…um…"

"Quite," Ryan said, meaningfully. "The man's got all the charm and personality of a rainbow trout."

Phillips let out a booming laugh, which drew stares from groups of people scattered nearby.

"You've only got yourselves to blame," he said, pointing an accusatory finger towards Ryan and then MacKenzie. "Both of you were asked if you wanted the job, and both of you turned it down. Now, look what's happened. Almost makes me wish Gregson were back…he might've been a raging sociopath, but at least he could hold a tune at the karaoke on a Friday night."

"Well, that's all right then," Ryan drawled.

"Forbes might not be that bad," MacKenzie interjected, to convince herself as much as anyone else. "People often try to assert their authority when they take up a new position… he's probably just nervous."

Anna nodded in support, and then looked into the bottom of her glass to hide her lying eyes. If ever a man had screamed, "Missionary Style, Mild Curry and Beige Y-Fronts", it was their new DCS.

"I reckon he's always been a bit of a stiff," Phillips said, trying to drain his glass without wetting his moustache. "Forbes used to work from the Ponteland HQ, years ago, before the office relocated to Wallsend. I remember him being strait-laced, even when he was a young bloke."

"I don't remember him, at all," Ryan said, and his eyes followed Forbes' retreating head, as he left the room.

"Might have been just before your time—and Denise's too, for that matter," Phillips told him. "He left to take up a promotion somewhere down south, I think."

Unspoken amongst them was a shared intention to find out all they could about DCS Andrew Forbes.

"Look, I'm just going to say one thing," Anna began, and almost laughed when three pairs of 'cop eyes' turned towards her. "He may not be charismatic, but Forbes could be just what your department needs. He's straight down the line, no messing around. The past two incumbents of his office weren't exactly sticklers for the law they're supposed to uphold. It must be hard for him to step into their shoes and try to restore a bit of dignity to the role."

"Aye, well," Phillips said, gruffly. "You might have a point there, lass. Does no good for us to start tarring the feller with any old brushes. He's no Gregson—or Lucas, for that matter."

"Thank God for small mercies," MacKenzie muttered.

"I don't need him to set the world alight," Ryan said. "I just need him to be law-abiding and sane."

"Tall order, in our line of work," Phillips warned him. "I'll settle for him not messing up the Gents."

"Spoken like a true prole," Ryan said, wickedly.

"Mind yourself, or else I'll mount an uprising. I've got two warrior women here, to help me."

"Where's the third?" MacKenzie wondered.

"Mel? Aye, I'm a bit worried about her," Phillips said, keeping his voice low. "Ever since we found that DNA match, she hasn't talked about much else."

He referred to trace DNA found beneath the fingernails of a female victim who'd suffered an unspeakable ordeal: first, at the hands of a gang of traffickers, and then, at the hands of an unknown assailant who'd tortured her and attempted murder. Thanks to her fortitude and sheer love of life, the woman had escaped to tell her tale—or, as much of it as her traumatised mind would allow. In a twist of fate, the DNA found on her person held a 98.6% match to DNA extracted from a hair follicle recovered from the body of Melanie's sister, Gemma Yates, fifteen years before. Unfortunately, there was no match to any name on the DNA database.

"I'm worried, too," Ryan said, softly. "I know better than most how these things can eat you up inside, and I didn't have to live for fifteen long years before bringing my sister's killer to justice. Knowing that Gemma's murderer is still out there, and still active, is beyond the pale."

"Mel keeps asking if there've been any developments and, I keep telling her, she'd be the first to know," MacKenzie said, sadly.

In deference to proper procedure, Ryan had entrusted the newly re-opened investigation of Gemma Yates' murder into MacKenzie's capable hands. He knew Melanie wanted to play a more active part, and he didn't delude himself about the number of hours she must have been devoting to the case on her own time, but he couldn't allow her to cross professional boundaries. Yates might have been a murder detective—and a very fine one, at that—but she was also a grieving family member, with a vested interest. The last thing he wanted was for them to find her sister's killer, only for the case to collapse at trial thanks to his own short-sighted management.

"I told her she's free to look into things in a voluntary capacity, as any family member might, but she must not abuse her position," Ryan reiterated. "It's one of the hardest conversations I've ever had, because I know damn well that if somebody had tried to tell me to back off when Natalie died, I'd have told them where to shove their well-meaning advice."

"And did, if I recall," Phillips intoned.

"And did," Ryan acknowledged, rolling his shoulders to shake off the memory. "I can imagine what Mel is going through, and I wouldn't wish it on my worst enemy. It doesn't change what has to happen, now."

MacKenzie nodded. "Between you, me and the gatepost, things aren't looking good," she said, casting a swift glance over her shoulder to be sure Melanie could not overhear and be disheartened. "There aren't any new leads, but I don't want to dampen her spirits any further."

Ryan sighed, and rubbed a hand over his chin.

"We're due to have a briefing on Monday," he said. "We'll go over it all then, and invite Melanie and her family in afterwards, for an update."

"Oh, but—"

"You thought she'd be in the briefing room?" Ryan guessed, and shook his head. "Can't do it, Mac. If that was ever—ever—to come out, the Defence would have a field day."

She nodded, because she knew he was right.

"Poor kid," Phillips said. "I hope the bastard pays, but nobody really knows what happened. What are the chances we'll ever know, or find the bugger, without a massive stroke of luck?"

"It's our business to know what other people don't know," Ryan murmured, thinking of the character he was embodying for the evening. "Never give up, Frank. He's out there, somewhere."

"Aye, but where?" Phillips worried. "Preyin' on some other lass, no doubt."

Ryan said nothing, thinking of his wife and daughter. "He'll pay for that, too. There's always a reckoning."

CHAPTER 2

Summer 2007

'The Boat'

Gemma weaved through the crowd, the effects of four sugary alcopops loosening her untrained body so that her legs wobbled and her head ached, a fact made worse by the hard, pounding music that beat a relentless drum in her ears.

She wanted to go home.

"Mel?" she whispered.

She peered through the billowing smoke and murky figures of dancing strangers who moved like marionettes, trying desperately to remember where they'd been standing before she'd left for the ladies' room.

Suddenly, she felt very alone.

Now, she noticed the leering eyes of men young and old, felt their breath on her bare shoulders as she pushed her way through the throng towards the revolving dance floor, slapping away the hands that made a grab for her, feeling tears rise to her throat.

"Mel!" she shouted.

She stumbled onto the dance floor, which creaked as it moved around in jerky circles, challenging even a sober person's balance. In Gemma's case, the effort was too great, and she slipped on the sticky floor, turning her ankle and falling hard to her knees.

"Here, let me help you."

Gemma looked up to find a man in his late twenties hunched down beside her, wearing an expression of concern. She opened her mouth to refuse, but there was something about his face, his eyes, that reassured her.

"Come on," he said, hauling her upward with a gentle hand.

He made a thorough scan of the room, eyes moving from face to face with laser precision.

"Where are your friends?"

"My—my friends?" she shook her head in confusion, thinking that none of her friends were there, that evening. "They're not here."

He almost smiled. "They've abandoned you?" he said, injecting a note of sympathy into his voice.

"Oh, they didn't—didn't—"

Without her realising, they'd reached the edge of the room, where he propped her against the wall and used his body to shield her from view. To the casual observer, they might have looked like two drunken lovers locked in an embrace.

"Now," he said, leaning down to speak into her ear so she could hear him above the din. "You're not really eighteen, are you? I can tell, you know."

Gemma froze, and tried to remember Mel's words of advice.

"I—yes, I am. I—um, I left my licence at home. In my bag. My drawer."

He smiled, enjoying the game.

"Really?" He folded his arms across his chest, drumming his thumbs against his own ribcage, heady with anticipation. "Do you have any other ID?"

Gemma closed her eyes and shook her head.

"That's a shame," he said, and took her arm in a firm grip. "I'm afraid I'm going to have to escort you out."

"What?" she whispered, trying to see past him to the dance floor, seeking her sister's face. "I can't go—"

"I'm sorry, you have no choice," he said, in an authoritarian tone. "You're breaking the law."

"I—I—"

I only wanted a single night, she wanted to cry. Just one night.

"I'm sorry, it won't happen again…" she mumbled.

"I should hope not," he said. "You don't know how dangerous these places are, for young girls like you. I see things happen, all the time, and it breaks my heart to have to speak to the parents."

"Wha—?"

Thoughts of her parents' disdain, their disappointment, made her stomach churn more than the alcohol.

"Why would you do that?" she asked him.

"Because," he said patiently, "it's my job."

He produced an authentic police warrant card, but his thumb covered the name printed on it—just in case. Gemma squinted down at the card, which she could barely read in the semi-darkness, but saw enough to understand what it meant.

She looked up at him in horror.

"Plain clothes operative," he explained, gesturing to his shirt and jeans. "We're trying to crack down on underage drinking in the city. It's getting out of control, and kids like you are getting hurt."

Her eyes filled with tears.

"I think it's time I took you home," he said, kindly. "Don't you?"

Gemma opened her mouth to tell him she couldn't leave without finding her sister, but loyalty kept her trap firmly shut. It was bad enough that she would face the wrath of their parents and the police; Melanie was already skating close to the wind and didn't need any additional black marks against her.

And so, she remained silent.

Melanie would assume she'd gone home and follow later. With any luck, she could keep him from finding out her sister existed at all.

"Time to go," he said firmly.

She bent her head in defeat, bowing to authority, trusting in it, as she'd been taught to do.

"No, not that way," he said, when she turned towards the main exit. "It'll take forever to push through all these people. Let's go the easy way out."

With a final scan of the room, and a wink for the bouncer who made a lewd gesture, he led her outside onto a covered deck that wrapped around the boat but was usually closed for health and safety reasons. The cold air hit her like a punch to the chest and Gemma began to shiver, the after-effects of excess alcohol, dehydration and shock at her unfortunate situation causing her to tremble violently.

"Nearly there," he said, hurrying her along. "You'll be home and tucked up in bed, before you know it."

"Thank you," she said, and he looked away to hide the fierce smile that spread across his face. "Please don't tell my parents."

"I promise, I won't be telling your parents a thing."

Nobody noticed a pair of young revellers leaving the boat, keeping to the shadows on their way along a side street where a police squad car was parked, off-duty.

"Here we go," he said, and she almost wept at the thought of having to ride home in the back of a police car.

What if somebody saw, and told her parents?

Oh, God...

"I feel sick," she said, and meant it.

He held back an expletive, and looked both ways down the street, calculating the risk. There wasn't really a choice: he couldn't allow her to be sick in the car.

"Don't worry," he said, between gritted teeth. "There's a bush, just here. Be sick in there."

He even held her bag, and took the opportunity to divest her of the mobile phone inside it.

When it was done, he frog-marched her back to the car and almost shoved her inside, too eager now, too impatient to get to where he needed to be.

The mood had shifted. Gemma could sense it, as an animal senses danger.

"Wait—"

Her bare legs squeaked against the back seat, and she realised it had been covered completely in clear plastic—even down to the footwells. A cage separated her from the driver and front passenger seats, and the doors locked automatically.

She looked up to catch him watching her in the rear-view mirror, and what she saw in his eyes caused her bowels to loosen.

He started the engine, turning the music up loud to mask the sound of her screams, tapping a finger against the edge of the wheel as he steered the car through the dark city streets. As they passed beneath a row of streetlamps, the light fell upon the card he'd discarded on the passenger seat and, as Gemma clung to the bars of the cage begging him to free her, she was finally able to read the words on the little piece of rectangular plastic.

Detective Constable Andrew Forbes.

The last person she would ever see.

CHAPTER 3

Spring, 2022

Bamburgh Castle

Detective Constable Melanie Yates stood in a corner of one of the anterooms at the castle, eyes glued to her smartphone while she scrolled through a spreadsheet she'd downloaded earlier.

"—Mel?"

She looked up with a start, and realised Jack had spoken her name several times before eliciting a response.

It was becoming a habit.

"Sorry," she mumbled, but didn't put the phone away. "I need five more minutes."

Detective Constable Jack Lowerson barely held back a sigh. He'd hoped an evening out, all dressed up with somewhere to go, might have taken her mind off things.

"Mel, we've barely socialised with the others," he said, quietly. "Why don't we head into the hall and say 'hello'?"

"Look, I just need five minutes! Is that too much to ask?"

His head whipped back as if she'd slapped him, and instantly she was contrite.

"Jack, I—"

But he held up both hands, fending off any further attacks, and took a step back.

"You know where to find us, when you're ready."

With that, he turned and walked away, balancing his own frustrated temper against natural sympathy for her situation. His love for Melanie was real, but he'd never claimed to be perfect, and was struggling to understand how he could help her.

Maybe he couldn't.

As he stepped into the King's Hall, he bumped into a man dressed in a plush Victorian suit, greying hair brushed back from an attractive but unremarkable face.

"Sorry," he muttered, and moved past him.

Andrew Forbes stood there for long seconds watching the woman on the other side of the small, oak-panelled room, thinking of the other times he'd watched her—or was it her sister?—unseen, years before. She'd been younger then, of course, but the passage of time seemed only to have improved her, if that were possible. The old excitement bubbled within, obliterating all else, and he took a moment to compose himself before venturing to join her.

"Excuse me," he began, and saw her jump in surprise.

"Y-yes?"

"Is it Melanie?"

She frowned then, eyes searching his face but finding nothing recognisable.

"Who's asking?"

"I beg your pardon," he said. "I'm Detective Chief Superintendent Andrew Forbes. The Chief Constable and I were looking for you, so that I could introduce myself. She's just nipped to the bar…can I get you anything?"

Mel couldn't remember the last time she'd had anything to eat or drink, but she had no appetite for either. Jack had tried several times to tempt her with some morsel or other, especially as she'd lost a significant amount of weight over the past few months, but she'd snapped at him to stop mothering her.

"No, thanks. Sir," she added, belatedly.

"Oh, don't worry about that," he said, waving away the formality. "At least, not until Monday, eh?"

He gave a little laugh, and she tried to force her lips into a polite answering smile, but they failed to comply.

"Nice to meet you," she managed. "I, er, I hope you enjoy working with us."

"Oh, I'm sure I will," he said, smiling again, the corners of his eyes crinkling at the edges.

"Ah! There you are, Mel." Chief Constable Morrison joined them, bearing two glasses of wine. "Would you like one?"

"No, thank you," she muttered, the phone she still held burning a hole in her palm.

Why were they standing there, making useless small talk?

"I think Ryan and the rest of the team are in the King's Hall," she said, hoping that would encourage them to move on.

"Yes, we've already paid them a visit," Forbes said, reading her body language without difficulty. "I'm planning to conduct personal meetings with each of my team over the coming week, but perhaps you can tell me what you've been working on?"

Her fingers clutched the phone a little tighter, fearful he'd take it from her.

"Um...well..." Her eyes frittered towards the Chief Constable, who met them with a knowing glint. "Obviously, there's my regular caseload. We have a few—ah—"

She struggled to remember the active cases she was supposed to be investigating.

"There's been a lot of clean-up work to do, following that recent trafficking bust I was telling you about a couple of months back," Morrison put in, taking pity on her. "Yates has been liaising with Vice, Fraud and Organised Crime to unravel any other like crimes arising from what was uncovered."

Forbes nodded. "Tragic case," he said. "I had a look at the file, when the alert came through. I understand there was a survivor?"

"They're all survivors," Morrison was bound to say.

"Of course," he corrected, swiftly. "But there was one, in particular—something about being lost in a cave, then abducted?"

"Yes, sir," Yates said, and he was pleased that she continued to treat him with the respect his position commanded. "Woman A was one of a number who were trafficked to the UK from Thailand. She barely survived an arduous journey and a shipwreck, days with debilitating injuries and risk of exposure in a sea cave. If that wasn't sufficient, a person whom she believed to be her rescuer was, in fact, an opportunist would-be killer, who'd become aware of her existence and took it upon himself to bag a ready-made victim. Apparently, he posed as a lifeguard."

Forbes shook his head, affecting an air of disbelief.

"To think that there are people out there who would use their power and position to undermine and take advantage of vulnerable people…sickening," he said, with a sigh. "Where's your witness, now? Gone home to Thailand?"

He asked the question carefully, very carefully.

"We have her in a safe house," Yates told him. "As far as we're aware, she's the only woman to have survived a man we believe to be an active serial killer, so there's every chance he'd try to silence her, if he could."

Forbes sipped delicately at his wine, the taste of failure still bitter on his tongue. Of course, he knew the woman was in a safe house; he'd tried several times to find out exactly where, but it seemed Ryan kept a tight ship.

Patience, he reminded himself.

"A serial?" he said, lightly. "Are you sure? They're extremely rare—"

"Only because the number we manage to uncover is depressingly small," Yates argued. "There may be many more out there who focus their attentions on highly vulnerable victims without a home, who've fallen between the cracks of society and may not even be missed. It's a fertile breeding ground for a certain kind of killer and their victims' lack of formal paper trail provides them with natural cover."

"Yes, it would be the smart choice for a killer to choose victims who are unlikely to be missed," he agreed. "You seem to have taken a personal interest in the case, detective?"

Yates exchanged another glance with the Chief Constable, who wore a resigned expression. Morrison knew as well as Ryan did that trying to prevent Melanie from investigating the death of her sister was a losing battle. So long as everything was seen to be correct and above board, that's all that mattered.

"I suppose so," Melanie admitted, looking him squarely in the eye. "Trace DNA was uncovered beneath our witness's fingernails following her ordeal. It was an almost perfect match to a small sample found in a hair follicle after my sister's body was recovered, fifteen years ago. We know it's the same person, sir, and he's been operating all this time."

"That's remarkable," he said, and then asked a rhetorical question. "Is he on the system?"

"Unfortunately, no," Mel said. "I wish he was."

Forbes nodded, sympathetically.

"Perhaps, in time?"

"We don't have any more time," she said, with an edge to her voice. "He's had long enough."

There was a fire in her eyes that lit one inside him; one that had been dormant for fifteen long years. He'd tried to replace her, tried to replicate that first, heady feeling with other women, other bodies, but nothing could compare with the first time, could it? He'd thought that experience was long gone, consigned to his memory and the few grainy photographs he'd managed to salvage from an ancient camera, which he allowed himself to look at on rare, special occasions, when his wife and children were away from home or asleep.

Yet, here she was, standing before him once again.

How was it possible? How had he missed a sister—and a twin, at that?

He would find out, he told himself, but not now. It wouldn't do to appear overly interested, and he'd already asked as many questions as he dared.

"Well," he said. "Anything I can do to help, just say the word."

"Thank you, sir. I appreciate that."

CHAPTER 4

June 2007

'The Boat'

Melanie came back from the bar loaded with another round of lurid-coloured drinks and realised her friends had decamped to another favoured spot of theirs: one of the darkened booths that lined the perimeter of the room and allowed for all manner of teenage sins, or alternatively a well-timed disco nap.

Moving through the crowds with practised ease, she peered through the shadows into every passing booth until she found the faces she recognised—some of which were beginning to look the worse for wear.

"What took you so long?" one of them asked.

"There was a queue," she said, setting the bottles on the table, which they attacked like a pack of thirsty hyenas.

Mel took a seat on the end of the sticky leather bench and reached for a bottle.

"Where's Gemma?" she asked.

"Gone to the loo," one of them replied.

She nodded and tapped her fingers against her knee in time to the music, soon caught up in their chatter. But, when Gemma still hadn't returned ten minutes later, she felt obliged to check. If she was throwing up, she might need someone to help. Although Melanie didn't relish the task, their newfound friendship demanded that she attend, as any good friend would.

"Back in a minute," she said, and rose unsteadily to her feet.

Then she hesitated, wondering which bathroom would be closest; The Boat had numerous facilities, and she didn't want to check every single one of them…

Deciding to try the nearest, Melanie made her way towards the neon sign and, had she not turned away exactly when she did, might have seen the flash of her sister's blue dress moving in the opposite direction as she pushed through the mire of sweating bodies, calling to her.

But she didn't see.

Instead, Melanie continued to the bathroom, where she was forced to wait in another queue behind a line of women who stood with their legs crossed.

Another five minutes ticked by, then Mel took her chance and stepped out of the line to walk to the front.

"Hey! You can't jump the queue!" one woman shouted, grabbing her arm in a bruising grip.

"I don't need the toilet, I'm looking for my sister—" she tried to say, but her protestation fell on deaf ears as word spread down the line and a war cry rose up against her.

"Yeah, me n'all," another cried out. "I don't need the toilet, I'm just lookin' for Brad Pitt!"

They all laughed, and Melanie held up her hands, moving back to lean against the grubby wall to wait. She stayed there for another ten minutes, growing more concerned with every passing minute, especially as her texts remained unanswered and when she'd tried calling, her sister's phone rang out.

Probably couldn't hear the ring tone above the music.

Eventually, she threw caution to the wind and pushed back from the wall to run ahead again, shouldering through the swing door into the ladies' room, ignoring the shouts behind her.

Inside, the area was filled with women in various states of undress: one stood by a sink with a friend, who was helping to repair a broken dress strap. Another was sprawled on the floor in floods of tears, wailing about, 'Tom and that bitch from McDonalds', while two friends attempted to pull her dead weight off the mucky tiles. Another woman stood beside a broken cubicle door with one foot artfully tucked beneath to hold it closed, protecting the modesty of a friend who was using the facilities.

There was no sign of Gemma, but she called out, anyway.

"Gemma! Are you in here?"

It was a popular name, and two other girls' voices called back to her, neither of which belonged to her sister.

"Never mind," she muttered, and made her way out again, ignoring the angry remarks from the women she passed.

Worried now, Melanie hurried back to the booth, pushing away token offers to dance from men she passed, their voices melting with the music until it was a persistent buzz in her ears.

When she reached the table, there was no Gemma to be found.

"Have you seen her?"

"Who?" one of her friends asked.

"Gemma! Where's Gemma?"

"Oh, her!" They laughed. "No idea. Maybe she went home?"

"She wouldn't go home without telling me," Melanie argued.

She turned around, scanning the darkened room, wishing she could stop the music and turn the lights up, just for a moment, so she could find her sister.

Now, she was faced with a dilemma: tell a bouncer and face inevitable questions about their age or hope that Gemma had gone home.

There really wasn't any choice.

Chest thumping, head spinning, Melanie made her way to the edge of the room, where a hard-faced man dressed in black stood with his hands clasped, an earpiece tucked into his right lobe.

"Excuse me!"

He turned to look at her and frowned slightly, sure he'd seen some bird who looked just like her.

The light played tricks, after a while, and it was almost one in the morning.

"Aye? What's the matter, love?" he asked, leaning down so that she could speak into his ear and be heard.

"I've lost someone!" she shouted. "It's my sister! I can't find her!"

That was an hourly occurrence, in his line of work, and he'd learned to treat such reports with a pinch of salt.

"Have you checked the loos, pet?"

She nodded.

"I've already checked. She isn't in there."

"You've checked all of them?"

"Yes!" she lied.

He was distracted for a moment by a young man falling drunkenly against him. After a quiet word and a none-too-gentle shove, he was given swift dispatch.

"Look, flower, I divn't nah what you want me to do about it," he admitted. "How long's it been, since you lost her?"

Melanie checked the time on her phone.

"Only half an hour, but—"

He laughed, and made a gesture with his thumb for her to move off.

"Howay, lass. She's probably wandered into the other room," he said. "Come back when you've got a real problem."

"You don't understand," Melanie persisted. "Gemma wouldn't—she's not used to places like this—"

But he'd already moved on to the next crisis.

"Help," Melanie whispered, feeling very young, and very frightened.

What should I do?

Her parents weren't at home, and the bouncer wouldn't help. Her friends were drunk or asleep, and she was surrounded by strangers.

Think.

Unbeaten, Melanie retraced her steps through the various dance rooms, moving from house to R 'n' B, to trance, none of which she really heard, until she reached the foyer. There, the same two bouncers who'd greeted them earlier stood yawning, counting the remaining hours until they could close up shop and go home.

Catching sight of her, one of them pushed back from the railing where he'd been leaning.

"Everything all right, petal?"

Almost in tears, Melanie relayed the situation.

"All right, now, all right," he said, giving her an awkward pat. "This kind of thing happens all the time—"

"Have you seen her?" Melanie demanded, bringing up a recent picture of Gemma on her phone.

Admittedly, she looked very different in the photograph to the girl who'd walked onto the boat, earlier that evening. Thinking fast, Melanie brought up a picture of herself dressed in the same blue dress, taken a couple of weeks earlier, when her hair had still been long.

"What about now?"

Humouring her, they looked at the picture and, after an infinitesimal pause, shook their heads.

"Sorry pet," he said, in a distant voice. "Haven't seen her. She'll turn up, at the end of the night. Just wait around here and you'll catch her."

"What if she's fallen into the water?" Melanie demanded. "What if some bloke has—has—"

"What? Taken her off for a quickie?" he said. "You're over eighteen and so's she. Old enough to know how to handle yourself, or you shouldn't be here."

Melanie felt tears clog her throat.

"We're both sixteen," she said, swallowing them back. "And I swear I'll tell everybody that you knew that and let me on board, anyway, unless you help me, now."

Both men exchanged a surprised glance. If word got out that they weren't checking identification properly, they'd lose their jobs, and the club could be shut down.

"Hinny, I don't think you're in any position to be—"

"Okay," she said. "I'll just call the police and see what they have to say about it."

"Now then, there's no need for that. We never said we wouldn't help..."

Without another word, they put a radio call out to every staff member on board, alongside a detailed description of Gemma.

That should do it, Melanie told herself, and watched idly as a police car turned at the top of the street, too far away for her to hail its driver.

She wondered who was being transported in the back, and what they'd done to deserve it.

CHAPTER 5

Spring, 2022

Bamburgh Castle

"Have you seen her?"

Ryan paused in the act of reaching for an hors d'oeuvre and turned to face a woman of indeterminate age—she could have been anywhere between seventy and ninety, by his estimation—who was dressed as Miss Marple and had sharp, bird-like eyes to match.

"I'm sorry?"

"Have you seen her?" the woman repeated.

"Who?" Ryan asked.

"The Pink Lady, of course," the woman replied, distractedly. "Usually, I see her around this time of the evening, but I haven't spotted her, yet."

She cast a glance in either direction, eyes widening while her bony fingers clasped a small handbag, knuckles almost white with the effort.

"Who's the Pink Lady?" Ryan tried to think of a historical character in the real or fictional realm who matched that description, so that he might help the lady to find her companion. "What's her name?"

"Nobody knows," the woman replied, cryptically. "She's rumoured to be a Northumbrian princess."

Thoroughly confused, Ryan abandoned the snacks and turned to face her.

"I thought you would know, being who you are," she continued, indicating his costume.

"Because...I'm Sherlock Holmes?"

She gave a hoot of laughter. "Don't be silly. You're that handsome detective, aren't you? The one I see on the news, sometimes."

Not only confused but embarrassed now, Ryan looked around for a friendly face to help extricate him from this peculiar conversation.

"Well, my mother thinks so," he said, giving her a smile. "Would you like me to help you find your friend?"

"Oh, she's certainly not my friend," the woman muttered. "She's not my friend, at all."

Thinking the poor old dear might be caught in the early stages of a memory disorder of some description, he tried a different tack.

"I'm—Ryan," he said, leaving off his formal title, for once. "What's your name?"

Before she could reply, a short woman of around fifty bustled over, dressed as a figure from Roman or Greek history, though he hadn't the faintest idea who.

"Angela! There you are," she said, breathlessly. "I was looking for you."

"I've been here, talking to this nice-looking young man," the older woman replied, with irrefutable logic. "It's been a while since you had a man, Gwen. Why don't you try this one?"

Ryan's lips twitched, while Angela's friend turned an immediate and unhealthy shade of puce.

"Sorry, she's—ah—"

"Cantankerous?" he offered, with a deliberate wink for Angela, who looked mischievous.

"You can say that again," Gwen said. "In any event, I need to steal her away for a minute. We're about to do the toasts, Angie, and I know everyone on the project wants to thank you publicly, as well as privately, for all your support."

Ryan might have been curious, but his stomach was rumbling, and miniature cones of fish and chips beckoned.

"I think Angela was looking for her friend in pink," he said to Gwen, who gave him a blank stare.

Here we go again, he thought.

"Something about a…pink lady?"

Gwen's face cleared, and she turned to Angela with a shake of her head.

"We've been through this a dozen times," she said. "The Pink Lady is just a ghost story—she isn't real."

The old woman became agitated. "No—no, I've seen her with my own eyes—"

"I'm sorry, we must be keeping you," Gwen said, apologetically, but Ryan shook his head. "No trouble. A lot of people claim to have seen spirits," he added, for Angela's benefit, and was pleased to see her frown disappear.

"Exactly," she said. "And I've seen this one every night for the past two weeks!"

"That's consistent," Ryan remarked.

"Yes, but the Pink Lady haunts the castle, not guest houses," Gwen pointed out, clearly having held the same conversation many times before. "Why would she suddenly appear, after all these centuries, at the Sandy Dunes Guest House?"

"I couldn't say," Angela replied. "Perhaps someone angered her, or she got lost on her way back from the other realm…"

Gwen rolled her eyes.

"What's the story behind this…princess, did you say?" Ryan surprised himself by asking.

"Legend has it, a beautiful Northumbrian princess of ancient times fell in love with a man, but he was of lowly birth, and her father disapproved of the match," Gwen explained. "To separate them, he sent the man overseas for seven years and forbade any contact between them, hoping that the time apart would diminish his daughter's feelings. Instead, the princess became increasingly depressed. In a last-ditch attempt, the king told the princess her beloved had married someone else, or died, depending on who's telling the tale. To cheer his daughter up, the king had his seamstress make up a lovely new dress in pink, which was the princess's favourite colour. Sadly, the princess climbed to the highest battlement and hurled herself onto the jagged rocks below, still wearing the dress."

"Charming story," Ryan remarked.

"It gets worse," Gwen said. "Tragically, the princess's lover returned home soon afterwards and was desolate when he found out what had happened. Now, it's said that the princess returns to the castle every seven years, dressed in a gown of pink. Apparently, people have seen her down on the beach, staring out to sea, waiting for her love to return."

"Well, a castle wouldn't be a proper castle without a couple of ghosts," he said. "I suppose they know to visit around Hallowe'en?"

"Funnily enough, yes," Gwen replied, with a small smile. "But one thing they've never done is migrate to Angela's guest house."

Ryan considered the lady in question, who had all the bearing of a fragile old lady, but all the cunning of a fox, if the twinkle in her eye was anything to go by. Perhaps his initial estimation of her had been wide of the mark, and Angela was mounting an elaborate ghostly marketing campaign, to drive business to her guest house.

Well, who could blame her?

"I hope you find what you're looking for," he said, with a smile for them both. "If you'll excuse me, I must find Watson."

As it happened, his fictional and real-life sidekick in the world of sleuthing was happily engaged in the important task of sampling three different kinds of Scotch egg.

"Now, here, you've got your standard pork sausage base," he was saying to MacKenzie, who wasn't a noted fan of sausage and egg wrapped in breadcrumbs. "Try a little nibble…"

She held up a hand. "I'll stick to my cheese and wine," she told him. "One of us has to be the classy one, in this relationship."

He made a sound of reproof, undermined somewhat by the breadcrumbs peppering his false moustache.

"Heathen," he mumbled. "There's a chorizo one here, and—ooh!—here's one made with Craster kippers."

She pulled a face. "You'd better have some strong mints for pudding, Frank, or you'll be getting no kisses from me."

It was enough to make him think twice about the kippers, but he risked a bite of the chorizo. Luckily for him, any sanctions were thrust from MacKenzie's mind when Lowerson approached them, looking downcast.

"Jack!" Phillips greeted him with exaggerated cheer, masking his assessment of the younger man's unhappy features with a blithe smile and a clap on the back.

"You look like you could use a drink."

Lowerson sighed.

"I won't argue with that," he muttered, and took the glass held out to him with a nod of thanks. "I'm sorry Mel isn't with me, she's—ah—"

He raised a hand, then let it fall away again.

"She's busy."

"She'll come through this," MacKenzie said, quietly. "It's a difficult time for her."

Lowerson stared down into the fizzing bubbles at the bottom of his glass.

"I know," he said. "I'm trying to help her, but I feel like I'm failing."

"You're not failing, lad," Phillips said. "All Mel needs is for you to be there, to listen, to be a shoulder when she needs it. You can't take away the pain she feels, or the grief, but you can ease it for her every time she looks up and finds you standing beside her."

He had a way of putting things that just made sense, Jack thought.

"You're right, Frank," he said, lifting his head. "I'm too wrapped up in my own feelings. I know she isn't really angry with me, she's angry at him."

"And herself," Ryan added, strolling across to join them. "Mel probably feels responsible for her sister's death—even though she knows, logically, that she couldn't have prevented what happened. It was in the hands of another."

He knew that feeling, and it was a hard one to shake.

"Her parents have always blamed her, and it's the reason she first joined the Force—to be able to find who killed Gemma and somehow make amends," Jack said.

Ryan frowned. "Why would her parents blame her? It makes no sense."

"The night Gemma died, she was out with Mel, underage drinking at a club in Newcastle," Jack explained. "Apparently, that wasn't Gemma's usual scene, and they got it into their heads that, if Mel hadn't led her astray, she might still be alive."

Ryan sighed, and thought of the terrible guilt Melanie must have carried. "It wasn't her fault," he said. "Besides, they were only kids."

"I know," Jack said. "But now, Mel's talking about what she might do when—if—she ever finds Gemma's killer. He's a dangerous man, whoever he is, and I'm worried."

Ryan exchanged a glance with the others, who wore matching expressions of concern.

"I know the impulse for revenge can be very strong," he said. "I've been there, I've lived it, and I've almost—almost—acted on it."

Phillips put a silent hand on his back, remembering.

"But it's a losing game," Ryan continued. "Even if Mel was ever to meet this man, and—what? Put a bullet in his head? A knife in his belly? He'd be dead, and she'd carry around the guilt of taking another life for the rest of hers, adding to the burden she carries already."

"She doesn't see it that way," Jack said.

Ryan knocked back the rest of his wine and set the glass down. "I'll talk to her, first thing Monday."

Jack was relieved. If she wouldn't listen to him, perhaps Mel would listen to her boss, a man they all looked up to, especially one who'd walked a similar path before.

"Thanks," he said. "I don't know what I'd do if I lost her."

At that moment, Ryan happened to spot their new DCS re-enter the King's Hall and experienced a funny little ripple down his spine. He couldn't account for it, other than some instinctive aversion to bureaucratic personality types, he supposed.

"You won't," he said, turning back to his friend. "Melanie has a village of people who care for her, and we're ready to fight, if need be."

Across the room, DCS Forbes turned his head, as though he'd heard them, and raised his hand in a kind of friendly salute.

Ryan didn't return it, but gave a brief, peremptory nod.

Forbes continued to smile and make all the right social noises until the end of the evening; until his fingers itched to take up one of the rusting armaments gracing the castle's stone walls and use it to slice a neat line across the chattering gullets of those around him.

While these pleasant thoughts roamed his mind, he distracted himself by formulating the early stages of a plan. For, one thing was quite clear: Ryan's team was a tight-knit group, bound not only by duty and shared experience, but by friendship and even love. Worse still, they'd taken all that and wrapped it around Melanie Yates like a forcefield, so strong it was almost tangible. Thus, in order to get to her, he needed to extricate her from their circle, and the best way he could think of to do that was to break it apart, so that she came to him.

Divide and conquer.

Nothing so easy.

CHAPTER 6

"Well, how was your night?" When Ryan and Anna returned home to the nearby village of Elsdon, they were greeted at the door by Ryan's mother, Eve.

"Interesting," they replied, in unison.

Eve opened her mouth, then shut it again. "Not exactly the response I was hoping for…"

"It was still great to get out," Ryan said, and curved a hand around Anna's waist to administer a kiss. "But it was an unusual night. I don't know whether it was the castle ghosts or my natural cynicism, but I couldn't shake a feeling of—"

"Impending doom?" Anna said, as she shrugged out of her coat. "Me too."

"Exactly," Ryan said, and kissed her again for good measure. "There was a tension in the air, even though, on the surface, everything seemed fine."

"Well, we didn't see much of Melanie," Anna reminded him. "It's hard not to worry about her—and Jack, for that matter."

"That's true," he said, as they made their way towards the kitchen. "But it seemed to be more than that."

Ryan began filling the kettle. "Perhaps the Pink Lady spooked me."

Anna gave him a lopsided smile. "I didn't know you were a believer…"

"I'm not." He laughed. "But I met someone who definitely does believe in ghosts. Goes by the name of Angela and runs the Sandy Dunes Guest House, in Bamburgh."

"Angela Bansbury?" Anna said, with surprise. "She's one of the archaeological project's major benefactors."

"Angela…Bansbury?" Eve queried, having been of the generation to watch Murder, She Wrote when it was first aired on television. "You must be joking."

Anna shook her head. "She's a local institution, as well."

"Thankfully, Bamburgh doesn't have the same murder rate as Cabot Cove," Ryan intoned.

At that moment, his father entered the room, having recently been upstairs checking on his only grandchild and—some might have said—his kindred spirit. As they always did when Ryan and Charles were together, Anna and Eve were struck by the physical similarities between father and son. Although he'd inherited his unusual shade of grey-blue eyes from his mother, Ryan had his father to thank for his height and military bearing, and for the shock of black hair that framed a chiselled face—albeit, in Charles' case, that hair was now a thick mane of grey.

"Emma's sleeping like the proverbial," he said, giving his son a quick, one-armed hug that took Ryan by surprise, followed by a more expansive embrace for his daughter-in-law, who didn't bat an eyelid.

"I'm afraid she was awake a little later than usual," Eve confessed, avoiding eye contact. "She—ah—well, you see, we were having such a good time singing along to Winnie the Pooh…"

"Aha," Anna said, with an indulgent smile. "Well, it's the privilege of being a grandparent to let Emma stay up past her bedtime, feed her too much chocolate and generally spoil her a bit. We don't mind."

"Easy for you to say," Ryan argued, "knowing fine well it's my turn to do the morning shift, tomorrow."

"Is it?" Anna said, blandly, with a wink for Eve. "Anyway, you were telling us something about Angela and the Pink Lady?"

"Mm," he said, pouring boiling water into a teapot. "She claims to have seen the ghost every day for the past two weeks."

"I didn't know Angela had been spending that much time at the castle," Anna remarked.

"Not at the castle," he said. "At her guest house."

"That doesn't make sense."

"Which is exactly what somebody called Gwen was telling her," Ryan said, reaching for the milk.

"I'm lost," Charles whispered to his wife. "Who's this 'Gwen', and why was she wearing pink?"

"Never mind, dear."

He mumbled something about getting more sense out of his granddaughter and went off in search of a newspaper.

"The Pink Lady has only ever been seen at Bamburgh Castle—if she's been seen at all," Anna continued. "It would be highly unusual for someone to have seen her elsewhere."

"Which is why I thought it could be a case of clever marketing," Ryan said, and began dishing out mugs of steaming tea. "People love a good ghost story."

"The Sandy Dunes would be the place for it," Anna said. "It's a crumbling old Georgian manor on the outskirts of the village. A bit chintzy, if you know what I mean, but full of character. I wouldn't be surprised if the place had a secret door or two."

"How does it fare, as a business?"

"Hard to say," Anna replied, taking a sip of her tea. "Bamburgh is very popular as a tourist destination, so you'd think there'd be plenty of punters looking for somewhere to stay. On the other hand, there are loads of cottages and hotels in the area, which might have been renovated more recently. Come to think of it, Angela isn't likely to have had any paying guests since the archaeological crowd arrived for the season, and they aren't paying for accommodation—only their meals."

"How come?"

"Angela is one of the benefactors, as I say. She's lets members of the dig stay for free, so I can't imagine she makes much of a profit—the guest house has ten bedrooms, including hers, so there wouldn't be much room for any other paying guests while they're there."

"That's very kind of her," Eve remarked, and reached for a piece of shortbread. "How many people make up the archaeological team?"

"Oh, at least ten, if you take into account seasonal interns, although they only stay a week or two at a time,"

Anna replied. "This year, there are six permanent members of the dig."

"I take it Gwen is one of them?" Ryan said.

Anna nodded. "Doctor Gwen Meakings is a former colleague of mine, from Durham University," she said. "She used to be part of the Faculty of Archaeology there, before moving to its corollary in Newcastle. She's experienced, but the project is headed up by Professor Alec Soames, who's been on the scene for years. He's been Head of Archaeology at Newcastle for as long as I can remember; in fact, he used to do a bit of work with—"

She broke off, and then spoke the name she had once loved like a father.

"—with Mark Bowers."

Ryan's jaw tightened, and he thought privately that the association with the late Mark Bowers was enough to consign the unfortunate Soames to his watchlist.

"What about the rest?"

"Ah...let's see. Obviously, I'm one of their visiting academics. I'm there to see if there's any crossover between the archaeological finds and my research into pre-Christian history in the area. Then, there's Doctor Petra Nowak, she's another visiting academic from the University of Warsaw; Doctor Oskar Fiske, who's visiting from the University of Oslo; John Adamu is one of Gwen's postgraduate students at Newcastle; and, then there's Jilly-Jane Thornton. She's what you might call a part-time archaeologist; she works for local government, most of the time. I think she managed to squeeze through the university door as a visiting fellow, or something of that kind, but I don't know that she's done much in the way of active archaeology for years. I think everyone was a bit surprised, when she showed up."

"Jilly-Jane?" Eve queried, again.

"I know," Anna said, with a chuckle. "She likes to be called 'JJ', for short."

"Can't blame her," Eve mumbled.

"How about interns?" Ryan asked.

"There's a couple of students, but they're not staying at Angela's guest house. They only come for a few days at a time."

Ryan yawned hugely, the effects of a busy week at work finally catching up with him. "Well, I thought you'd like to know, in case you wanted to ask Angela about her experience with the ghost—as part of your research."

"Oh? What are you researching?" Eve asked.

Anna took a deep breath and voiced the private dream she'd been working on for a while.

"I'm considering expanding my career a bit," she told her mother-in-law. "I love my work at the university, but it can be inflexible, especially as Emma is still so small."

Eve nodded, remembering when Ryan and Natalie had been young. "It's hard to juggle family life, sometimes," she sympathised.

"Exactly. Which is why I'm thinking about varying my writing from non-fiction historical texts into the realms of fiction," Anna said, in a rush. "I don't know whether I'll be any good at it…"

"You'll be wonderful," Ryan interrupted, forestalling any self-doubt she might have felt. "I know it."

Eve's heart warmed to see the love shining from her son's eyes, and she reached across the table to squeeze Anna's hand—partly, in support of his assertion, and partly as an unspoken 'thank you' for bringing such joy to the only child she had left.

"So," she said, crisply. "What do you plan to write about?"

"Well, I have in mind a Northumbrian ghost story," Anna said. "I could write a companion guide to the myths and legends of the region, but I really want to write something spine-tingling in time for Hallowe'en. Maybe, after that, some kind of historical fiction."

"I think it's a great idea," Eve enthused. "I hope you'll let me read it, when you've finished."

Anna was nervous.

What if it was no good?

What if her family didn't have the heart to tell her?

"On one condition," she said. "You have to tell me the truth. I need to know, if it's a terrible story."

Eve smiled. "It's a deal. Mind you, if anybody gives you a nasty review, you can always have a poltergeist chase them off the pages of your sequel."

Anna's lips curved.

"Don't give her ideas," Ryan said, darkly. "I'll have to watch my back, in case I end up meeting a nasty demise."

"Think of it as an incentive to keep putting the loo seat down," Anna told him, flexing her fingers meaningfully. "It wouldn't hurt to put that picture up in the hallway, either…"

"See?" he said to his mother, while bending down to bestow a kiss on his wife's upturned lips. "You've created a monster. She'll be popping us off, left right and centre."

"Better on the pages than in real life," his mother laughed, and then reached up to pat his cheek. "On which note, I'll say goodnight."

After Charles stuck his head around the door to wish them the same, Ryan and Anna checked their daughter was still sleeping peacefully and then retreated to their bedroom, where Eve had left the sidelights on for them to cast a warm, welcoming glow around the room.

"Your mother is so thoughtful," Anna said, as she sank onto the edge of their bed.

"Don't be fooled," Ryan said softly.

He closed the door, then walked across to join her with slow intent, sinking to his knees in front of her. Watching her eyes dilate, he reached for the boots she still wore, his fingers brushing the inside of her thigh.

"My mother's hoping for more grandchildren, that's all," he said, peeling the boot from her leg with slow precision before reaching for the other one.

Anna smiled, then closed her eyes as his fingers trailed back over her skin.

"Maybe, one day," she managed.

"We could practise, in the meantime," he whispered, and lowered her back against the bed. "You'll need some inspiration—in case you ever write a love scene in one of your books."

"Books, plural, now, is it?" she said. "Very selfless of you, I must say, to help with my research."

"I can be very giving," he said, and brushed his lips against her. "I hope you're taking notes."

She laughed softly and then gasped his name as her mind and body succumbed to the moment. Her last, fleeting thought was to wonder how many other women could claim to have found themselves in the same scenario with Sherlock Holmes.

At least he'd taken off the hat.

CHAPTER 7

"How was your evening, darling?"

DCS Forbes kept his back to his wife as he undressed. "Very enjoyable," he replied, which wasn't entirely untrue. "I was sorry you couldn't be there."

Now, that part was a lie.

Jenna Forbes sat up against the pillows, displaying a low-cut vest top she often wore for bed. In the early days he'd enjoyed the view, but not since the children.

Now, the sight of her sagging décolleté repulsed him.

"It would have been so nice," she said, and tried valiantly to mask her disappointment. "I just couldn't get a childminder at such short notice."

He made a small sound of sympathy, though, in truth, it was the precise outcome he'd hoped for. He'd known about the charity ball for over a month, ever since Morrison had first offered him the promotion, but he'd only sprung the news on his wife the previous day.

He liked to keep their time together short and perfunctory, wherever possible.

"Well, you know, I only went along to meet my new staff," he said, wearily. "Otherwise—"

"Oh, I know, darling," she said quickly, not wanting to upset him.

Andrew was so sensitive.

"There'll be other times," he assured her, and she gave him a wan smile.

"Of course. Maybe we could—"

He yawned loudly. "I'm going to jump in the shower, then I'm afraid I've got a couple of work e-mails to send," he told her. "Don't wait up, love, I'll try not to disturb you later."

If she thought it was strange for him to be answering work e-mails at that hour, and at the weekend, she didn't question it. Over the years they'd been together, Jenna had gradually lost her sense of what 'normal' looked like to other people; she only knew what 'normal' was for their family, the one he had created and conditioned.

"Okay," she said, banking down her disappointment.

For all that he was, to many people, a very average man, Jenna loved her husband and thought him a charming, sophisticated person whom she was still attracted to, despite all their years of marriage. She supposed it was a pity his sex drive was so low—he only ever wanted to be intimate very late at night, in the dark, once a month, at best. She wished he would be more adventurous, more amorous, but he assured her he loved her, so she tried to be understanding. It was a small price to pay for having a perfect husband, beautiful children and a happy home.

All she'd ever wanted.

"There are some snacks in the fridge," she told him, with a bright smile. "Don't work too hard."

"I'll try not to," he said, throwing a smile over his shoulder as he made his way to the bathroom.

Forbes stayed in the shower for as long as he could, thinking of the woman in the blue dress and of her sister. Then, when he could be reasonably sure his wife was asleep, he crept back into the bedroom and tugged on a pair of dark jogging pants and a matching top, before padding along the landing to check on their two children.

Both were fast asleep.

He moved downstairs, his feet silent against the carpeted floor, and made directly for his study—a small room at the back of the house, overlooking the garden. He took out a keyring with numerous keys of different shapes and size, selected one that would unlock the door, then stepped inside, locking it securely behind him.

Once inside his little sanctuary, he moved towards a large cabinet made of heavy oak, set against one wall. He selected another key and bent down to open one of the doors, behind which was a stack of neat papers and files. Tugging them out, he crouched down and reached towards the back, feeling around with his fingertips until he located a small hole he'd bored into the base. He crooked a finger and lifted the wood to reveal a small cavity, inside which he'd tucked away a metal box.

He didn't reach for it straight away, but remained perfectly still, listening intently for any sound on the floorboards above his head, where his daughter's bedroom lay, or the tread of his wife's footsteps.

Silence.

Satisfied that he wouldn't be interrupted, Forbes reached inside, carefully lifting the box from its hollowed-out bed. He held it reverently, with all the care he might have shown a newborn baby.

How long had it been since he'd allowed himself to look?

A month? Two?

He selected another key which unlocked the box and, with all the eagerness of a small boy at Christmas, snatched up its solitary contents.

Another ordinary-looking key.

But this key gave access to his most prized possessions, the culmination of a life's work—or what was left of it. How he could have misjudged the dosage when sedating his last victim was a source of deep personal embarrassment; he was highly experienced and highly skilled at his…what should he call it? His hobby. It was the only time a woman had ever escaped him—in fifteen years—and although he'd always planned for the worst-case scenario, he'd never imagined ever needing to implement his exit plan.

But he'd always do whatever was necessary.

In the case of the Thai woman, it had been necessary to incinerate the outbuilding where he'd built his kill room and destroy its contents entirely. He'd only been able to save his most precious memorabilia, which he'd stashed in the safest place he could think of, but the memory of watching his photographs and trinkets go up in flames was enough to send him into a rage all over again, and he was in too fine a mood to be angry.

There was so much to look forward to.

Clutching the key in his sweaty palm, Forbes locked the study behind him, stood in the hallway for long minutes until he was certain his family wouldn't stir, and then slipped out of the house.

It was time to move the little canvas rucksack.

Forbes didn't like to keep his special possessions in any one place for too long but, until he could find an appropriate location to site his next den, the little rental garage would have to do. It was dank and smelled strongly of vermin, but he didn't care. All he needed was somewhere private where he could sit in a chair and enjoy taking a trip down memory lane.

He flicked on the single strip light, heard the scuttle of mice scarpering for cover, and then shut the garage door behind him. Inside, he made his way to the middle of the concrete box, to an armchair covered in plastic sheeting, which he removed. Resting on the chair was a larger version of the locked box he kept at home, and his body began to respond to the anticipation of what he would find inside.

"Slowly," he told himself. "Make it last."

He couldn't afford to come to the garage too frequently; he might be seen, and his wife might find him gone from the house.

The risk was too great.

Oh, but the pleasure...

Forbes lowered himself into the chair and retrieved a small packet of hand wipes from the pocket of his jacket, which he set on the arm. Then, he took out the little key and took his time turning it in the lock, teasing his senses, then breathed out the air he'd been holding in his chest when the box clicked open.

Inside, perfectly wrapped in plastic, were his treasures.

His fingers hovered, unsure which to touch first, and sweat beaded on his lip, which he wiped away with the sleeve of his hoodie.

He closed his eyes, remembering the first time he'd seen her.

The girl in the blue dress.

His fingers reached inside the plastic, easing between its folds until they brushed against blue satin, blood-stained but preserved for posterity. A feral smile spread across his face, and, in the semi-darkness, he no longer looked human; he was a clown, a wooden puppet with exaggerated features, terrifying to behold.

When his eyes reopened, they were almost black.

CHAPTER 8

The following Monday dawned brightly, the sun casting a mellow pink hue over the rooftops and spires of the city of Newcastle, lending the River Tyne a molten sheen as it undulated gently towards the sea. The world seemed peaceful, so far as it could be, with crime rates at an all-time low in the area and, as he steered his car into the staff car park at Northumbria Police Headquarters in the east of the city, Ryan allowed himself a rare moment to relax. He turned off the engine and leaned back against the headrest, thought of his wife and family, then of his 'work family', and counted himself a very fortunate man.

A sharp rap on the window disturbed his momentary solitude and sent his eyes flying open again, whereupon he was greeted by the sight of Phillips—or, at least, he assumed it was his sergeant, and not a cloned version of the man—dressed entirely in Lycra, while straddling a mountain bike.

He reached for the button to wind down the electric window.

"Mornin'!" Phillips said, and gave a cheery wave.

Ryan didn't respond immediately, but made an inspection of the man's attire, which left very little to the imagination.

"Frank?"

Phillips tipped up his sunglasses and propped them on the rim of his helmet. "Oh, aye, you probably couldn't tell it was me, with these on."

Ryan was speechless. "You—what—why?"

His sergeant continued to grin, as though nothing was amiss, while Ryan struggled to compute the scene that lay before him.

"It's my new thing," Phillips declared, patting the handlebars of the bike he'd picked up online. "Before I pick up one of those fancy-schmantzy home-workout bikes, I thought I'd try the old-fashioned way and see if I can shift these last few pounds."

He rubbed his belly, which was constrained by a layer of tight black fabric but was liable to explode over the elastic of his matching bike shorts at any given moment.

"What happened to the boxing?" Ryan asked weakly, keeping his eyes firmly above waist level. "The boxing was fine."

And there was no Lycra in sight.

"Oh, I still get down to Buddle's once or twice a week," Phillips said. "But this little beauty here takes me on the open road, where I can feel the wind on my face…"

He sucked in a gulp of air to punctuate the feeling, and promptly choked on a bug.

"I'm—alreet—" he wheezed, waving away Ryan's move to help him, while hastily dismounting from the bike to double over and cough up the offending creature.

At which point, from his seated position in the car, Ryan was treated to a rear view of Phillips' shorts, which had ripped neatly down the back seam sometime during the journey from his home in Kingston Park, revealing a jaunty pair of banana yellow boxer shorts beneath the film of Lycra.

"You couldn't make this up," Ryan muttered. "Frank—"

"I'm alreet," Phillips repeated, coughing again for good measure before straightening up. "There, that's better."

"Frank, I should tell you—"

"I know what you're goin' to say," Phillips interrupted him, with a knowing smile. "You're thinkin' of road safety, and all that. Well, you've no need to worry, I'm gannin' canny on the roads, can't be too careful with some of these maniac drivers."

"No, I was going to say—"

"You're wonderin' how long it takes me to get into the office?" Phillips interrupted again. "Well, it took a while this mornin' as it's my first time cyclin' in, but it'll get quicker an' quicker, you mark my words."

Ryan scrubbed a hand over his face, and then unfolded his long body from the car. "Frank, you've got—"

At that precise moment, a couple of female constables crossed the parking lot and gave a loud wolf whistle.

"Oh, aye, you'd be lucky!" Phillips called back, then turned to his friend with incredulous eyes. "Y'nah, it's been a real eye-opener, this mornin'. I've had horns honkin' at me, women hangin' out of car windows while they were stopped in traffic, all tryin' to get my attention. You'd think they'd never seen a muscular bloke in bike gear before. It puts it all in perspective, when you think about what women have to put up with from us men."

By now, Ryan was grinning openly.

"What're you laughin' at?" Phillips asked. "Look, I nah you're usually the one to get the wolf whistles, son, but there's a lot to be said for an older man in his prime. The lasses love a bloke they can hold onto…"

"Jesus, Mary and Joseph."

Before Ryan could respond, this bald statement came from MacKenzie, who'd chosen to drive into work after dropping Samantha at school. She slammed out of her car and crossed the tarmac to meet them, her face a picture of comic horror.

"Frank, please tell me you didn't cycle all the way across town with your arse on display."

Phillips adopted a dignified expression. "There's bound to be a bit of the old gluteus maximus on display, while I'm pedalling," he said. "I can't help it if the women of the city get an eyeful. There's no need for you to feel jealous, love—"

MacKenzie looked at Ryan, whose shoulders shook with mirth, and then back at her husband.

"Frank, can't you feel a draught?"

Phillips thought about the question. "I s'pose it's a bit nippy, but—"

MacKenzie shook her head, and then resorted to base tactics by giving him a playful smack. "How about that?"

"Well, if you weren't my wife, I'd call that sexual harassment in the workplace, for starters, and I've got Ryan here as my witness…" Phillips replied, before the truth hit him like a pain in the posterior.

He looked between them. "My arse is hangin' out of these shorts, isn't it?"

"In a word, yes," Ryan told him, keeping a straight face.

Phillips spun around, so his back was concealed by Ryan's car.

"You could have told us!"

Ryan rolled his eyes.

"Now what am I goin' to do?" Phillips asked them, in a stage whisper. "There's no way I can make it down to the changin' rooms without gettin' an earful of abuse, lookin' like this."

Ryan wondered why it was that Frank felt perfectly comfortable wandering through the corridors of the Northumbria Police Constabulary in a skin-suit, but was mortally embarrassed by the prospect of having a sliver of underpants on display whilst doing so.

"Think of it this way," he said. "You can always come dressed up as Doctor Watson tomorrow, and they'll forget all about today's little mishap."

"Oh, aye, you'd love that, wouldn't you…"

Ryan chuckled. "Trust me, Frank, so long as I don't have to look at your near-naked rump ever again, I don't care if you come dressed as the Queen of Sheba."

On which note, he and MacKenzie began sauntering towards the main entrance.

"C'mon, Frank," MacKenzie called back. "We haven't got all morning!"

"Oi! Why, you pair of no-good, low-down—"

Phillips muttered something filthy beneath his breath, took a hasty glance in either direction and then streaked across the tarmac in a blur of black and yellow.

CHAPTER 9

From a window on the second floor of Police Headquarters, Jack Lowerson let out a long peal of laughter and turned to Melanie with a smile.

"You have to come and see this," he said. "Frank's had a wardrobe malfunction."

At her desk across the room, Yates barely looked up from her computer monitor.

"He's—" Jack laughed again. "Now, he's running like greased lightning across the car park…Mel, this is priceless—"

She snapped. "Jack, can't you see that I'm busy?" she almost shouted, drawing awkward stares from their colleagues at neighbouring desks in the open-plan office. "I don't care what Frank is doing—all right? I have work to do."

She turned back to her screen and tapped angrily at the keys in front of her, leaving Jack to stare at her back, the smile slipping slowly from his face.

Catching the tail-end of their little tête-à-tête, DCS Forbes stepped fully into the room and gave them all a cheerful smile.

"Morning, everyone," he said. "Jack? I wonder if I could have a moment?"

Lowerson banked down the hurt, boxing his feelings away for the present, and returned his new superintendent's smile.

"Of course, sir."

"Let's go to my office," Forbes suggested. "Via the break room? I don't know about you, but I'm parched."

Jack nodded, and they made their way towards a little galley kitchen further down the corridor. As they entered, there was a meaningful pause while Forbes waited for his subordinate to do the honours, which Lowerson did, out of a sense of obligation.

"Ah, coffee or tea?"

"Coffee, if you don't mind," Forbes replied. "Milk, no sugar."

Jack went about the business of setting up the filter, while Forbes watched him, scrutinizing the younger man with narrowed eyes.

This was the man who shared Melanie's bed, was it?

He was attractive, in a gelled, teeth-whitened sort of way, but hardly in her league. From what he'd heard, Jack Lowerson showed significant promise as a detective and would be in line for the promotional pathway very soon, according to Ryan's most recent report. Then again, judging by past events, Jack Lowerson was also a man prone to poor judgment, at times, and had been too often at the mercy of his own pride.

He could use that.

Yes, he could certainly use that.

As they made their way back along the corridor, Forbes considered the best approach.

"I've heard a lot of complimentary things about you," he began, as they stepped inside his new office.

"Thank you, sir," Lowerson said, and brightened a bit at the thought of having gained the respect of his peers. "That's good to know."

"You enjoy the work?" Forbes walked around his desk and sank into an ergonomic chair, indicating that Jack should take one of the sagging visitors' chairs opposite.

"Yes, sir," he replied, perching on the edge of one of them.

"Plenty of collars, a few road bumps here and there," Forbes continued, with a wink that suggested he didn't worry too much about those. "And outstanding scores in your written examinations."

Jack smiled.

"With a track record like that, I'd have thought you'd be on the pathway to becoming a DI, by now."

Jack didn't know how to respond. It was true, he'd like to progress up the ranks, but he was sure Ryan would put him forward for the DI pathway when he felt he was ready.

When would that be? his mind whispered.

"Well, we'll have to see what can be done about that, won't we?" Forbes cut in, as if he'd read his mind.

"I—thank you, sir."

"Don't mention it," Forbes replied. "I'll have a word with Ryan, and see what we can do to expedite things."

It was all happening so fast, Lowerson hardly knew what to think.

"Unless, of course, you don't feel you're up to the challenge?" Forbes added, with an air of doubt. "If you're not ready…"

"I'm ready," Lowerson said quickly.

"That's settled, then," Forbes said, with a slow smile. "Leave it with me."

When Ryan stepped into the open-plan workspace belonging to the Major Crimes division of the Criminal Investigation Department, Melanie Yates pushed back her chair and made a beeline for him.

"Sir? I was hoping to speak to you about today's briefing."

Ryan had been expecting the conversation, but that didn't make it any easier.

"Mel, we've already discussed this," he said, as gently as he could. "You and your family will be apprised following the briefing, and I believe your parents are coming in to join us later this morning for that very reason."

Yates swallowed back the words she wanted to cry, the frustration she longed to unleash.

"Sir—with respect—I deserve to be a part of the investigating team."

Ryan heard the heartbreak, the sense of betrayal, and, in that moment, hated the job he was tasked to do.

"I'm sorry," he said simply. "You know how your inclusion on the investigating team would be construed by the Crown Prosecution Service, the Defence, and a jury, if we find your sister's killer. We have to do everything strictly by the book, Mel, or not at all."

Her jaw clenched, and she looked away before answering. "I know—I know you're just saying what you have to say," she muttered. "But—maybe—if we kept it between ourselves—"

His brows knitted together in a dark frown. "Are you saying what I think you're saying?" he queried, in a low voice. "Mel, you know that isn't how we operate."

She drew back, running an agitated hand through her hair. "You can't expect me to do nothing," she said, her voice rising dangerously. "I can't just sit around, pretending to care about all these other cases, when I know he's out there, killing someone else, or planning to."

Ryan laid his jacket over the back of his chair, very slowly, very deliberately, to give her a moment to calm down. From the corner of his eye, he spotted MacKenzie, who took her seat nearby and had enough tact to keep her eyes averted.

Unlike the rest of the vultures in the room, he thought.

"Let's go for a walk," he said.

"I have—" Mel broke off when she saw the patient look on his face, and nodded. "All right," she said. "Where?"

Ryan gave her a small smile.

"At times like these, I take the advice of my alternative therapist—you might know him? Goes by the name of Frank Phillips, and swears by a smoked bacon sandwich at least once a week."

That brought a reluctant smile.

"I'm really not hungry," she said.

Ryan had eyes in his head, so he didn't need to speak to Lowerson to know that she'd lost weight. He could see for himself how clothes that previously fit like a glove now hung from her slender frame.

"See how you feel when we get to the canteen," he advised, and stepped back to allow her to precede him.

Ryan kept up a stream of easy chatter as they made their way down to the staff canteen, so that she began to relax and the cortisol in her body began slowly to drain away. Presently, the scent of baked beans and some sort of meaty casserole assailed their nostrils, and they pushed through a set of double doors into a large room dedicated to keeping Her Majesty's law enforcement officers fed and watered.

"What'll it be?" he asked her.

"Oh, you don't have to—" Mel said, hurriedly.

"I know," he replied. "But I'm happy to."

When she gave a limp shrug, he turned to the serving staff and ordered a couple of bacon stotties with 'the works', a couple of coffees and two large bottles of still water.

"If you don't want any of that, you don't have to eat it," he said. "If there's something you'd prefer, just let me know."

She shook her head, while the smell of frying bacon began to permeate her nostrils.

"So," Ryan said, once they'd taken a quiet table on the far side of the room. "I've got twenty minutes until the briefing on Operation Heartbeat. Let's try and make the most of it."

Her fingers circled the cup of coffee, but she didn't drink. "It's as I said upstairs," she began. "I want to be included."

"You are," he said. "Everything we do, we do in your best interests."

The simplicity of that statement was enough to bring unexpected tears to her eyes.

"Thank you," she said, hoarsely.

He took a swig of coffee, allowing her to regain her composure, and thought about what he needed to tell her.

"I won't pretend to know how it must feel to have lived with hatred for fifteen years," he said eventually.

"Hatred?"

Ryan nodded. "You know what I'm talking about," he said deeply, commanding her attention. "The festering, fulminating, all-encompassing hatred we feel towards the person who's stolen the one we loved. It's a fungus, Mel, a gangrene that eats away at your heart, body and soul, if you let it."

She said nothing, but her eyes shone with understanding.

"Like I say, I don't know what it's like to live with that for fifteen years; my hatred for Keir Edwards—or, let's give him his proper title, shall we? My hatred for 'The Hacker', was instantaneous, a blue-flamed, white-hot anger that led me almost to kill the man and take an eye for an eye. I had my hands around his throat…I came close to taking a life, that day."

He paused to take another drink.

"At least you knew who he was," Mel muttered. "You had a face. A name."

He nodded slowly. "Is that better?" he wondered aloud. "I suppose so. I had a name and a face to be angry with, even when so-called justice was done, and he was put behind bars. But it doesn't end there, Mel. One of these days, you'll have a face and a name to transfer all the anger you've been holding on to, but it won't feel better. It'll never feel better, until you forgive yourself."

She gave a bitter laugh, and took a small sip of coffee, surprising herself by then taking a long gulp of the warming liquid.

"Forgive myself?" she said, affecting an air of bravado. "I didn't do anything wrong."

Ryan's lips twisted. "I know that, and I know you know it, too—logically. But the heart and the mind are two different realms, aren't they?"

Again, tears clouded her eyes, and she blinked them away.

"You can talk to me, if you want to," he said. "I could write a pamphlet all about sibling guilt."

She gave him another reluctant smile.

"Gemma..." She cleared her throat. "Gemma was my twin, my look-a-like, until I reached an age where I wanted my own clear identity. I didn't want to look like her and, since I'd never be as smart or as good as her, I concentrated on being the opposite of those things."

Ryan reached idly for his sandwich and took a bite. A moment later, she mimicked the action, fiddling with her plate while her mind was far, far away in the past.

"She would never have gone out clubbing, the night she was abducted, if it wasn't for me."

She spoke the words as if they were a universal truth.

"I see," Ryan said, chewing thoughtfully. "So, your sister didn't have a mind of her own?"

Melanie was defensive. "Gemma was very intelligent," she snapped. "Of course, she did."

Ryan nodded. "So, you bullied her into going?"

Again, Melanie was shocked. "I would never have bullied her!" she said, gripping the bacon sandwich between her fingers so that a bit of ketchup oozed out. "Gemma asked to come with me, that evening."

Ryan took another bite. "So, what gives you the right to appropriate her agency?"

Melanie stared at him. "What? I'm not, I—"

"From what you've told me, Gemma made the last independent choice she wanted to make, which was to spend time with her sister, doing something new and fun for her," Ryan said, mildly. "It ended badly, not because of anything you or she did wrong. Until then, she was having fun, wasn't she?"

Melanie remembered the laughter, the dancing.

"Yes," she whispered. "But we were underage. We shouldn't have been there at all—"

"Mel, what do we always say about 'victim blaming'?" he interrupted. "We're trained never to do it, because of the simple fact that it's never a victim's fault if someone hurts them. It doesn't matter if you were wearing nothing but underwear, it doesn't matter if you were sixteen or eighteen, or if Gemma didn't usually go clubbing. None of those facts are relevant to the plain and simple truth, which is that somebody else decided to take something that wasn't his and to destroy it. You aren't responsible for the actions of others."

"I should have been with her," she said, brokenly. "It should have…should have…"

"Been you?" Ryan said softly, and set his sandwich back down on his plate. "I know that feeling, and it's a hard one to shake. When we love someone, we'd put ourselves in danger to save them; we'd gladly swap places. But, let's imagine that Gemma's sitting on that chair right beside you."

Melanie looked at the empty seat, in reflex.

"What?"

"Just play along," he said. "It's a little exercise a psychologist friend of mine taught me, once. Close your eyes and imagine Gemma's right there, sitting beside you."

She sighed but did as she was told. To her surprise, after a few seconds of concentrated effort, she could almost feel her sister's presence.

Her eyes flew open.

"Now, ask Gemma whether she would want to swap with you," Ryan said quietly. "Ask her if she blames you."

A single tear trailed down her cheek, but Melanie turned back to the empty chair.

"Do you?" she whispered.

No, came the silent reply.

Another tear spilled, and Ryan handed her a napkin.

"Love runs both ways," he said. "Gemma wouldn't have wanted to see you suffer like this. She loved you because you are who you are—a strong, capable person."

Melanie met his eyes. "I don't know how to work with the anger," she admitted.

"Channel it," he replied, with absolute conviction. "Your body's running high on too little sleep, too little energy and too much cortisol. Do you want to be weak, when you finally track this arsehole down? Do you want him to see you beaten?"

Her eyes flashed, and it was all the answer he needed.

"Use the gym, pound the pavements…speak to Frank and he'll show you how to use violence with precision in boxing, down at Buddle's Gym. Speak to Mac, and she'll show you how to kick-box the feelings into touch. Speak to Anna, and she'll tell you how to use the past to inform the present. Speak to me, and I'll tell you anything I can, I'll do all I can to bring him in and put him behind bars. But, above all else?"

She waited.

"Above all else, speak to Jack. He loves you, and wants to help."

Melanie gave him a tremulous smile, nodded, and then looked down at the sandwich she still held in her hands. She raised it to her lips and began to nibble the edge, while her stomach gave an enormous rumble of relief.

"I think your alternative therapist has a point," she said, after a minute or two. "This stuff has magical healing powers."

Ryan smiled. "Just don't tell Frank I said that," he replied. "I'm still not forgiven for the time I abandoned half a stottie, up at Seahouses."

Mel was astounded. "You…left half a stottie?"

Ryan swore beneath his breath. "Not you, as well!"

Mel shook her head. "You either commit to the stottie, or you don't," she said, gravely, and took a huge bite of her own to prove the point. "It's a way of life."

He grinned, wondered briefly what his old southern mates would make of his new life, up north, and then polished off the last bite with a bit of a flourish.

It seemed he'd chosen to commit.

CHAPTER 10

While Phillips peeled off his defective bike shorts to the accompaniment of whoops and cheers from his fellow police officers, fifty miles further north Anna sang along with Julie Andrews to *Supercalifragilisticexpialidocious* while she and Emma pootled along the winding country lane towards Bamburgh. It was a road she knew like the back of her own hand, that part of the county being only a few miles south of Holy Island, where she'd been born and grew up. During her early childhood, there had been many times when her own mother had driven Anna and her sister, Megan, along the same road to have a picnic on Bamburgh's sandy beach, recounting tales of Vikings or of Grace Darling, the young lighthouse keeper's daughter who'd risked her life to save others, when the *Forfarshire* was shipwrecked in 1838. Now, a small museum had been set up in Darling's name in the village, not far from where she'd been laid to rest in the little churchyard of St. Aidan's, and Anna often made a point of laying some flowers at the site whenever she happened to be in the area.

She squinted against a sudden shaft of sunshine that broke through the clouds far above, enjoying the play of dappled light against the windscreen as it filtered through the passing trees, and when they rounded another hedgerow the castle came suddenly into view, a mighty, golden edifice that must have struck fear and awe into the hearts of any would-be invaders.

"Look at that, Emma," she said. "It looks like a fairy tale castle, doesn't it?"

"Ooh," her daughter replied.

Anna smiled and continued towards the village, slowing the car as they reached Front Street. The village was approached via three main routes: Lucker Road, running from the A1 dual carriageway to the west; Links Road, running parallel to the coast and connecting Bamburgh to the village of Seahouses, to the south; and Radcliffe Road, which ran parallel to the coast in a northerly direction. The outskirts were mostly residential, with the occasional stone-built property and a couple of smaller modern developments, but the centre was blessedly unspoilt, its roads lined with quaint cottages arranged in a triangular formation around a central green. There was a smattering of independent shops, a tearoom by the name of The Copper Kettle, and a couple of good restaurants, alongside a few pubs that doubled as inns for passing travellers—but the bulk of the real estate was devoted to the many holiday cottages and guest houses serving the tourist population that landed on the tiny village all year round, to enjoy its superior setting and bask in its history, which seemed to be a living, breathing thing in that part of the world.

Rather than heading towards the castle, which stood to the east of the village, Anna steered her car north along Radcliffe Road, slowing as she reached a set of pillared gates on the very edge of the village, surrounded by open farmland on three sides. A battered wooden sign swung from an ornate metal bracket and read, 'SANDY DUNES GUEST HOUSE', which was certainly an apt name, given the property's idyllic setting overlooking a long stretch of dunes and, beyond them, the sea. Turning through the open gates, Anna followed a curving, tree-lined driveway until she reached the main house, which stood well back from the road and was resplendent in the morning sunshine. It was Georgian, built of fine sandstone that had mellowed with age and the effects of the salty air, and boasted large windows to maximise the views on all sides. Ivy and wisteria grew on the front of the house and over its entrance portico, while the gardens had an overgrown, romantic feel—partly owing to a lack of management, and partly owing to its owner's deliberate preference for wild, untamed things. A stone archway on the far side of a semi-circular driveway gave access to a couple of stone cottages, for the gardener and other staff, plus a discreet car parking area that was currently empty—Angela's guests having decamped for the day to begin excavation works at the castle—aside from a solitary old Land Rover in an unforgettable shade of mint green that belonged to the lady herself.

It was a grand old dame, Anna thought, much like its owner.

It was a house she had never visited before, but had glimpsed from the road and frequently admired, so it was with some degree of interest that Anna approached the imposing front door, with Emma tucked snugly against her hip.

There was an old-fashioned bell pull, which she tugged and heard the corresponding jingle of a bell on the other side of the wall.

"Hear that, Emma? We sing about jingle bells at Christmas, don't we?"

When nobody answered, Anna let a wriggling Emma stand on her own two feet, took the baby's hand in a safe grip and tried the bell pull once more.

Still no answer.

She tried the handle, in case it was left on the latch for paying guests to come and go, but the door wouldn't budge. It was a large house, run by an old lady, so it was possible Angela hadn't heard the bell or was enjoying the sunshine in her back garden, Anna reasoned. So she gave Emma's hand a gentle tug and they followed an attractive flagstone pathway around the perimeter, passing beneath the stone archway as they made their way around to the back. As Emma's little feet stomped the ground, Anna glanced idly through ground floor windows, smiling at the amount of chintz and lace in each of the formal rooms, which were high-ceilinged with an abundance of character features and kept as neat as a pin.

"Nearly there," she said to the little girl. "Would you like a carry?"

"No," Emma said, clearly, and Anna smiled. Not only was her daughter a beautiful little black-haired carbon-copy of her father, it seemed she had inherited his independent streak, as well.

She'd look forward to the teenage years…

Eventually, they rounded the edge of the house and a tiered garden spread out before them, a patchwork in shades of green, punctuated by flowering plants of all shapes and colours.

"Beautiful, isn't it?"

"Ah ha," Emma agreed, toddling off to pat the petals of a nearby flower. "Pretty f'ower, mamma!"

Anna smiled and lifted a hand to shade her eyes, looking out across the lawns and stone urns to see if there was any sign of Angela, but found none.

"This way, Emma."

She waited for her daughter to take her hand again, then they made their way towards a set of ornate French doors leading from the garden to the back of the house.

"Let's try knocking, shall we?"

Anna raised her knuckles to tap the wood and Emma copied, bashing her little fist against one of the lower panels.

"Careful," Anna warned her. "Not too hard!"

Emma grinned, devilishly, a trick she'd learned from her father.

"Ruffian," Anna said, playfully, and then sighed. "I think Mrs Bansbury must be out. We'll have to come back another time."

Emma tapped on the pane again, this time with her pointing finger.

"There!"

"What's there, sweetheart?"

"There," Emma repeated, and tapped a bit harder, rattling the door.

"Emma, I've already told you to be gentle," Anna chided, coming down to the little girl's height to prise her fingers away from the glass. "I don't want you to hurt yourself—"

She trailed off, having seen what her daughter had seen through the grubby glass panel.

The French doors led directly into a sunroom, but the doorway connecting that room to the hallway stood open and, through it, she could see the sweep of an elegant staircase. At its base, there was what appeared to be a jumble of clothes… but it wasn't.

It was a person.

Crumpled like a sack of potatoes, limbs twisted at abnormal angles.

"Oh, God," Anna whispered, and automatically tried the door but found that locked, too.

"God," Emma repeated, clear as a bell. "What's God?"

Anna was in no mood for a theological debate.

"I'll tell you later," she said, scooping Emma up into her arms. "Mummy has to make a phone call, now. Let's go."

Anna turned, intending to hurry back to her car and put a call through to the emergency services, and almost barrelled into a man rounding the corner of the house. He was around sixty or seventy, with the rugged, weather-beaten look of one who had spent much of his life outdoors.

In his gloved hands, he carried a shovel and some thick bin liners.

CHAPTER 11

Shortly after ten o'clock, Ryan, Phillips and MacKenzie assembled themselves in one of the smaller meeting rooms at Police Headquarters. Lowerson had elected to remain with Yates. The room was stuffy, the main window having been painted shut by a team of local authority decorators whose instructions had obviously been to, "slap the paint on, pronto," a fact made worse by a general odour of strong chemicals wafting from the carpet-tiled floor, which had recently been fumigated.

"It's hotter than Satan's oxter in here," Phillips declared.

Ryan rifled through his mental file of 'Frank-isms' but came up with nothing.

"I give up," he said. "Satan's—what?"

"Oxter," Phillips repeated, obligingly.

Ryan made a silent appeal to MacKenzie, who merely smiled.

"In Ye Olde Geordie, it means, 'armpit'," she explained.

"What else would it mean?" Phillips asked, and gave a funny little shake of his head, no doubt lamenting Ryan's lack of education.

"Well, obviously, now you mention it, it's very obvious," Ryan said. "Just like, 'gadgie' and 'radgie', 'netty' and 'spelk'... nothing so simple to understand."

"Exactly," Phillips agreed. "That gadgie'll be geet radgie if he gets a spelk while he's on the netty—easy-peasy."

Ryan stared at him, wondering how many more years it would take before he was proficient in the language thereabouts.

"You're saying that—a man?—will be...very angry if he... gets a splinter while he's on the toilet?"

"Isn't that what I just said?"

Ryan gave up on any further debate about semantics. "Mac? Talk to me—preferably, in a language we can all understand."

She decided it probably wasn't the moment to try some of her old Gaelic.

"Right enough," she said, and drew out her notepad. "Well, as you both know, the investigation into Gemma Yates's death has been formally linked to our ongoing investigation into the kidnapping and attempted murder of Lawana Chen—code-named 'Woman A', for her own protection, while the Ghost Squad investigation is ongoing."

She referred to the internal investigation that had been launched following Lawana's recovery, alongside twenty or so other women—including her daughter, Achara, code-named 'Woman B'. They'd been trafficked into the United Kingdom by a ruthless gang whose tentacles had spread into the corridors of several police command divisions, including their own. While that investigation continued, and the

CPS continued to prosecute a wide network of dangerous men and women involved in the racket, it was far safer for Lawana and Achara to remain anonymous.

"The location of Woman A and Woman B is known only to a small circle of people, including ourselves and their trauma counsellor," she continued. "We want to keep it that way."

The other two nodded.

"Do Jack and Mel know?" Phillips asked.

MacKenzie pulled a face. "Jack does, because he's on the task force," she replied. "But he hasn't told Mel, and he won't. It's best to keep things very separate, and she has no need to know."

"Good." Ryan approved. The last thing he needed was for Melanie to take it upon herself to pay Lawana or Achara a visit, in a misguided attempt to help the investigation.

"How're they doing?" Phillips asked, thinking of mother and daughter. "They'd been through hell and back, the last time I saw them."

"Better," MacKenzie was pleased to report. "Unfortunately, Lawana's physical rehabilitation is taking longer than expected, owing to the extent of her spinal injuries, but, really, it's a miracle she can walk at all."

"She's a fighter," Phillips said. "What about the lass?"

Achara had suffered a different kind of trauma, but no less horrifying.

"We managed to find a Thai-speaking counsellor," MacKenzie said. "She works with both women every week and, judging from her reports, it seems the biggest challenge for both of them is battling severe post traumatic stress."

"Understandable," Ryan said.

"Very," she agreed. "But it makes interviewing them quite difficult. The language barrier can be overcome, but both women are suffering from short-term memory loss associated with severe trauma—especially Lawana, which is a shame, considering she's our star witness."

Lawana Chen was the only living person to have seen their unknown perpetrator, a man the press had already christened, 'The Shadow'—as if he were a superhero and not a violent killer.

"That could change, in time," he said.

"Maybe," MacKenzie replied, without much enthusiasm. "I had a word with her therapist to ask that very question. She doesn't think they've made much progress unlocking Lawana's memory in the months that have passed since her ordeal; in fact, she's of the opinion Lawana's regressed even further, as a kind of defence mechanism."

Ryan rose from his chair, stretching out his long body to shake off the disappointment. It was hardly Lawana's fault that her mind chose not to remember the horror it had experienced; it wasn't her fault that their hopes rested upon her to remember the tiny, seemingly insignificant details that could make all the difference. But, set against that, all Melanie Yates's hopes rested on the woman being able to remember those details, so she could try to narrow down an otherwise insurmountable search for a man who might as well have been a shadow, for all they knew of him.

He stuck his hands in his pockets, and reverted to the things that had always served him well in a difficult investigation: process, diligence and tenacity.

"Okay, so we've hit an obstacle," he acknowledged. "But there are things we can do to help unlock Lawana's mind. If she'll allow it, I think we should contact Gregory again and ask for his help. I've never met a head doctor as good as him."

"Doctor Gregory?" Phillips said. "Aye, he could be a good shout. Worked wonders with Samantha, when she couldn't remember what happened to her ma."

MacKenzie nodded her approval, too. "He's a safe pair of hands," she agreed.

"I'll contact him," Ryan decided. "Let's hope he's in the country."

"Bit of a gad-about, isn't he?" Phillips joked. "Must be alreet for some…"

"I think his last 'glamorous' trip took him undercover inside a remote mental institution in the Catskill Mountains," Ryan said. "I'm not sure it was all fun and games, Frank."

"Aye, well, I'd take it over having to supervise a gaggle of teenage lasses down at the school disco," Phillips said, and folded his arms across his chest defensively. "Makin' small talk with parents you don't know, havin' to nod and smile while they're gannin' on about playin' golf, who's got this car or that car, who's havin' a bleedin' affair with so-and-so, don't you know…it's enough to send anybody over the edge."

"Everyone has their own vision of hell," MacKenzie said, with a small chuckle at her husband's pained expression. She wondered what he'd have to say when he found out there was another school social coming up, and she'd signed them both up to be parent helpers…

"At least there won't be any more for a while," he was saying, with obvious relief.

She looked down at her notepad, to hide a smile.

"Coming back to Lawana," Ryan said. "What has she been able to tell us, so far?"

MacKenzie took out another sheet of paper, where she'd summarised key information she'd been able to elicit from Lawana during a series of interviews held over the past few months.

"Obviously, the most damning piece of evidence is the DNA match," she said. "That's something we hold in reserve, if and when a match is flagged."

"Nothing as of Saturday," Ryan had to say.

MacKenzie shook her head.

"I have alerts set up, obviously, but I often check manually, just in case. The indisputable fact is that he just isn't on the system," she replied, with an unhappy shrug. "That tells us he doesn't have any previous."

"Also tells us he isn't a copper," Phillips remarked, and the other two nodded.

As a matter of standard procedure, every officer's DNA was stored on an internal database, which allowed forensics teams to distinguish alien DNA from that belonging to a member of an investigating team who might, unwittingly, have contaminated a crime scene. It helped with the process of elimination.

"So, we know he's kept his nose clean," Ryan said. "He's careful, probably methodical and disciplined, to have avoided detection for so long."

"Doesn't help us much," Phillips grumbled.

Ryan disagreed. "It always helps to know the enemy," he said. "The more we know of his character, the easier it will be to find him."

MacKenzie turned back to her list. "Aside from the DNA match, I've tried to build up a physical description of the perp based on what Lawana has been able to tell us," she said. "Unfortunately, the description she's given of her assailant has changed a few times—she's described him as being very tall, broad and muscular on one occasion. But, the next time I've spoken to her, she's described him as being considerably shorter, with more of a wiry, athletic frame."

"Standard problem with eyewitness accounts," Ryan said. "A victim is often left with an impression of their assailant being far more physically menacing than they turn out to be, in real life. The mind plays tricks."

"We've worked with an artist to try and put together an approximation," MacKenzie said. "It's in the file, if you want to have a look, but it's very rough. I don't think it would be good enough to use."

Ryan reached for his laptop, tapped a few keys and brought up the visual. Immediately, he saw what she meant. The lack of accurate and consistent description had made it very difficult for the police artist to produce anything they could use as a photofit, or even anything they could release to the press. To counteract the problem, several sketches had been created, bearing very little similarity to one another.

"Let's try again, after Gregory has spoken with her," he said. "Perhaps we'll have more luck once the memories start coming back."

MacKenzie nodded. "I tried focusing Lawana's mind on the room, instead of the man," she said. "She was held captive in his little bunker for over twenty-four hours, and he turned on the lights when he—ah—visited her, so there should be some scope."

"There's another characteristic we can add to our list," Ryan murmured. "Arrogance. Complacency. He was quite happy for her to see his kill room, not only because he probably enjoyed ramping up her fear, but because he never imagined she would escape. He thought he had nothing to worry about."

"He'll be worrying now," Phillips chimed in. "There's an eyewitness and a DNA match. He'll have to stay quiet for a while, or risk exposure."

Ryan strolled across to the window, and was about to pass comment when there came a brief knock at the door.

Their new DCS entered the room, bearing coffees.

"Morning, sir," Phillips said, rising to his feet alongside MacKenzie, who murmured something polite. Ryan nodded to the man, but didn't make any particular move to welcome him.

He hadn't been invited.

"Morning, all," Forbes said, in his most cheerful tone. "I thought refreshment might be in order. I'm spending the next few days getting to grips with the department's caseload, so I thought it might be worthwhile for me to sit in on a few of your briefings, if you don't mind?"

His tone suggested there should be no reason whatsoever for them to mind and, since the man was their boss, they could hardly refuse.

They settled themselves again, and Forbes took the chair Ryan had previously occupied. It was a small thing, but it was noted.

"Please, don't let me interrupt you," he said. "Carry on as you were."

He reached out a hand for the stack of papers Ryan had left on the desk in front of him, but before his fingers could grasp the pages, they were retrieved.

"Thank you," Ryan said, moving them out of reach. "I'll be glad to put together a summary note for you, following our briefing…sir."

Forbes linked his fingers, and smiled again. "Of course."

The atmosphere in the room having shifted completely, Ryan adopted a more business-like tone.

"Mac? Please carry on."

She nodded. "Ah—right. So, as I was saying, I spoke to… Woman A about the room where she was held, to try to build up a picture of her surroundings. We've had mixed success, so far."

"I understand the crime scene was largely destroyed," Forbes remarked.

"It was," MacKenzie confirmed. "However, our forensics team were nonetheless able to recover fragments of photographs and other paraphernalia they're still in the process of cataloguing and assessing."

Forbes worked hard to keep the surprise from his face. Everything should have been destroyed, but he supposed there was always a margin for error, as he'd learned to his cost.

"Were any of the photographs helpful?"

"They may be, if we can match them to any known missing persons," MacKenzie said. "The problem we have is the images are so damaged, their quality is too low to scan and run against the database digitally. Without that facility, it's a matter of manually checking them against every missing person who could be a physical match for the individual in the photograph, which is time-intensive. It's made all the harder when you consider that we don't know how old the photographs are; if we assume they're trophy images of the killer's past victims, we have no way of knowing whether those victims are more recent than Gemma Yates, or older than her. It's hard to narrow the field of enquiry when we don't know the date range of our killer's activity."

He clucked his tongue, sympathetically. "Hasn't Woman A been able to give you an accurate description?"

He was certain she'd have been able to describe him in full, nauseating detail and the prospect of imminent discovery had cost him a few sleepless nights, in the beginning. But, as the days and weeks had passed, he'd learned not to worry so much.

"We were just discussing this before you joined us," MacKenzie told him. "Unfortunately, our witness hasn't been able to give us an accurate description. Trauma has affected her memory. The best we've got is an age range between late-thirties and early-fifties."

"Quite a range," he said, and wondered whether to be offended by the fact she'd thought him somewhere in his early fifties.

"It's still something," MacKenzie said, optimistically. "We plan to keep working with her to try to elicit further details, but it's slow progress."

He sighed, as though commiserating with their plight. "The difficulty is, of course, that there are other cases to think of, and limited resources…" he said.

"We're aware," Ryan said, mildly. "We'll continue to manage our resources in the most efficient way—as always."

Forbes smiled, but it didn't reach his eyes. It was funny, he thought, how some people were more instinctive than others. In his experience, most of them didn't realise the danger until it was much too late, which had worked in his favour, time and again. But, in this case, it seemed Ryan had the measure of him from the outset. He could have no idea of the extent of his knowledge, of course, and he'd need to make sure things stayed that way. Furthermore, it was clear that preventative action needed to be taken, before the poison could spread.

Ryan must be separated from his team, and quickly.

"We managed to get a partial CCTV sighting of Woman A's assailant on the ANPR cameras outside the South Shields area," MacKenzie was saying. "Digital Forensics have worked hard to try to enhance it but this guy's a pro. He kept his head down, he covered the registration plate with mud, and the van was a standard, dark-painted transit, most likely torched by now."

Forbes almost nodded, before remembering himself.

"It confirms he's an operator," Ryan said, choosing to focus on what they did know, rather than what they didn't.

"With a man like that, how do you hope to catch him? He sounds…highly intelligent," Forbes said.

Ryan took him by surprise, and laughed. "The same way we always do," he replied, and, for an uncomfortable moment, Forbes might have believed that he knew. "We look under every stone, we speak to every possible witness, we check, then we check again and again. We never stop until we find him—and, when we do, he's going to wish he'd never been born."

Ryan said it so casually, and with such breath-taking conviction, Forbes almost believed him.

"Besides," Ryan added, for good measure. "Let's not forget we're dealing with another, garden-variety killer. The press might call him 'The Shadow' but I call him 'The Fruitcake.'"

Phillips let out a hoot of laughter, MacKenzie grinned, and Forbes took a sip of his coffee to hide the hot wave of anger that coursed through his body.

They'd see who'd be having the last laugh.

Oh yes, they'd see.

CHAPTER 12

"Who're you?"

Anna might have asked the same question, and clutched her daughter more firmly to her breast.

"I'm an acquaintance of Angela's," she said. "I was just visiting, but there's no answer at the door, and I think—I think I can see her lying at the bottom of the stairs. I need to call for an ambulance—"

She backed away from him, eyeing the shovel he still held.

"We'd better get inside," he said, leaning the shovel up against the wall to bend down and retrieve a key hidden beneath a nearby plant pot. "We can use the house phone, if need be."

Anna had no intention of following this stranger inside, especially not with Emma to think of, but she wanted to see for herself whether Angela was alive and, if not, to ensure nothing was touched or moved.

It was a quandary.

"You go and check Angela," she suggested. "Emma and I will come as far as the connecting door—I don't want the baby to see anything she shouldn't."

It happened to be true.

"All right." He nodded, and stepped through the doorway.

Anna waited until he'd moved well ahead, then followed him, keeping a sensible distance. She held Emma so that her face was turned away and watched the man drop down beside Angela's inert body. He removed his glove and pressed two fingers to the side of the woman's neck, before rearing back, as if in shock.

"She's—I think she's dead—" he intoned over his shoulder.

"Call for an ambulance—and the police, too," Anna told him, and he rose quickly to do that very thing.

After he'd disappeared through one of the doorways off the hallway, Anna took one last, thorough look at the body on the marble floor, noting the placement of surrounding furniture—life with a murder detective having apparently rubbed off—and then headed out of the French doors to retrace her steps. As she half-walked, half-ran around to the front of the house, stealing the occasional glance over her shoulder as she went, she was unable to escape the feeling of being followed.

But nobody was there.

Emma protested at the strength of her motherly hold and Anna relaxed her grip, securing the child into her car seat before racing around to the driver's side. Once inside, she activated the internal locks and fumbled for her mobile phone.

She had her own call to make.

The briefing concluded, Phillips and MacKenzie moved off with renewed gusto to find an errant killer, while Ryan remained to collect his papers, unknowing that the spider remained in that very room.

"I wondered if we might take the opportunity to have our one-to-one discussion," Forbes said, in a tone that reminded Ryan strongly of an old, unlikeable master from his boarding school days.

He flicked his gaze to a large, plastic clock on the wall.

Ten-forty-five.

"I'm sorry, I have another important meeting in fifteen minutes," he said. "I'll be happy to arrange a more convenient time with your PA."

There was nothing inherently wrong with the response, but still, the lack of deference angered Forbes.

"That's a pity," he said. "I was hoping to discuss plans for Lowerson's promotional pathway."

Ryan looked up briefly at that. "Jack is a talented detective," he said. "He could go as far up the hierarchy as he—and the powers that be—will allow."

Forbes smiled thinly. "Well, speaking as"—he paused to give a little, self-deprecating laugh—"one of the aforementioned 'powers', it seems to me to be past time for Lowerson to be thinking of going for his DS badge. Don't you agree?"

Ryan didn't blink, and merely reached for his mobile phone, which he took the time to 'unmute'.

"Jack is more than capable," he replied. "However, speaking plainly, there have been errors of judgment that have inhibited his progression. They're behind him now, I hope."

"Quite," Forbes said. "In which case, I see no reason why he can't pick things up again. I've taken the liberty of making some enquiries and, given that we're already full to brimming with detective sergeants in Northumbria Constabulary, perhaps it may be worth him considering a transfer to South Tyneside Command."

Ryan frowned, caught off-guard by the prospect of losing his friend to another police command, when his phone began to peal out a rendition of Back in Black.

"Interesting choice of ringtone," Forbes said, turning to leave. "Give some thought to what I've said, won't you?"

Ryan watched him go, unreasonably irritated by the man's odd, loping style of walk, but set it aside to take the call from his wife.

"Hello," he said, leaning back against the empty conference table. "Everything all right?"

"It's Angela," Anna said, without preamble. "She's dead."

Ryan might once have been perturbed by that sort of blunt news, but, given that death went part and parcel with the job, his tone reverted to 'business' mode. Process and procedure, facts and evidence…alongside the occasional manhunt, to keep things spicy. That was his daily grind, and he wouldn't have it any other way.

"What happened?"

"I took Emma with me into Bamburgh," Anna said. "We drove out to see Angela, as I planned, to talk about her sightings of the Pink Lady—you remember?"

"How could I forget?"

"Well, her guests were out for the day, I suppose, and there was no answer at the front door—"

"Was it locked?"

Anna paused to think. "Yes," she replied. "I tried the handle, thinking Angela might leave it on the latch during the daytime for her guests to come and go, but it was definitely locked."

"All right," Ryan said. "What happened next?"

"I wandered around to the back of the house, in case Angela was in the garden and couldn't hear me," she explained. "The weather is beautiful up here, today."

Ryan smiled, and thought of the sun bouncing off the water.

"Is that where you found her?"

"No, I couldn't see anybody in the garden," Anna replied. "I was about to leave, when—when Emma spotted her through the French windows. You can see straight through the sunroom to the hallway and that's where she was lying, at the foot of the stairs."

"Is Emma okay?"

"She's fine," Anna said, stealing a glance at her daughter through the rear-view mirror. She'd already fallen asleep in her car seat, the morning's exertions pottering around Angela's garden having taken it out of her.

All the same, Anna kept her voice low.

"Emma doesn't understand what she saw," she said. "She thinks somebody had fallen asleep on the floor, and I made sure she wouldn't see anything unsettling."

Ryan half-smiled at the innocence of children, and hoped it would remain that way for a long time to come.

"All right," he said. "Did you check the body?"

"No," Anna said. "I would have, if Emma hadn't been with me, and if I'd known how to get in the house. The back door was locked as well."

"Then, how do you know she's dead?"

"A man—a stranger arrived," she said, looking out of the car windows, in case he should loom from the shadows somewhere. "He was carrying a shovel and some heavy bin bags."

"He—what?"

"It sounds bad," she agreed. "And, I won't deny it gave me a bad moment, after seeing Angela lying there. I didn't get his name—there wasn't time—but I guess he's Angela's gardener, judging from the clothes. He asked who I was, I explained, and he found a spare key beneath a plant pot. He was the one to go inside ahead of us and check for a pulse. Then, he went off and called for an ambulance—"

And, indeed, she could see it approaching now, turning through the stone pillared gates before continuing along the driveway towards her with flashing blue lights.

"I kept a distance from him but I managed to get a good look at things, in case anything was moved after the fact."

"Cynic." He approved.

"I learned from the best."

"Look, I have to go in a moment," Ryan said, with an eye for the time. "Do you need me to head over, later? Were there any obvious signs of foul play?"

Anna heaved a discontented sigh. "That's just it," she said. "Angela looked like she'd fallen. I couldn't see any obvious signs of abuse, and there was no bloodshed—apart from a small knock on her head, which could have happened when she fell."

"Still, something doesn't feel right to you?"

"It sounds ridiculous, I know," she muttered. "It's just—Angela didn't strike me as a doddery old woman, you know? She was sure-footed, if anything, and she knew her own mind."

"It's not ridiculous, and, as far as her not being in any way doddery, I agree with you," Ryan said, remembering his last conversation with the lady. "But accidents can happen to anyone. It only takes a split second for a life to change."

Anna knew it very well, and for that very reason chose to live each day to its fullest, in the sure and certain belief that nobody could predict the future.

"Look, unless something comes to light that suggests otherwise, it doesn't look as though there's any reason to think that Angela's death was suspicious," Ryan said, walking to the door and knocking the lights off with his elbow, while his hands held case files and a phone. "Just to be sure, I'll have a word with the local police team, once they've had a chance to assess the scene. How does that sound?"

Anna nodded, and raised a hand to signal to one of the paramedics, waving them towards the front door which now stood open thanks to her gardener friend.

"Thank you," she said. "And, Ryan?"

"Mm?"

"Don't let any accidents happen to you, all right?"

"Same goes," he said. "I'll see you later."

Anna ended the call and sat in her car for long minutes, thinking of how it took many years to build the fabric of a lifetime, to fill it with memories and laughter, with tears and challenges and work and love and all the other things in between, only for it to end in the blink of an eye.

"Mamma?"

She jumped a bit, not having realised Emma had woken up. "Yes, sweetie?"

"Pretty f'ower," she said again, and pointed out of the window towards a cherry blossom tree.

Anna nodded, and resolved to think of the gift of living in the present, in that very moment with a little girl whose eyes shone with wonder.

"Yes," she said softly. "It's very beautiful, just like you."

CHAPTER 13

Ponteland

Summer 2007

Melanie Yates lay on the bed in her room, her body curled tightly into the foetal position.

Four days had passed since Gemma's disappearance from The Boat and, with each day that passed, her stomach ate more of its own flesh as worry had consumed her—body and mind. She hardly noticed, just as she didn't notice the shadows beneath her eyes, nor the fact her nails were bitten almost to the quick.

The house was silent but for the occasional crash in the kitchen downstairs. Her mother swung wildly between bouts of inconsolable weeping and eruptive anger, and their crockery had borne the brunt of it. Melanie had felt the sting of her mother's palm across her face when the police had called her parents to tell them the worst news they could ever wish to hear.

I'm sorry to inform you that your daughter has been classified formally as 'missing'.

We're pursuing all lines of enquiry...

Trite, empty platitudes designed to give hope to the hopeless. Words she would say to other families, years later, but not then.

Then, she heard the words as though from a great distance, her head fuzzy and clouded by lack of sleep and a grief that had already begun to take hold.

Would your daughter have run away? she'd heard the police ask.

No, Gemma would never have run away. The thought would never have entered her mind.

Did your daughter meet anybody—a boyfriend, perhaps?

No, Gemma had no time for boys. She gave her time to learning, to helping others, never herself...Melanie's the one who wastes her time with boyfriends.

Was it usual for her to go clubbing, underage? they'd asked, and Melanie had heard her mother's reply, from behind a closed door.

Gemma would never have done it. Never! It had to be Melanie who encouraged her. It must have been her fault.

It must have been her fault.

Must have been her fault...

"Must have been my fault," she whispered, and closed her eyes as her body began to cramp, bile rising to her throat as it tried to reject the unpalatable truth; the certain knowledge of what was to come, and who was to blame for it.

Her sister was dead, and there was nobody to blame but herself.

The Family Room at Northumbria Police Constabulary Headquarters in Ponteland was painted in a shade of taupe that was, no doubt, designed to be inoffensive to the poor, unfortunate souls consigned to sit on its sagging visitors' chairs, reading the assortment of leaflets scattered on its cheap coffee table.

Grief counselling.

Yoga for wellbeing.

Church groups.

Melanie stared at the last one, her eyes burning with tears unshed, hating the dog-eared paper and what it represented, hating the room with its stench of loss and despair.

Hating herself.

She rose and walked to the window, giving her parents a wide berth, and fumbled with the catch until it flew open. When it did, she gulped in the clammy summer air and wondered how she could continue to breathe in and out when, somewhere out there, she was certain…she knew…she knew…

"Mr and Mrs Yates?"

A woman of around thirty-five entered the room, dressed in navy slacks and a plain white shirt.

Caroline Yates gripped her husband's hand like a vice, eyes wide with fear.

"I'm DCI Morrison," she said. "I'm one of the team who's been working on your daughter's disappearance."

She glanced at the young girl by the window, whose eyes were grave with a knowledge not yet imparted.

Morrison drew in a tremulous breath and steeled herself to do what must be done.

"I know that you came here today to receive an update about your daughter's case," she said, swallowing hard. "Unfortunately, in the past ten minutes, we've received a report of a body having been recovered. I regret to inform you that we have reason to suspect the body is that of your daughter, Gemma. I'm so sorry."

The girl turned away to stare blindly out of the window, while Caroline and Mark Yates stared at her, mouths gaping like fish as they tried to make sense of what she'd told them.

Mark began to shake his head back and forth in automatic denial, even while his face began to crumple. Caroline continued to stare, as great, rolling tears began to run down her face.

"Gemma. No. No. It's not Gemma."

"I'm sorry," Morrison repeated, and reached for a box of tissues, which she set on the table in front of them.

"I don't believe you," Caroline said suddenly, eyes wild with grief as she thrust upward from the chair to face the messenger, ready to kill her for what she'd told them. "I don't believe you."

"We'll need one of you to help us to make a formal identification," Morrison continued in the same gentle tone, hardening herself to the horror of moments such as these. "I wish I didn't have to ask it of you, but I do."

"Caroline—" her husband whispered, in a voice thick with emotion. "Caroline, come and sit down."

"Don't tell me to sit down!" she cried, spinning back around to face Morrison. "This—this person you've found. It must be someone else, because it can't be Gemma. Do you understand me?"

Morrison said nothing, because there was nothing she could say that could possibly take away the woman's pain.

"Yes, we'll look at the body, because I know it won't be Gemma," Caroline continued, her voice unnaturally high. "I'll do it now—"

"We'll need to arrange a time, Mrs Yates," Morrison said, and her quiet voice seemed to be the woman's undoing.

Caroline stared into the other woman's eyes, saw the sympathy, the patience, and hitched an enormous shuddering breath.

"Oh, my God," she whispered. "You're not wrong, are you?"

Again, Morrison said nothing, but she took the woman's trembling arm in a gentle grip and steered her back down into a chair, where her husband mustered enough strength to reach across to try to console her.

"How?" Caroline managed. "How—how did—how was she, when, when you found her?"

Morrison looked across to the window again, where the girl leaned against the wall, her legs having lost the strength to support themselves.

"Perhaps this conversation would be best conducted without your daughter present," she suggested.

As if coming out of a fugue state, Caroline and Mark turned their heads towards the window, then back again.

"Yes, that's a good id—" Mark began.

"No, she can stay," Caroline growled, in a tone so low they strained to hear. "Melanie should stay and hear everything you have to say."

"I really don't think that's wise, Mrs Yates."

Caroline began to laugh hysterically, through her tears. "Wise? Wise? I'll tell you what wouldn't be wise, shall I?" she snarled, rising from her chair again to prowl around towards where her daughter stood, almost cowering. "It wouldn't be wise to put yourself in a dangerous situation at all, would it? Only a fool would do such a thing, wouldn't they?"

Desolate, beyond hope, Caroline raked bitter eyes over her living daughter and saw only a visual reminder of the one she had lost.

"Gemma would never have been out at all, that night, if it wasn't for you."

There, Melanie thought. At least she's said it, out loud.

"Mrs Yates, it doesn't help to place blame," Morrison said, with a swift frown for Melanie's father, who was slumped in his chair, seemingly defeated. "In any case, Melanie wasn't to blame for what somebody chose to do to Gemma—"

"What did they do?" Caroline asked. "Tell me what they did to her."

"Mrs Yates, I think we should talk further when you've had an opportunity to deal with the shock," Morrison said.

"I want to know what happened to my daughter!" she shouted. "What have they done to her? What did they do to my baby? Tell me!"

Morrison looked away, at a spot on the wall to allow herself a moment's composure, and then looked the girl's mother dead in the eye.

"We don't know yet, Mrs Yates. We'll be conducting a thorough post-mortem to ascertain the extent of Gemma's injuries."

Overwrought, her life shattered, Caroline fell back down into the chair and wished for one thing.

Oblivion. Escape.

There was vodka at home.

She began to laugh hysterically, and Mark cast a worried glance towards his daughter.

"Melanie, love, why don't you go and—and—"

He could barely find the words.

"Come with me," Morrison said softly, and held out a hand to the girl. "Let's give your mum and dad a minute to themselves. We'll get you a cup of something sweet, and maybe something to eat. You look as though the wind could carry you off."

Melanie walked like an automaton, her face devoid of expression, her eyes dark and haunted.

At the door, she turned one last time to see her parents clutching one another, bodies racked with pain, never to be the same again.

All in the blink of an eye.

CHAPTER 14

Wallsend, Newcastle

Present Day

"I hate these rooms."

A few minutes before eleven, Melanie Yates stood by the window in the Family Room at Police Headquarters in Wallsend, remembering a time many years ago when she'd stood by another window, in another room with the same heavy, cloying air of sadness and the same shade of ugly taupe covering its walls. Then, she'd been a girl. Now, she was a woman, and told herself that her heart was not so easily wounded, her eyes not so quick to cry—and her mouth not so quick to smile, either.

"We could use a different room, if you like."

Yates turned away from the window to face Chief Constable Morrison, who'd taken the time out of her busy schedule to pay the Yates family a personal visit. It remained one of her greatest regrets that she—and the successive teams who took over the Gemma Yates murder investigation—had never been able to bring justice to the family. She would never forget the first time she'd met Melanie, and how she'd watched her young mind struggle to bear the weight of her parents' grief as well as her own.

She remembered feeding Melanie a sandwich, watching and waiting until she forced every morsel down, so scared was she that the girl would keel over, without anybody to care if she ate or starved herself to death as penance for the terrible crime of being a teenager, and having snuck out to go clubbing.

She'd done the same thing herself, many moons ago, but without such disastrous consequences.

"Here's fine," Melanie said, and Morrison snapped her mind back to the present. "I've been in this room dozens of times."

"Usually, on the other side of the fence."

Melanie nodded. "I can handle it."

"I know that better than most, Mel. You can handle anything life throws at you—you've been doing it for a very long time."

Mel looked away sharply, determined she would not cry.

Not here.

"I—" She cleared her throat. "I never thanked you. For your kindness—back then."

Morrison decided to cross her own personal boundary, and stepped forward to put a hand on Melanie's arm.

"You've nothing to thank me for," she said, and gave her arm a gentle rub. "I'm only sorry I couldn't—" She shook her head. "I'm sorry I couldn't find him for you, Mel. I wish the outcome had been different."

Melanie nodded. "I know. You did everything you could. They all did."

She spoke of every murder detective who'd worked the case, passing it around like a parcel, each one hoping to be lucky enough to unlock the mystery and claim the collar. She didn't know all their names; not all of them were recorded on the files. When public interest had waned, so too had resource allocation, and soon people had stopped talking about being the one to find Gemma Yates's killer and moved onto the next outrage, the next victim, consigning her sister to the slush pile.

"I know our failure was the reason you joined up," Morrison said, and Melanie didn't bother to deny it.

"I was arrogant," she said. "I thought that, if I could train to be one of you, I'd do it better. I'd be the one to notice that one significant clue everyone else had missed." She laughed at herself. "I was a fool."

"You've never been a fool," Morrison snapped, and Melanie raised surprised eyes at the tone. "Never speak about yourself in that way."

Sandra Morrison paced about a bit, noting the cracks in the walls of their 'new' building, the depressing art prints and yellowing posters, and resolved to overhaul the space to make it more welcoming. People had enough to deal with, without being subjected to grim interior design and sanctimonious flyers about the benefits of veganism and mindful sleeping.

"The years roll by, don't they?" she murmured, turning back to face the woman she remembered as a girl, who watched her with the same soulful eyes. "It seems only yesterday that we were sitting in the cafeteria together, while your parents dealt with the shock. How are they, these days?"

Melanie could have lied—she'd done so, in the early years—but there was no need to put on airs for her Chief.

"The same as ever," she said, and began to tidy the room as she talked, unaware it was a coping mechanism she'd developed whenever she was forced to think of her parents. "For more than ten years, my father barely spoke, and my mother turned to booze."

Melanie looked up, expecting to find judgment on Morrison's face, but instead found quiet understanding.

"Mum hit rock bottom," she continued. "Mostly, she functioned, but when the bad days outnumbered the 'good' ones, I suppose she had to make a choice between living or dying."

It was never just the victim who died, Morrison thought. Killers desecrated whole families.

"She got some help?"

Melanie laughed, but it was an ugly sound. "She found God."

Religion and politics were always touchy topics, especially for the British, Morrison thought. But, for her part, she'd always chosen to distinguish between religion and faith.

But she didn't bother to say that to Melanie, who'd obviously had it up to the eyeballs.

"The problem when people find God, is that they're desperate for everyone else to find him too," Melanie continued, and walked across to pour a glass of water from a nearby dispenser. She waggled a polystyrene cup, and Morrison nodded.

"Yes, please. I take it, you didn't find God?"

"I wasn't looking for him," Melanie said, and handed her a cup. "Funnily enough, I don't take a lot of comfort from kingdoms in the sky."

Morrison could imagine everything Melanie had left unsaid. The sermonizing, the relentless effort to bring her into the 'fold' of the Church, the touting of forgiveness—which would have seemed like hypocrisy, set against a backdrop of the many years when Caroline Yates had not practised forgiveness, least of all with her own flesh and blood. No amount of bake sales or collection pans for the needy could replace the years Melanie had gone without a mother's love; something she'd desperately needed, and was plain for all to see.

"The death of a child is a wound that never heals," she said, and felt a familiar, long-forgotten clutch in her chest that was pushed aside. "Everyone has their own way of coping, and a lot of people turn to faith, as you know. That's only all right if their choice causes no harm to others."

"Church or no Church, the day my mother lost Gemma, she—" Melanie broke off, suddenly unable to speak.

"She lost you, too?"

"She never lost me," Melanie whispered, brokenly. "She discarded me."

Morrison was moved to embrace the woman, to try to absorb some of her pain, but there came a knock on the door and the moment was lost.

Shortly afterwards, they were joined by Melanie's parents, by MacKenzie, and, finally, by Ryan, who apologised for being a couple of minutes late. Caroline and Mark Yates exchanged the necessary pleasantries like a pair of automatons, without any spark behind their eyes.

"I'll leave you in a moment, but I wanted to stop by and offer my best wishes to you both, once more," Morrison said. "I know your daughter's murder has seen many changes of hands, but Ryan and MacKenzie have my utmost confidence, as I'm sure they have Melanie's, too."

She paused, meaningfully, and Yates nodded.

It wasn't that she lacked confidence in her colleagues, it was that she wanted to be a part of their work.

It was her right—rules and regulations, processes and procedures, be damned.

"We're at peace with our daughter's loss, Chief Constable," Caroline said, in a placid tone that grated on Melanie's nerves. "We understand her passing was all part of God's plan."

Melanie closed her eyes.

God's plan?

"There's a reason for all things," her mother continued, and Melanie felt years of anger well up inside, white hot and ready to burst from every pore.

"There was no reason," she said, very quietly.

"Pardon?"

Their company forgotten, Melanie raised mutinous eyes.

"None of this was 'God's Plan,'" she said, firmly. "Gemma's death was the work of a psychopath, and nothing more."

Something flickered in Caroline's eyes.

"I used to think like you," she said, with a trace of pity. "I used to carry my anger on my sleeve, until I realised that everything in creation is His work. Gemma was only with us for a short time, but that was all in his plan."

Melanie felt sick, as though the room was closing in, contracting in time with her racing heartbeat.

"Why don't we discuss where we're at with the case?" Ryan suggested, keeping a sharp eye on Melanie's suddenly pale complexion. "Mel? Why don't you take a seat, here, beside me."

With the kind of natural grace that he was known for, he pulled out a chair for his colleague, set a short distance away from her parents, whom, he correctly surmised, she would not have wanted to be too near.

"Thank you," she said, and slumped onto the lumpy foam padding. "I—we—want to know what progress you've made, and what other actions you plan to take."

"Of course," MacKenzie said, taking one of the other chairs so the five faced one another in a rough circle, Morrison having excused herself to attend to other business.

MacKenzie proceeded to set out the work that had been done so far, the long hours spent re-visiting the casework.

"I understand that it will be very frustrating for you to hear that our witness hasn't been able to tell us any more about her ordeal, or give us a useful description," she said, with a sympathetic eye for Melanie, in particular.

"She's told us he's male," Melanie said, keeping a tight rein on her anger. "Hardly a revelation. Does she understand how much she could help others, if she told us what he looks like? Does she understand? Maybe she's too frightened to say—"

"It isn't that," MacKenzie said, with quiet authority, and the look she gave Melanie was similar to one she might have employed with her own daughter, when she was considering a tantrum. "Woman A is very keen to help us, and is equally frustrated by her own limitations, at the moment."

"Remember, she has her own axe to grind," Ryan added. "She wants to see this man brought to justice, just as much as you do."

"We have a plan to help her," MacKenzie continued, speaking now to Melanie's parents. "We know a psychiatrist and criminal profiler by the name of Doctor Gregory. He has an excellent professional reputation and we've worked with him before—my own daughter benefited from a hypnosis session with him, and was able to remember key details about her mother's death. Our hope is that he may be able to unlock Woman A's mind and help us all, in the process."

Melanie gave a brief nod.

It was a good plan.

"When—?"

"We really don't see any need to continue with this, any further."

All eyes turned again to Caroline Yates, who reached across to take her husband's hand, giving the impression of a united front—though the man said not a word.

There was a short, awkward silence, during which Melanie stared at her mother with frank disbelief.

"Do you mean, you'd rather not attend any further briefings like this?" MacKenzie enquired, politely. "Of course, we appreciate these can be triggering, so we fully understand if you'd rather not."

"No, we mean that we're prepared to drop the investigation, altogether. Whoever killed our daughter is unlikely to be found, after all this time, and, you said yourself, the DNA evidence has elicited no identity match."

"Mum, please, don't give up—" Melanie whispered.

But Caroline wasn't listening. "I'm sure you're all very good at your jobs," she said, with a smile for the officers in the room, except her daughter, whose eyes she avoided. "However, as the Chief Constable said from the outset, many, many others have tried before you, and, without wishing to be rude, why should you be so different?"

She shook her head, and reached for her bag, preparing to leave. Her husband noted the cue, roused himself enough to let out a resigned sigh, and began shrugging into his jacket.

"For many years, we waited for a phone call that never came," Caroline explained, rising to her feet. "We waited by the phone, day after day, hoping to receive the news that he'd been captured. It never came. I refuse to carry on in that terrible purgatory—and besides, we've already forgiven him his sins, haven't we, Mark?"

Her husband neither confirmed nor denied, but his tired, myopic eyes slid across to where his daughter eyed him with open contempt.

"Your mum knows best," he muttered. "No sense in raking everything up, again. Why not let sleeping dogs lie, eh?"

His lined face appealed to her, his eyes begging her to agree, to keep the peace between them all.

Melanie had reached her limit. "You want to give up? Fine. That's fine," she told them. "But I haven't given up; I'll never give up trying to avenge Gemma."

"Perhaps that's your own guilt talking," her mother said, and silence fell upon the room.

Ryan opened his mouth to defend his friend, but MacKenzie laid a hand on his arm. This fight went deep, to the very core of the Yates family, and it was for Melanie to decide how and when to end it.

Across the room, Yates nodded slowly.

"I'm well aware who you feel is to blame for that night," she said. "You've spent a very long time making sure I'd never forget it, haven't you?"

Caroline looked at her daughter, then away again. "Don't be ridiculous. I'm sure you're embarrassing your colleagues with all this nonsense."

"Am I?" Melanie laughed shortly. "Well, we can't have that, can we?"

"Would you like us to give you some time alone?" MacKenzie asked.

But Mel shook her head. "I don't think there's anything else to say."

With that, she turned and left.

CHAPTER 15

DCS Forbes found Melanie Yates outside the fire exit, on the far side of the building.

She was seated on the floor, knees bent with her head resting against the exterior wall. Her arms hung limply at her sides, giving an overall impression of defeat.

Vulnerable. Alone.

Just how he liked his women.

"DC Yates?"

Her body jerked, and she would have scrambled to her feet, but he held up a hand to stop her.

"Please, don't let me disturb you," he said quickly. "I came out for a bit of air, myself. This job can get on top of all of us, sometimes."

Mel looked into his eyes, searching for any sign that he was being disingenuous, but found nothing but open understanding.

"Yeah…I suppose it can."

He took a step closer, tucking his hands into the pockets of his trousers.

"I gave up smoking a while ago," he lied, never having touched a cigarette in his life. "But I still like to pop outside for a notional fag break, from time to time."

She gave him a watery smile. "I tried a few, when I was a teenager," she said, remembering. "Glad I didn't bother, in the end."

He waited a beat, listening to the faraway sounds of the city, before speaking again. "Rough morning?" he asked kindly.

Melanie didn't know why she found it so easy to talk to him. By rights, his position alone should dictate a strictly professional footing, perhaps with the occasional pleasantry exchanged in the corridor. But their new DCS had an unassuming, unthreatening air about him that put her at ease, and she found that she liked him all the better for it.

"I—yes. My family came in today, to discuss my sister's murder investigation."

"Of course," he said, and his voice dripped with sympathy. "That must have been difficult."

"I've had easier mornings," she said lightly, coming to her feet in one fluid movement. "But, hey. That's the job I signed up for, and it shouldn't be any different simply because it concerns my own family."

He admired her bravado, at the same time as he knew he must break it.

"We're all human," he said, and decided to take a chance by sharing something with her that could accelerate a bond.

Where there was a bond, there was trust.

And, where there was trust, the rest was open season…

"You know, I wasn't sure whether to mention this, in case it would be a source of sadness to you," he began. "But, as we're speaking of your sister's investigation, I should tell you that I was one of the detectives who worked on it, back in the early days."

"You were?"

He nodded, and it happened to be true. He'd made it his mission to be assigned to the case, and had taken every opportunity to derail pertinent lines of enquiry.

"Not for very long," he added. "A promotional opportunity took me away from Northumbria down to Thames Valley, but for a couple of months I worked alongside everyone else to try to find the man who killed her."

She looked out across the car park to the Pie Van, where an orderly queue was already beginning to form ahead of the lunchtime rush for pasties and hot beef sandwiches.

"Thank you for trying," she said, laconically.

He watched the play of emotions on her face, and felt the old need rise up. He imagined taking her there, crushing her against the wall or dragging her to the floor.

Patience, his mind whispered.

"I sat in on the briefing today," he said instead, and his voice betrayed nothing of his inner thoughts.

She wondered how many more members of Northumbria CID, besides herself, would have access to the investigation.

"I was surprised not to see you there."

Her head whipped around at that.

"There are…good reasons why I can't be involved," she reminded him. "Legally."

He raised an eyebrow, and took another step closer, so they stood only a metre or two apart. Close enough for him to smell her skin, and imagine…

"Well…we all know there's a difference between following things to the letter, and being seen to follow things to the letter."

She didn't know how to respond to that, having heard the opposite viewpoint from Ryan, only that very morning. Yet here was a man more senior, more experienced in the police hierarchy, telling her that exceptions could be made from every rule.

It was beguiling.

"Ryan is a good detective," he tagged on, reluctantly.

He knew they all worshipped the man as though he was a demigod, so he might as well play along. That way, it would seem that neither of them would want to go against the mighty Ryan's wishes.

"It's his job to make sure things are kept ship-shape, and I wouldn't have it any other way. But, you know, I come from a different school of thought."

She waited.

"I believe in taking an eye for an eye," he said. "If it were my sister who'd been killed, I'd want whoever did it to feel the same pain—not to have an extended holiday in a prison somewhere, where he'd probably get off early for good behaviour. I'd want something much more…final."

She'd thought about it, many times.

"Look," he said, keeping his voice low and conspiratorial. "What if I kept you in the loop—privately of course?"

She searched his face again, like a wounded animal looking for another trap.

"Why would you allow me to see the file, sir?"

"Because I'm a fair man, or so I like to think," he said, and his fingers itched to touch her. To hold her.

To kill her.

"I would be so grateful," she said. "I'm going mad, wondering and hoping…not knowing…"

"Perhaps the team could use some fresh eyes on the facts, eh? Sometimes, you need to be especially invested in a case to bring it to its just outcome."

She smiled for the first time in a long while, and she'd never know what it cost him not to act, then and there.

"Thank you, sir. I won't forget this."

He nodded. "We'll just keep it our secret," he said.

"Mel—?"

They both turned as the external door opened again, and, this time, it was Jack Lowerson who stepped out into the shade of the early afternoon.

"Oh," he said, catching sight of the superintendent. "Sorry, am I disturbing a meeting?"

"Not at all," Forbes trilled, and congratulated himself on his restraint in not reducing the young man's face to a bloody pulp. "We were just talking of this and that. Police philosophies, and such."

He exchanged a knowing look with Mel, and, to her shame, she smiled again, already a co-conspirator to the deception.

Love makes you do foolish things, and she'd do anything for Gemma.

"Well, it's lunchtime, so I'll leave you two to enjoy your break," he said, and turned to leave.

After the fire door had clicked shut behind him, Jack took Mel's hand in his own.

"I was looking for you everywhere," he said, rubbing her cold fingers between his own. "Mac said the family meeting was difficult?"

"I see that gossip travels fast," she snapped.

Lowerson frowned. "She didn't mean it like that, at all," he said. "You know Mac isn't like that. She only mentioned it to me because she was concerned about you."

Mel looked down, and then away. "I know," she said wearily. "I know people are worrying about me."

"Don't you think we have a right to?" he asked, carefully. "We love you, Mel, and this is one of the hardest times in your life. Please, let us help you."

She turned to him suddenly. "Jack, if I asked to see the file—not to do anything with it, just to see it…maybe to work on a few things by myself…would you let me?"

He was shocked. "Mel, you know I couldn't do that," he said, shaking his head in confusion at her apparent loss of reason. "I'll tell you about any major breakthroughs, I've already told you that's allowed, but I can't give you sight of the file. You know I can't."

She moved away from him. "Fine," she said. "Forget it."

"Mel, I'm always on your side—"

"I said it's fine."

She didn't need Jack to show her the file, anyway. If he wouldn't help her, she knew someone else who would.

CHAPTER 16

After learning that the enigmatic Doctor Gregory was in London, for the time being at least, Ryan arranged for him to pay them a visit as soon as possible. Following that, he dealt with the management of several other major crime investigations, mediated the usual staff squabbles, signed off leave requests and absence forms, before finally settling down to do a bit of research on their new superintendent.

A cursory online search for 'Andrew Forbes' elicited several puff pieces in the local press, detailing his past heroics and commendations, although nothing lately as he'd risen up the ladder and was no longer responsible for the kind of infantry work that would necessitate him dealing with cases on the ground. Now, Forbes was the man behind the microphone, the one in a dress suit with a serious face for the cameras and an air of quiet confidence designed to reassure the public.

"Boo!"

"Hello, Frank."

Phillips sank down into an empty chair. "How the heck did you know I was coming? I was tiptoein' all the way across the room…"

Ryan snorted. "I've heard quieter herds of stampeding elephants," he said. "Besides, I can smell that beef and onion pasty a mile away."

Phillips cursed his love for meat and gravy, and the spent packaging in his jacket pocket that gave him away.

"You know it's my only weakness," he said.

"Uh huh. Haven't you got any work to be doing?"

"It's comin' up to four o'clock," he said. "It's my turn to collect Samantha from school today, so I'll be headin' off shortly. She's had a dress rehearsal for the school play."

Ryan paused to ask the question Phillips was obviously waiting for. "Who's she playing?"

Phillips' face lit up with pride. "She's goin' to be Juliet." He beamed. "The lead part! Isn't it grand?"

"That's wonderful," Ryan said, and felt a similar pride for the little girl with red hair and dimples. "Who's playing Romeo?"

Phillips' smile slipped, little by little. "I hadn't thought of that."

Ryan rolled his eyes. "Here we go…"

"Aye, and Romeo & Juliet's a bleedin' romance, n'all!" Phillips blustered. "Well, all I can say is whichever little whelp is hopin' to steal a kiss from my lass can just think again…"

"I'm pretty sure, at their age, it's all very basic acting," Ryan said, to assuage his fears. "They're probably studying Shakespeare in English class. It'll be very innocent…"

Phillips rubbed the stubble on his chin, wearing the same concentrated expression he might have worn had he just faced a hardened criminal.

Eventually, he let out a harrumph.

"Feels like, everywhere I turn, there's some little snotty-nosed kid sniffin' round. Take last weekend," he said. "We popped over to the stables, as usual, so she could muck out and have a ride of her horse, Pegasus."

"What's wrong with that?" Ryan asked.

"Nowt's wrong with that," Phillips said. "But, as for that stable lad, who keeps on tryin' to show her this move and that move, tellin' her all there is to know about horses and ridin'…well, we've all read Jilly Cooper."

Ryan hadn't had the pleasure. "The author?"

"Aye, you know the one."

"I do, but I haven't read anything of hers, yet. Is it good?"

Phillips remembered a very pleasant weekend lost in the pages of Riders, many years ago.

"Aye. Well. That's another conversation. Look, the point is, it's all about…I mean, well…it's all about…"

"You can say it…" Ryan laughed.

"Sex!"

"Ah. You're worried that she'll find out about S.E.X.?" Ryan teased him, in a stage whisper.

"Aye! No! I mean, well, it's normal and all that," Phillips said, growing red in the face. "We had another bleedin' letter from school, tellin' us they're goin' to be gettin' another talk about it, next week. How many talks do they need to have, eh?"

Ryan opened his mouth to answer, but Phillips railed on.

"All she needs to know is not to try it until she's thirty. No! Make that thirty-five, to be safe. I might be dead and gone, by then, so I'll not have to meet the feller."

Ryan burst out laughing.

"Alreet for you to laugh about it," Phillips grumbled. "You've got all this to come."

Ryan's smile slipped, slowly.

Emma?

No…

"That's…entirely different."

Phillips waggled a finger at him. "Ahar, not so funny now, is it? Well, I'll tell you, it only gets worse the older they get. We were watchin' The Last Kingdom the other night, and she walked in right when…you know…"

"They were getting jiggy?"

Phillips pursed his lips. "Aye. Then, I was tryin' to turn the telly off, and I managed to turn up the blasted volume…"

"And you were worried about her finding out about the birds and the bees from some poor stable lad," Ryan said. "It sounds to me like you and Denise are doing a pretty good job of opening her mind, as it is."

Phillips scrubbed his hands over his face, remembering the panic.

"Then, she started with a hundred-and-one questions. Asking all about what they were doin' and why they had no clothes on…"

Ryan laughed, imagining Phillips' mortification. "And you said—?"

"That they were having a 'special cuddle.'"

"A what?"

"You heard."

Ryan laughed again.

"Next thing, she started asking if everyone needs a special cuddle, especially if they're sad…I'm tellin' ya, it's a minefield!"

Ryan wondered whether to tell his friend that Samantha had probably heard all sorts of things in the playground, and was likely pulling her parents' legs, for the fun of it.

"You know, you could just try telling her the truth."

Phillips nodded miserably. "I know. Denise says we're havin' 'The Chat' tonight, and I'm in for it, if I try to duck out."

Ryan laid a hand on his friend's shoulder, as a king might have done to a warrior on the eve of battle.

"I'll pray for you."

"You don't believe in God."

"Oh, yeah. Well, good luck, mate."

As Phillips moped off towards his car, Ryan spent another half an hour looking into his boss's previous movements, but could find nothing that gave any cause for concern. On the face of it, DCS Andrew Forbes had a solid track record. Born and bred in Newcastle upon Tyne, he'd graduated from the police training academy and taken a job at Northumbria, whereupon he'd risen to Detective Constable by the time he was thirty. He'd married in his late-twenties and become a father around the same time, at which point he and his family had moved down to Oxfordshire so he could take up a promotion as Detective Sergeant, then Inspector, at Thames Valley Police. More years had passed, until he'd taken a further promotion to Detective Chief Inspector with South Tyneside Area Command, two years ago.

Now, he was Superintendent, at the age of forty-three.

Not bad.

His children were fifteen and thirteen, respectively, his wife a stay-at-home mother, though both were of school age. Ryan wasn't the man to sit in judgment about anybody's family unit, nor their personal arrangements, but he wondered whether Mrs Forbes's lack of employment was her decision, or her husband's.

Some men liked to be the bread-winner, to retain the economic and decision-making power.

But that was idle speculation.

Ryan logged off his computer, telling himself that Phillips was right, after all. It did no good to tar people with old brushes, nor look for shadows where none were to be found.

CHAPTER 17

Bamburgh Castle was glorious in the early evening sunshine.

Rays of light broke through the gathering clouds far out to sea, beaming down upon the castle's ruddy-brown volcanic stonework so that it blazed like a fiery beacon on the Northumbrian coastline. Ryan had spent enough time with a scholar of history to have picked up a few pertinent facts and, to his delight and dismay, he was happy that he could recall some of the many titbits Anna had imparted about Bamburgh over the years. For instance, as he followed the Links Road north, cruising along the coast towards the village with the castle looming up ahead, he could recall having been told that the site upon which the castle now stood was first an old Celtic fort known as Din Guarie and probably the capital of the kingdom of Bernicia during the fifth and sixth centuries. It had a chequered history, passing between Britons and Anglo-Saxons, Vikings and Normans, before falling into the hands of the English monarch in the late eleventh century. It crumbled into disrepair during the seventeenth century, but was restored during the eighteenth and nineteenth centuries, eventually being purchased outright by Lord Armstrong—the same wealthy industrialist who'd built Cragside and its surrounding forest, from nothing but moorland. Owing to its long battle history, the site was rich in archaeological pickings—not to mention shipwrecks, as with much of the treacherous coastline in those parts.

The castle grew larger and more indomitable as Ryan approached, steering his car along the road that wound past the grassy foothills at the base of the craggy mound upon which the fortress had been built. His destination was on the other side of the village, on Radcliffe Road, having promised his wife that he'd stop by the Sandy Dunes Guest House to speak with one of the local police officers who'd attended the scene at Angela Bansbury's house, earlier that day.

In and out in ten minutes, he thought. Fifteen, tops.

He'd be home in time to put Emma to bed.

When Ryan pulled up outside the handsome Georgian villa at five-thirty, it seemed that most of the village had congregated there, judging by the rows of parked vehicles occupying much of the driveway and courtyard beyond. Among them, he spotted a single squad car but no forensic vehicles, Angela's body having already been removed to the mortuary.

Slamming out of his car, Ryan paused for a moment to watch the sun setting over the distant hills, not minding the chill rolling in from the evening's fret. He stood tall and dark, his face unmoving as he allowed himself a moment's peace, and to anybody watching he might have resembled one of the many statues scattered around Angela's bohemian garden, carved from stone and mellowed with time.

The wind shook a few petals from a nearby cherry blossom tree and he smiled, catching one of them in his palm.

"Pretty," he murmured, unconsciously echoing his daughter, and took out his notebook to slide one perfect bud between its pages for posterity.

He waited until the sun slid off the edge of the Earth, then turned and made his way to the front door. He rang the bell and, within seconds, it opened.

"I'm sorry, we're fully booked."

The woman who stood on the threshold was somewhere in her forties, and possessed a round face that was, at that moment, distressed and bore the ravages of tears.

"I'm not a customer," Ryan assured her, and reached for his warrant card. "DCI Ryan, Northumbria Police. I'm here to speak with Detective Constable Reed?"

"Oh, I see. Please come in."

"Are you one of the guests?" Ryan enquired of her, as he stepped inside an impressive marble hallway and wiped his feet.

"No, I'm Angela's housekeeper, Pauline," she said, closing the door behind them. "I do a lot of the guest management for Angela…or, perhaps I should say I did…"

She looked as though she would break down again, and Ryan was swift to distract her.

"You appear to have a full house," he said, cocking an ear towards the sound of several voices coming from the direction of one of the entertaining rooms further down the hall.

"Yes, we have the archaeological team staying with us at the moment," she explained. "They got quite a shock when they heard what had happened to Angela. Such a terrible shame, her falling down the stairs like that. It's no way to go, poor old dear."

She shook her head, then the penny seemed to drop.

"I was led to believe Angela's death was an unfortunate accident," she said, keeping her voice low as they approached the living room. "But, if you're a chief inspector, does that mean…something else?"

Her hand clutched at her neck, in fear.

"It doesn't mean anything, for now," he said. "I'm here as I was in the area and happened to know the lady—briefly. A matter of professional curiosity, that's all."

She didn't appear convinced, but pushed open a panelled door to reveal a large, airy room filled with people.

"…the fact is, she could have had a heart attack and fallen down the stairs," one woman was saying. "I know a man who had a heart attack in his car and drove straight into the side of a bus shelter. It was sheer luck that nobody happened to be waiting in there, at the time."

"Well, of course, anything's possible," another was saying. "She seemed fit as a fiddle, if you ask me."

"Well, Pauline did mention that Angela had heart trouble," the other averred. "And she was a good old age…"

"I think it's best if we avoid speculation—" This attempt at crowd management came from a woman of around thirty, whose mid-brown hair had been pulled into a practical ponytail, away from a face that was obviously tired, but remained alert.

Ryan knew, simply by the cut of her jib, that she was a copper.

"Excuse me," Pauline interrupted them, and all eyes turned to the stranger by the door. "This is Detective Chief Inspector Ryan, from Northumbria Police. He's here to speak to DC Reed."

Reed, whose first name turned out to be Charlie, turned to Ryan with open curiosity, quickly masked by a professional smile.

"DCI Ryan," she said, weaving through the sofas and chairs to greet him. "Thank goodness you're here."

Her words spoke volumes, and his lips twitched.

"Would you mind if we used one of the other rooms, Pauline? We have some sensitive material to discuss—I'm sure you understand."

"Of course, if you'll—"

"Now, just a minute."

This imperious edict came from a man who was as wide as he was tall, with a wiry grey beard coating a rotund face with small eyes that were almost lost in the folds of skin surrounding them.

"I think we have a right to know if there's been anything suspicious about Angie's death."

Ryan took a step forward. "I'll be the judge of that," he said, quietly. "In the first place, you can tell me your name."

"This is Professor Alec Soames!"

This outraged outburst came from one of his archaeological colleagues, a woman of around sixty with a weather-beaten face and a pinched expression around her mouth that Phillips might have likened to a cat's arse.

"I'm sure he's able to speak for himself," Ryan said mildly. "You are?"

"JJ Thornton," she said, and paused, presumably waiting for some sort of recognition.

When none was forthcoming, her face fell into yet more hard lines.

"I demand information," Soames repeated, moving to the centre of the room, a leader to a motley crew of students and scholars who feared and revered him, in equal part.

Ryan turned to Reed, who stood beside him with the weary expression of one who'd wasted much of her afternoon placating a crowd who believed their voices to be more important than hers.

"Have these residents been informed of the tragedy?" he asked, in a voice that carried.

"They have, sir," she said.

"Have they each given their statements?"

"Yes, sir."

"Do any of them happen to be the late Angela Bansbury's next of kin?"

"No, sir," she said.

"Then there's nothing further to discuss," he said, to the room at large. "If and when we have any further enquiries to make, or information to give, you'll be the first to know."

Without further ado, he turned, leaving Pauline and DC Reed to follow—and Professor Soames and his cronies to stare after him in varying degrees of admiration and outrage.

"Thank you for agreeing to meet." Ryan was ever the professional, so the first words he spoke to DC Reed as they were shown into a small library room were an expression of thanks.

"It's no trouble," she said, although she would have to call her childminder and ask if they could spare another hour. "To be honest, sir, I don't know that there's much here of interest to you."

"No?"

"The scene was very ordinary, other than the fact Angela was found at the bottom of the stairs," she said. "The forensics team completed their assessment by early afternoon and the police pathologist gave his approval for the body to be moved. Their preliminary opinion was that it was a case of accidental death, although obviously they'll update that assessment if new evidence comes to light. All of the statements from Angela's staff and guests seem to tally, in terms of agreeing that nothing appeared out of place."

"Staff?"

"She kept a housekeeper, a cleaner and a gardener, who came in twice a week. As I understand it, Angela had this guest house as well as a number of other holiday cottages around the village, which were used as holiday lets. It was very lucrative and must have kept all of her staff busy."

That explained how she could afford to offer the guest house for free, each year, to the archaeological team, Ryan thought.

"How about the body—you said there was nothing suspicious?"

"There was a small head wound, which appeared to be consistent with the fall," Reed told him.

"Could it have been caused by blunt force?"

"I'm not a pathologist, of course, but in my opinion the extent of the injury wasn't enough to indicate the use of a weapon," she said. "As I say, it was more like a knock to the head, sustained during her fall, most likely."

"Any swelling?" he asked. "Bruising?"

She thought back, and then brought up some images taken on her smartphone.

"Here we are," she said, handing him the phone to see for himself. "There's a small amount of bruising around the site."

"Which means she was still alive when the wound was inflicted."

"Sir?"

He looked up, briefly. "Blood flow," he reminded her. "Circulation stops when a person dies, which means there would be no blood circulating around the wound to form a clot, or a bruise."

Reed nodded.

"No obvious sign of any other trauma," he said. "The body is obviously twisted, the ankle broken, by the looks of it. I agree, there don't appear to be aren't any strangulation marks or other injuries that might have been inflicted by a third party."

She shook her head. "We found no sign of any blood spatter in the surrounding area, or on the stairs," she said. "Nothing to indicate a struggle."

He continued to scroll through the images as she spoke, and made a small sound of acknowledgement. It seemed that, for once, he was going to be able to walk away from a scene without having to designate the case 'suspicious'... which made a pleasant change, he had to admit.

"What about her situation?" he asked, still scrolling. "Next of kin?"

"None that we know of," Reed said. "She was unmarried, without any children, either."

Ryan nodded. "See if you can find a will," he said. "It'll be a quick way of finding out."

Reed planned to do that very thing.

"Any reason to think somebody might have wished her harm, Detective?"

"None at this stage, sir," she replied, watching him covertly.

She had eyes in her head, and he was the best thing she'd seen in a good long while. As a single, divorced, working mother who also happened to be a police detective, her love life resembled a barren wasteland, so she told herself she had to get her kicks where she could...

Her eyes refocused and she realised, with acute embarrassment, that he'd asked her a question and was awaiting her reply.

"Sorry, I didn't catch that?"

"I asked if you knew what colour Angela was wearing, today?"

"Colour?" she parroted. "Ah, I think it was a navy cardigan over a navy top, and a long, patterned skirt in shades of green and blue."

"Nothing pink?"

She shook her head.

"Were any of the guests wearing pink when you first met them today?"

She gave him a quizzical look. "No, not that I remember, sir. Why do you ask?"

He held up a picture she'd taken of the staircase, and, at first, she didn't know what she was supposed to be looking at.

"The—the stairs?"

"There's a pink thread, or scrap of material, on the skirting board running along the stairwell—here," he said, zooming in the image to show her. "What time did you attend the scene?"

"Shortly after ten-thirty," she said, without hesitation.

"And you took these pictures?"

"Yes, I did. I arrived before the forensics team, so the pictures were taken before they or any of the guests returned to the house," she said. "If there's a thread there, it was also there when Angela fell."

He nodded.

"I wonder if it's still there now. Let's have a look," he said and, without waiting for a reply, led the way from the library towards the staircase.

Finding the hallway empty, Ryan reached for a light switch and flicked on more overhead lights, to illuminate the stairwell. Then, he retrieved a pair of nitrile shoe coverings from his jacket pocket alongside a pair of matching gloves, which he drew on, and was pleased to see Reed doing the same. Then, they made their way up the stairs, moving slowly to look for the piece of offending pink material.

After a careful inspection, they found nothing.

"The forensics team gave the all-clear, so the guests have been allowed to move up and down the area since their return," Reed said, worriedly. "Did I do the wrong thing?"

He shook his head, rising from his crouched position on the half-landing where the material had originally been.

"Not if they'd given you the all-clear," he reassured her. "If the team did a thorough job, they'll have bagged the material for the lab. Who was the Senior—Tom Faulkner?"

He referred to their most senior crime scene investigator—or Scenes of Crime officer, depending on who you spoke to.

"No, it was a woman called Nicky Duggan," Reed told him.

Ryan hadn't heard of her, which meant she was probably new to the team that very week. "Do you have her details?"

"Yes, but—" Reed thought of the time, but one look at Ryan's face told her he wasn't the kind of man to be overly concerned with nine-to-five scheduling.

"If you call her now and ask the question, it won't play on our minds all evening," he reasoned, and she had to agree with that.

Reed made the call, while Ryan took a brief tour of the upper floor of the guest house, finding most of the guest rooms locked. By the time he returned to the library, Reed had an answer for him.

"Nicky wasn't overly happy to be disturbed at home, but I begged a favour and she checked her log from today," she told him, keeping her voice low until he closed the heavy panelled door behind him. "She says there's no record of any pink material being found."

Ryan began to smile, and then let out a rich peal of laughter.

"What's funny, sir?"

"Nothing, except the fact that I'm getting complacent, in my old age. I thought this would be a simple house call, a plain, old-fashioned accidental death—terribly sad, but nothing more."

"I'm sorry, sir, but I must be feeling tired. I don't understand what difference this makes?"

"All the difference," he said, growing serious again. "It means that, between your arrival and the arrival of the forensics team, somebody saw fit to dispose of that scrap of material."

"Why would they…ah."

"Exactly," he said. "Why would they do that?"

Reed nodded. "They wouldn't, unless it was relevant."

"I need to know your movements since you arrived here," Ryan said. "I want a complete timeline, so we have an accurate window where somebody could have slipped inside and stolen evidence."

She nodded.

"I'll do it, right away."

"Oh, and Reed? I'm designating the lady's death 'suspicious.'"

"Fine," she said. "Bagsy not being the one to tell Professor Soames."

With that, she scuttled from the room and put a call through to her childminder.

CHAPTER 18

Jack Lowerson watched his girlfriend surreptitiously from the other side of the room, where he'd laid out two place settings at their dining table, lit a candle between them and had uncorked a very nice bottle of red wine. In the oven was one of Marks & Spencer's finest 'Meal for Two' dinners, which had served them well in the past.

Unfortunately, she didn't look to be much in the mood for a cosy dinner.

"Mel?"

She didn't hear him, too engrossed was she in her files, as always, so he tossed away the tea towel he'd been using to polish the wine glasses and mustered the courage to approach.

"Mel?" he repeated, softly, so as not to startle her.

She jumped, all the same.

"Dinner's ready," he said, keeping a smile pinned on his face.

If he smiled, maybe one of these days, she'd join him.

Instead, she stared at him, almost straight through him.

"I thought you might be hungry."

"I'm not," she muttered. "Thanks, though."

He supposed he should be grateful that she'd thanked him for the effort, but it was hard not to feel rejected, once again.

"All right," he said. "I'll—you know what? I'll just put it in the warming drawer, in case you feel peckish, later."

She sighed, clearly irritated by his company, and he felt angry, all of a sudden.

"You know, I'm trying my best, here," he said, between gritted teeth. "I love you, Mel, and all I ask is a bit of consideration from time to time."

"Oh, sure," she sneered, her own hurt and frustration finding an outlet—albeit, the wrong one. "So, you're just like every other man, eh, wanting a woman to fawn all over him? Well, you knew from the start, that's not me."

Her accusation was so unjust, it stole the breath from his body for a moment, until he found his voice again.

"That is deeply unfair," he said, with genuine hurt. "You know fine well I don't want you to simper over me—"

"Doesn't sound like it to me," she raged, setting the file to one side. "So, you made dinner and I'm not hungry. Is that a crime? Should I force the food down my gob, just to make you feel better?"

He said nothing, and seconds ticked by, during which time a flush crept up her neck.

She'd gone too far.

"I'm sorry, I—"

"Eat, or don't eat, it's up to you," he said, very coolly. "You're a grown woman with a mind of your own—one

I happen to admire, by the way, despite what you seem to think. I also happen to love you, despite the fact you've been bloody awful to live with—"

"I—?" She was insulted, offended, but couldn't deny the truth of it.

"Your sister was murdered, and it was a terrible thing. We all feel for you, particularly me," he continued, in the same calm tone that made even more of a mockery of her own. "I've done, and will continue to do, everything I can—whether that means trying to force feed you, so you don't collapse, or work on the cold case to try to help you find the closure you desperately need. But, remember, you're not the only one who's suffered tragedy."

Tears burned the back of her eyes, but they were tears of shame.

"What do you kn—"

She stopped herself, only a fraction too late.

"What would I know?" he finished for her. "Gee, Mel, I don't know. Maybe I'd know a bit about how it feels to have your heart devastated by the loss of a loved one. In your case, it was a sister. In my case, it was—"

"Don't say Jennifer Lucas," she muttered, folding her arms.

"I wasn't going to. If you'd let me finish, I was going to say, 'my mother.'"

She looked away, embarrassed.

"I'm sorry. I know it's awful what happened with your mother."

Lowerson's mother had murdered the woman who'd made his life, and theirs, a misery—but, instead of owning up to her crime, had allowed the world to think her own son had been responsible. His mother was serving time behind bars, now, and although she'd lost her liberty, he'd lost so much more.

"There are many kinds of loss," he said. "Every one of us has suffered; Frank lost his first wife to cancer, and mourned her for years before things worked out with Denise. Even little Samantha lost her mother, and was witness to the murder when she was only a baby. She was orphaned, Mel, which is worse than either one of us has suffered."

She opened her mouth to stop him, to stay the diatribe that was both true and justified, and which shamed her to her core, but he ploughed on, determined that she should listen.

"Anna lost both of her parents too, and was a child of domestic abuse before then. She's been attacked and under threat numerous times, since then, but she still lives her life as though it's worth living. Ryan lost his sister, and has shouldered trauma and stress every day of his working life, more than any of us has had to bear, and he does it for that reason. MacKenzie was kidnapped and almost killed, and she lives with a debilitating injury that prevents her from running as she used to, from doing a lot of the things she used to love. For years, she's battled the post-traumatic stress of being a survivor, where others weren't."

"Please," Mel begged him. "Stop."

A single tear rolled down her cheek.

"I don't know if I should," he said, pacing away from her as though he was tired of being too near. "All this time, I've been treating you with kid gloves, thinking that's what you needed. I told myself to give you time, to let you find your own way, but I see now that it's enabled you to become obsessive and downright self-centred."

She hugged her arms around herself and said the only thing that was in her mind to say.

"I agree."

He tried to hide his surprise, but failed. "You—right. Well, good." He ran his hands through his hair, leaving it jutting out at odd angles.

"I don't know how to stem the tide of anger," she said. "It's overtaken me, Jack. All I think about is killing him, making him suffer as he made my sister suffer."

He took a deep breath and let it out again slowly. "It wouldn't help," he said.

"Ryan told me the same thing," she said. "This morning, he gave me a stellar pep talk detailing all the reasons why I need to detach and, for a while, I felt better."

"What changed?"

If she'd thought about it, she'd have realised it was her conversation with DCS Forbes that changed her mood back to anger, but she didn't make the connection.

"Nothing," she said. "It's just fifteen long years of frustration bubbling to the surface, and there's nothing to be done about it."

There was one thing, she thought.

Kill the monster who lived in her nightmares.

"What if we never find him?" Jack asked her, already fearful of her response. "Mel, there's a chance we won't, which means you'd have to find a way to live with it."

She said nothing for a long moment, then shook her head slowly.

"We will find him."

She had to believe it, or lose the final part of herself to a man she'd never met.

Or so she thought.

CHAPTER 19

The next day

"I thought you didn't believe in ghosts."

Phillips made this observation from the passenger seat of Ryan's car, as they made their way along the dual carriageway in the direction of Bamburgh.

"I don't," Ryan confirmed.

"But you think the Pink Lady might have shoved Angela Bansbury down the stairs?"

"Yes."

Phillips took a sip of his tea and watched the passing scenery. "Glad we've cleared that up. Do you want me to ring for an exorcist?"

"Not unless they can exorcise the demon that's obviously inhabiting your arse, at the moment. Frank, that's criminal!"

Ryan made a point of jamming the windows down on both sides, but Phillips only gave him a sheepish smile.

"Don't blame me," he said. "It's all the cabbage Denise has been makin' me eat. Cabbage curry, cabbage soup, cabbage bloody stew…I thought she might have sprinkled a bit in my coffee this mornin', n'all."

"Well, you can tell her that she's found a new interview strategy," Ryan said. "From now on, there's no need for any fancy techniques when we're dealing with a difficult suspect; all we need to do is load you up with cabbage, send you in there with them, and lock the doors for twenty minutes. They'll tell us everything they know, just so they can get out of there."

"It's not that bad, man." But, he had to admit the fresh air was welcome.

"I've smelled corpses less pungent than your bouquet, Frank."

"It's the price you have to pay for my scintillating company."

"Scintillating, or suffocating?"

Phillips gave a hoot of laughter. "I'd say you've got bowel trouble to come, but I've got a sneakin' suspicion you're gonna be one of those jammy gits who barely puts on weight so doesn't have to think of cabbage diets—and keeps all his own hair."

He patted his own thinning mane.

"Frank, the day I willingly consent to a cabbage diet is the day they bury me six feet under."

"It might be, if you gas yourself out like I almost did," Phillips quipped.

"Just get it out of your system before we get to Bamburgh. We need to at least try to appear professional, when we interview people."

"Well, if you insist."

And thus, for the remainder of the journey, Ryan drove with his head half-hanging out of the car window, to the accompaniment of an occasional toot.

While Detective Constable Reed went about the business of finding Angela's next of kin, Ryan and Phillips relished the opportunity for a day out of the office, under the guise of interviewing those who had been among the last to see Angela Bansbury alive.

"So, you're tellin' me there's about an hour when somebody could've slipped inside the house to snaffle that bit of pink fabric?" Phillips said, as they huffed their way up a small incline towards the main entrance of Bamburgh Castle known as the 'Great Gate' and, beyond it, to the main archaeological dig site.

"Reed got there around ten-thirty, not long after the paramedics and the first responders, then the forensics team arrived at around eleven-thirty, or thereabouts. That gives about an hour's window."

"Surely, somebody would have been seen," Phillips argued. "The way Angela was lying, they'd have had to jump over her to get up the stairs and pick up that scrap on the half-landing. The paramedics were tending her, to begin with, then there were the first responders and DC Reed…"

"Actually, I have a theory about that," Ryan said. "There's a second stairwell that would traditionally have been used by the servants of the house. It runs from the utility corridor, near the kitchen, and comes out onto the first-floor landing. You can follow it up to the second floor, too. Anyway, if someone went up that way, they could double back down the main stairs to remove the material when the coast was clear for a minute or two. It's a large house, easy to get lost in, especially with various people coming and going."

"I s'pose," Phillips admitted.

"There's another theory," Ryan said. "Anna told me the gardener picked up a key from beneath a plant pot, outside. I mean to ask the guests whether any of them knew about that or, if not, how they came and went."

"They probably all had keys, or knew how to access one," Phillips said. "That still doesn't solve the problem of not being seen."

"People only stand out when they're not supposed to be there," Ryan said. "The guests had been staying there for more than two weeks; any one of them wouldn't have been out of place. Besides, the police team weren't standing guard directly over the body—they were guarding the house, so they weren't watching the stairs. Once the paramedics left, it would be easy enough for someone to slip around the back and access the house that way. They could be in and out in a couple of minutes."

"How would they get around to the back?"

"Easily," Ryan said. "You'll see for yourself how thick the woodland is along the driveway. Nothing easier than parking up on the main road, or walking from the castle, for example, then slipping inside and keeping to the shadow of the trees."

"Seems a lot of effort," Phillips remarked. "Just over a scrap of material."

"It represents more than just material," Ryan reminded him. "It may have belonged to the infamous 'pink lady' Angela was telling me about, before she died."

"Not this again…"

"I don't think she was a spirit, for God's sake," Ryan said. "But it might have been a woman dressed up to resemble a spirit."

"Or a man."

"What?"

"A man can just as easily slip on a nice little pink number and put on a convincing show."

Ryan nodded. "Fair point."

"Pity we don't know her dress size."

"Why's that?"

"So that we could try and gauge which one of them could fit into it, o' course."

Ryan grinned to himself. "I'll tell you what," he said. "You have a good look at each of them, and tell me which one you think could have worn it best."

"Cheeky beggar," Phillips muttered. "You're lucky I like you so much."

CHAPTER 20

"Quite something, isn't it?"

Ryan and Phillips stood at the very end of the West Bailey, which jutted out atop its dolerite plateau above the expanse of sand far below. Immediately to their left was another entranceway known as 'St Oswald's Gate', which was accessible via a steep climb from the underside of the castle's mount. Beyond it was the village, spread out like a model village in miniature with the bowling green and children's playground now sitting where, once, armies of men had stormed. To their right was the sea, an endless line of deep blue ocean that lapped gently enough against the beach but grew wild and unpredictable off-shore, with foaming white crests visible even from their vantage point as the waves rolled and fell as the wind whipped them to a frenzy.

"Aye, it's not bad," Phillips conceded, and Ryan smiled to himself.

In Frank's world, that was high praise. And, why not? As far as castles went, this one was hard to beat.

"Go on, admit it," Ryan said.

"Admit what?"

"Admit that, standing here, you could quite fancy yourself as one of those old kings of Northumbria," he said, spreading his arms out to encompass the views.

Phillips sniffed. "Seems like a lot of hard work, if y'ask me."

"I can see it now," Ryan continued. "King Frank of Bernicia."

"Oh aye, if you were about, I'd be more like Baldrick to your Blackadder."

Ryan laughed. "You do come up with some cunning plans," he said. "Not sure how many of them have ever worked, mind you."

"I'm a benevolent king," Phillips said, affecting a regal air. "But I sometimes make examples of particularly insolent courtiers, as a warning to the rest. Besides, I'd be Good King Frankius of Bebbanburg, if it's all the same to you."

Ryan laughed again, and made a bow.

"I grovel in mortification—my liege."

"Ah, get away with yer," Phillips said, and gave his friend a playful shove. "Howay, who're are we s'posed to be lookin' for, anyway?"

"You can't really miss him," Ryan said, casting his eyes around the bailey for any sign of Professor Alec Soames. "He looks a bit like Henry VIII, in his later years, since we're talking about kings…"

Sure enough, the very man stepped out of the clock tower, where he kept a semi-permanent office—the same one, they would later find, had once been occupied by Professor Jane

Freeman, who had come to an unfortunate end whilst sitting at the very same desk.

They decided it was probably tactful not to mention it.

"Professor Soames?"

The man looked up, seeking the source of his interruption, and frowned heavily when he spotted Ryan.

"I think he likes you," Phillips joked.

"I thwarted his attempts to fish for information, last night," Ryan explained, under his breath. "He's used to getting his own way, I think."

They wandered across to meet him, wearing polite smiles.

"Good morning," Ryan said, as they approached.

Soames looked down his broad nose—though, given that Ryan was almost a foot taller, the gesture was lost on them both.

"I wonder if we might have a word."

"I'm very busy," Soames said.

"This won't take long," Ryan told him. "Perhaps we can walk and talk."

Soames grunted, and began ambling towards the East Bailey, where they'd recently re-opened an old archaeological trench from the 1960s.

"This is Detective Sergeant Phillips," Ryan said, and Soames gave another grunt. "We'd like to ask you some questions about your movements, yesterday, and your relationship with Angela Bansbury."

Soames stopped dead and turned to them.

"I've already given an account of my movements to your colleague—whatshername?"

"Detective Constable Reed," Ryan said.

"That's the one," he said, and immediately forgot her name again. "Anyhow, I told her all about it, yesterday. Why on Earth should we have to go over it all again."

"I'm sure you wouldn't want to obstruct a murder investigation," Ryan said, very smoothly.

Soames' eyes widened, and the rolls surrounding them wobbled dangerously.

"Murder? I thought...I was given to understand Angela's death was an accident?"

"It appeared that way, at first, but evidence has come to light that warrants further investigation," Ryan said. "We'll be re-visiting everyone's statements, including yours."

"Right," Soames said. "Well, I suppose, in the circumstances, that's fair enough."

"Thank you," Ryan said, gravely. "Perhaps you'd begin by telling us how you know Angela?"

Soames scratched his thatch of wiry hair, then smoothed it back.

"Well, through the charity, of course," he said.

"The charity?" Phillips enquired.

"The Bansbury Charitable Fund," Soames explained. "Angela's family have lived in or around Bamburgh for generations, and her ancestors were wealthy merchants who bought up a fair bit of property in the village which she still retains, plus more besides, I'm sure. Anyhow, through her charitable trust, Angie supported a number of good causes, including our little research project."

Ryan made a note to himself to find out who the trustees of the charitable trust were.

"Very generous," he said, for the time being. "Do you plan to continue the excavation, now that she's passed away?"

Soames looked at him as though he'd spoken gobbledegook.

"Of course," he said. "The Trust continues in perpetuity and provides a generous annuity, the funds of which are solely used to fund our annual dig."

Ryan nodded. "What are you working on at the moment?"

"We recently re-opened an old trench that was last excavated in the 1960s," Soames explained, his natural aversion to Ryan momentarily overruled by passion for his subject. "My research has led me to believe there's far more to uncover in that part of the ground than was previously thought, so it's worth our time and effort to go over the area again."

"What do you think you'll find?" Phillips asked.

"Well, what we're really interested in is plugging the gaps in the castle's history," Soames told him. "We know quite a bit about the Anglo-Saxon history to the castle, because, back in those days, Northumbria was the largest and most powerful of all seven kingdoms. It had a natural harbour, of course, which made it an excellent site both defensively and otherwise. Ida the Flamebearer, first of the Saxon kings, laid the timbers of the first wooden stockade on the site here."

"Good name," Phillips said, and Ryan cast him an amused glance which spoke volumes.

Frank the Flamebearer.

"So, you don't know what happened after then?"

"Just the opposite," Soames said, with a hint of impatience. "We know the Danes followed, then the Normans, before it became the property of the English monarch. It was always an important border garrison, given how close it is to Scotland. It's the history prior to Anglo-Saxon times that we're most interested in—we'd like to know the extent of Roman occupation, in these parts."

"Wasn't there a roundhouse discovered here, recently?"

Soames seemed surprised that either of them would be educated enough to know about it, but inclined his head.

"The latest of many important finds."

"Coming back to yesterday," Ryan said, now that he'd given the man a good head of steam. "When was the last time you saw Angela?"

Soames puffed out his face, much like a blowfish, and let the air out again with a long whistle.

"Must've been around seven-thirty, yesterday morning," he said. "We gather for breakfast at seven, daily, and make our way here by eight-thirty, on the dot."

"All of you?" Phillips asked.

"Yes, indeed. We keep to a schedule, Detective, because we have limited time and resources. Besides, each of us is eager to discover the next find."

"How did Angela seem to you? Did she appear well?"

"Well, I suppose she did seem a little tired, but then, she was getting on a bit, and it was early morning."

Ryan nodded. "Nothing else bothering her?"

Soames' eyes frittered away, then back again.

"Nothing whatsoever," he said, and scratched his head again. "Why d'you ask?"

"Just trying to get a picture of things," Ryan said, easily. "After you'd seen her at breakfast, what did you do then?"

"As I say, we all decamped to the castle, as usual. We were gone by eight-fifteen."

"No stragglers, or anyone who said they'd catch up?" Phillips asked him.

"Nobody," Soames said, firmly. "We all have better things to do with our time than going around terrorizing old ladies. Now, if you don't mind, I really need to get back to my work."

Ryan bade the man farewell and watched him trundle towards the dig site. He waited until Soames was out of earshot before turning to his sergeant.

"What d'you make of him?"

"Bit trumped up," Phillips said, succinctly. "Got a bit of an opinion of himself, hasn't he?"

Ryan nodded. "He's got an ego, that's for sure, but he wouldn't be the first or the last."

"Didn't like it when you asked him about whether anything was bothering Angela—did he?"

"No," Ryan murmured. "He certainly didn't."

"Something lurking there," Phillips surmised.

"If there is, we'll find it," Ryan said, with a smile that was pure hunter. "Next?"

"Lead on."

CHAPTER 21

While Ryan went in search of secrets, another man stepped off the train at Newcastle Central Station in search of other kinds of secrets, hidden in the outer limits of the human mind.

Doctor Alexander Gregory was, at first glance, not dissimilar to Ryan in build and appearance; they were of a height but, where Ryan was athletic, Gregory had lost weight since his time in America and appeared more wiry, though he hoped to change that. They both had dark hair, but Gregory's was curlier, and his eyes were not blue-grey but a bold green, albeit deeply shadowed thanks to a chronic lack of sleep, which was a by-product of listening to other people's problems.

He made his way out of the station and set his leather holdall on the floor beside him, then leaned back against the stone wall overlooking the short stay car park and waited.

He didn't have to wait long.

There came a couple of swift honks.

His face creased into a smile as he caught sight of Detective Inspector Denise MacKenzie, who pulled into the car park and waved at him through the windshield of her car. He remembered her from the last time he'd visited the North East of England, when he'd worked with her daughter, and his lasting impression had been of a striking, red-headed woman with intelligent eyes, an incisive mind and a razor-sharp tongue.

Her husband was a lucky man.

He made his way towards her car and let himself into the passenger seat.

"Doctor Gregory," she said, with a bright smile. "Thank you so much for coming up at short notice."

"Hello, DI MacKenzie," he said, returning her smile. "Please, call me Alex."

"In that case, I'm Denise."

She started the car again and waited for a gap in traffic before they could get on the road. Central Newcastle was busy at that time of day, but it wasn't too long before they were zipping through the streets towards the junction that would take them north, towards an undisclosed location.

"Ryan didn't tell me very much on the phone," he said, once they were on the open road. "Aside from sending me a summary of the case, to date, and a potted history of the subject, he told me nothing of what you're hoping to unlock from her mind."

"That depends which subject you're talking about," MacKenzie said. "Our first port of call is a Thai woman known as 'Woman A', whose real name is 'Lawana'—that information is extremely sensitive, given her status."

"I understand—I signed a non-disclosure, if it helps."

MacKenzie thanked him. "It does help," she said. "There are people who would pay good money—even kill—to know her name, and where she is, now."

Gregory nodded.

"Lawana is a survivor of one of the most traumatic experiences I've had the misfortune to investigate, in all my career," MacKenzie said, softly. "She's tough, she's a fighter, but she's battered and her mind is bruised—badly. It's closed in on itself, for protection."

He nodded, understanding perfectly.

"I read about some of the details," he said. "It was horrifying."

"To be honest, Alex, a part of me would rather leave her to it, and let her mind paper over the cracks so that she can try to forget," MacKenzie admitted. "But it isn't so simple. She holds information, without even realising it, that could bring a killer to justice. At the moment, all we have is a DNA sample but no matched identity. We could wait another fifteen years before the bloke gets pulled up for something completely unrelated, and the DNA flags for a match, or it may never happen."

"And, of course, his other victim was the sister of one of your colleagues—Yates, is it?"

MacKenzie nodded. "Which brings me to your second port of call," she said. "Mel has asked if you could run a hypnosis session with her, too, to see if there's anything she remembers that she might have forgotten over time."

"I don't see why not—if she's willing."

"If anything, Alex, she's too willing."

"I see," he said, slowly.

MacKenzie chewed her lip, wondering how much to say without appearing to betray her friendship with the younger woman.

"Mel's had fifteen years of uncertainty, then her hopes were raised when we found that DNA sample, only to be dashed again when there was no ID match. She talks about nothing else, she thinks about nothing else, and it's interfering with her ordinary life. She's also talking about revenge."

"Anger is an extremely destructive emotion," he said. "It's corrosive."

She nodded. "I was angry, for a time, after my own ordeal," she said. "I felt robbed of retribution. But I had a shift in mindset—I'm still alive, and that's the only thing that matters."

Gregory nodded. "I'll see what I can do," was all he said.

He never made promises.

By the time they pulled up outside the unprepossessing, white-painted bungalow on the outskirts of Morpeth, to the north of Newcastle, the sun was almost at its peak in the sky.

"Lawana is very willing to cooperate," MacKenzie said, as she brought the car to a standstill. "However, she's also very frightened."

"I'll do my best to keep her mind safe," Gregory said. "She can only face what she chooses to face; I can't, and won't, force anything more."

MacKenzie was satisfied with that.

"She lives here in the safe house with her daughter, Achara," she continued. "They're protected by twenty-four-hour security, at Ryan's behest, and the whole building has heightened security in any event, with coded access. An English Thai-speaking special care worker lives in with them both, to help them acclimatise and take care of everyday things like shopping, until the immediate threat has passed."

"How are they both finding it?"

"They're torn," MacKenzie said. "It's been a few months, now, and Lawana wants to go home to Thailand, whereas Achara wants to stay here in the UK. It's complicated."

Gregory nodded. "Okay, good to know the background. Shall we go and meet them both?"

"This way."

They approached a pair of locked electric gates that were almost as tall as the house, and MacKenzie pressed the intercom button. After a brief conversation in which both she and Gregory showed themselves clearly for the CCTV camera, they waited while the gates opened and then waited again while they closed, MacKenzie casting a keen eye around the vicinity for any sign of a tail.

They knocked on the door and allowed themselves to be scrutinised, repeating their names once more and waiting patiently for a series of locks and dead bolts to be opened.

"Hello, Mac," the woman who greeted them said. "And, you must be Doctor Gregory."

"Hi, Carrie. May we come in?"

"Please," the other woman said, looking over their shoulders by force of habit. "Come in."

"Lawana's waiting for you in the sitting room, with Achara," Carrie told them. "She'd like Achara to be there with her."

Gregory wouldn't normally have argued with any request for a support partner during what may prove to be a traumatic session, but there were exceptions.

"How old is Achara?"

"Sixteen," MacKenzie murmured, and he gave a slight shake of his head.

"Given the subject matter, the potential content that may come out, I'm not sure it would be advisable for Achara to hear it," he said. "No matter how much she may have seen of the world herself, it's clear that her mother's trauma has been exponentially worse. There's no telling what she might say, and then we'd be adding to Lawana's secondary trauma."

"I'll explain that to her, in her own language," Carrie said. "But she knows her own mind."

Gregory smiled.

"Let's hope so."

CHAPTER 22

"What does the 'JJ' stand for?"

The woman who called herself 'Doctor JJ Thornton' sent Phillips a fulminating glare. "Does it matter?"

"This is a police investigation," Ryan said. "We don't deal in monikers."

She glared at them both, and he was forced to admit that his charm apparently didn't extend to academic archaeologists, if their track record that morning was anything to go by.

"Jilly-Jane," she said, between gritted teeth.

Both men worked extremely hard to keep straight faces.

"I see," Phillips managed, in his most professional tone. "And, are you a regular member of the dig team, or are you joining them for this summer, only?"

"Oh, I plan to be a regular member," she said, with a hint of smugness Ryan found unpalatable. "Professor Soames has assured me that I will be."

"My wife, Doctor Taylor-Ryan, tells me that you divide your time between archaeology and another job—is that correct?"

"Archaeology can be hard to break into," she said, defensively. "It's all about who you know, isn't it? I've always been held back."

Her skin bore the marks of sustained alcohol abuse, judging by the myriad of broken capillaries dancing over her cheeks and nose, and they stood out like angry scratches as her mood shifted towards brittle anger.

"Of course," Ryan said, placating her as best he could. "Could you tell us your movements yesterday?"

"I got up at around six-thirty, I went down to breakfast at seven and we all left around eight-fifteen. I was here for the rest of the day, until we heard the news about what happened to Angela, and came back here at around four-thirty. We gave our statements to DC Reed, had some dinner, and sat around the living room until you turned up."

"You're sure everyone left at the same time in the morning?" Ryan asked.

"Positive," she said, simply. "I'd know if they didn't, because I'm the one tasked with keeping a daily record of our collective efforts. It makes me aware of people and what they're doing."

"Very observant," Phillips said. "In that case, did you see anything unusual or concerning?"

She shook her head. "No, I didn't."

"Do you know of anything that might have upset Angela, or threatened her?" Ryan prodded.

Her eyes slid across to where the rest of her team were busying themselves in the trench a few yards away, then back again.

"No, nothing."

When she moved off a short time later to re-join her party, Ryan and Phillips exchanged another eloquent look.

"I'm startin' to get the funniest feelin' that some of these history buffs aren't bein' a hundred per cent honest with us," Phillips said.

Ryan smiled without any particular mirth. "You and me both, Frank. I know that history is open to interpretation, but murder seldom is."

They spent more time interviewing the remaining archaeological team, all of whom confirmed more or less exactly what Professor Soames had told them at the start of the interview process: they'd all left by eight-fifteen, the previous morning; nobody knew of anything concerning relating to the late Angela Bansbury other than her recent reports of having a daily visit from the Pink Lady; nobody had seen anything suspicious, and nobody had slipped away at any time, each of them having been present on castle grounds throughout the day, a fact corroborated by one or more of them.

Which meant they were each in possession of a rock-solid alibi.

"Well, that's that," Phillips said, as they made their way back down towards the village, around midday. "Couldn't have been any of them who pushed her."

"We don't know that Angela was pushed," Ryan said. "But we know she was serious about having seen the Pink Lady. At first, when she told me about it, I thought it was some sort of marketing ruse to cash in on the myth. However, she'd have no need to perpetuate the myth to people she knew very well, and who weren't a target audience, so the only logical conclusion is that she truly believed she'd seen the ghost."

Phillips agreed. "So, we're back to our theory about someone dressin' up as the Pink Lady to give the old woman a fright?" he said. "If it wasn't one of these lot, it had to have been one of her staff."

"Process of elimination," Ryan agreed. "Let's go and chat to them, now."

"Ah, now, just hold your horses there, son."

Ryan raised an eyebrow. "What?"

"Look around you," Phillips said, gesturing towards the picture-perfect village up ahead. "Tell me what you see."

"Ah…" Ryan shrugged, not quite sure where the conversation was heading. "I see tourists, sunshine…"

"You see ice cream and tea rooms," Phillips informed him, bluntly. "In tea rooms, there's tea cakes and scones, quiches and cakes aplenty."

Ryan folded his arms across his chest. "Absolutely not," he said. "Even if we did have time—which we don't—Mac would have my guts for garters if she found out I'd let you loose in The Copper Kettle."

Phillips had already caught the scent of freshly baked goods, and was following it like Winnie-the-Pooh might have followed a honey pot.

"She doesn't have to know," he whispered, a bit manically. "I've got strong breath mints in the car…"

Ryan took his friend's shoulders in a firm hold and gave him a shake. "Frank, you don't know what you're saying, it's crazy talk—"

Phillips grabbed Ryan's shirtfront and clung on. "It's the cabbage," he wailed. "I can't take it anymore, I need sugar—"

"Look," Ryan said, glancing to either side, as if he expected MacKenzie to sneak up on the pair of them. "We'll make a bargain, just this once."

Phillips nodded, eyes half-mad with sugar fever.

"We'll have lunch in the tearoom, if you promise never to wear Lycra ever again."

Phillips made a show of thinking about it, then stuck out his hand.

"Deal."

Phillips made as if to run off, but Ryan held him back. "One last thing," he said.

"What? What?"

"I was never here, understand? I never saw a thing, I never ate a thing, I never encouraged a thing..."

Phillips nodded vigorously. "Mum's the word."

CHAPTER 23

After some gentle persuasion, Lawana agreed not to have her daughter sit in on the session with Gregory and, instead, to make do with her Thai translator and MacKenzie. Upon first meeting Gregory, she was hesitant, and spoke in a stream of fast Thai that sounded like music to his untrained ears.

"She'd like to know your credentials," Carrie said.

Gregory smiled and took a seat opposite where Lawana lay semi-reclined on an orthopaedic sofa, a necessity following the permanent injury to her spine. She was a tiny woman, reed thin with scars on her face and neck that would take a long time to heal. He might have thought her frail, had he not already known about her grit and determination to survive.

"Of course," he said, and ran through an impressive list of academic and real-life experience. "I can provide her with immediate references, if she'd like to speak to them."

This was relayed to Lawana, who seemed to consider it, then turned to MacKenzie.

"She'd like to know whether you vouch for him."

MacKenzie didn't hesitate. "I do."

There was another exchange.

"That will be sufficient."

"Thank you," Gregory said, keeping his voice light. "First, I need to talk you through the process."

He proceeded to discuss the potential benefits and pitfalls of hypnosis; how it didn't always work and had varying degrees of success. If the session was successful, it could mean re-living painful emotional experiences and she should think carefully about whether she was willing to embark on that journey. He stressed the fact that she should not feel pressured in any way—and MacKenzie reinforced this last message, on behalf of the police team.

Lawana listened, her dark eyes moving between them, and there was a short silence after the message was translated, while she deliberated.

"She says she's still happy to proceed," Carrie confirmed.

Gregory went about the business of setting boundaries, of agreeing a 'safe' word which, if either of them spoke it, would end the session immediately.

They chose, 'má-lí', which meant 'jasmine'.

Then, he created a restful ambiance, and reminded the other women in the room not to interrupt the flow of their session, unless it was urgent. He asked Carrie to repeat his words exactly as he said them, and to repeat Lawana's replies exactly as she gave them, too. MacKenzie sought permission to record the session, which was agreed.

When all was ready, they began.

"I want you to close your eyes, Lawana."

Gregory spoke slowly and evenly, and was pleased that Carrie emulated his pacing as much as she could in her translation.

Lawana closed her eyes, though her fingers remained clasped tightly over her chest.

"I want you to imagine you're in an empty room," he said. "The room has four plain, white walls, and a plain white floor. Can you see it?"

She nodded slowly.

"I want you to imagine there's a single door on the wall in front of you…behind that door is the most beautiful place you've ever been. What's behind the door, Lawana?"

It took a moment for her to relax enough to visualise but, after a couple of attempts, she gave him an answer.

"It's a beach," Carrie translated. "A wide, sandy beach with palm trees and turquoise water…she visited once, when she was young."

"Good," Gregory said. "Imagine you're walking along that beach, Lawana…imagine lying down on the sand, feeling it run between your fingers. Imagine every ounce of stress leaving your body…first, from your toes, then your feet, your legs…"

He took her through a process of meditation, until her body visibly slumped on the sofa, and her fingers unclasped.

"Remember this safe space, Lawana. Whatever happens now, you always have this place to come back to at any time," he said. "When you want to come back to the beach, say má-lí. What do you need to say?"

"Má-lí," she whispered.

"Okay, good," he said. "We're going to leave the beach, now, but only for a few minutes. You can come back to it at any time."

She frowned, her eyes were still closed.

"Through the trees, there's a building, Lawana," Gregory said, very carefully. "It's made of tumbledown stone. Can you see it?"

Her fingers began to twist and pick at the material of her blouse, and she nodded.

"Can you describe the building, Lawana?"

At first, he thought she wouldn't say anything, and he opened his mouth to try again when her reply came—so softly, they strained to hear.

"It's…" Carrie paused, trying to interpret the woman's reply. "It's a building of grey stone, like an old barn. Most of the roof has fallen in, and birds are nesting in the rafters."

"What kind of birds?" Gregory asked, focusing her mind on the mundane with deliberate restraint, so they didn't rush inside the room that awaited them all beneath the foundations of that old barn.

"Pigeons," came the reply. "Hundreds of pigeons."

"Can you smell them?"

Lawana nodded, her nose wrinkling.

"Rabbits, too," Carrie said softly. "The floor is covered in bird and rabbit dung…she feels it beneath her hands, she can smell it—"

Gregory recalled that Lawana had dragged herself along the floor for half a mile to escape her tormentor, fingers bloodied and torn, body battered and broken.

She began to grow agitated.

"She says—she says she has to hurry to get away—"

"Nobody is there now," Gregory said, quietly. "Nobody is inside, and you can leave at any time."

Lawana's chest still rose and fell rapidly, but she nodded.

"Can you see a door, Lawana?"

She began twisting her hands again.

"Yes."

"Where is it?"

"Up ahead, at one end of the barn. It's old, made of very heavy wood. It has a padlock on the back."

"Imagine that door opening for you," Gregory said. "Imagine you don't need a key to enter or leave—and remember, you can leave at any time. Can you open the door?"

She nodded, little more than a jerk of the head, and spoke again in fast Thai.

"She says he'll be coming at any minute."

"Nobody is coming," Gregory said, in the same even, unflappable tone. "You can enter or leave at any time."

He repeated the last message over and over, to remind her that it was no longer real—merely the fragments of a memory he was helping to piece together.

"Can you open the door?"

Lawana nodded, clutching her hands to her chest.

"She says she's frightened."

"Of what?"

"The monster."

"What does the monster look like?"

"Evil, with cruel eyes."

"What colour eyes?"

"Brown," she replied, without hesitation, and Gregory glanced over at MacKenzie, who nodded silently.

That was new information.

"What colour is the skin around his eyes?"

"Milky white."

That part wasn't new information, but it was useful to have it confirmed again.

"What about the monster's eyebrows? Can you see them?"

There was a pause, then Lawana shook her head.

"No. He's in shadow. He lives in the shadows. He's Shadow Man."

Evidently, news of the press's ridiculous title for her attacker had reached Lawana and infiltrated her consciousness.

"You can help to bring him into the light," Gregory said. "Do you want to open the door, or leave it closed?"

He waited, they all waited, until Lawana spoke softly again.

"I want to break it down."

In the end, Gregory spent three hours with Lawana, after which time he drew things to a close—not because the woman was displaying alarming levels of trauma, but because he feared the session had run on for too long and she'd be left mentally and physically exhausted.

When Lawana had chosen to break down the metaphorical barrier, she'd done just that, raging headfirst into her old memory of the room where she'd been held. She described it in detail, including the placement of a small ceramic sink, the bed, the makeshift toilet and his habit of bringing a plain black rucksack. She could not recall further details of his face—that was a bridge too far—but she could remember the faces of the women who'd stared at her from the walls, both living and dead, their images covering the walls. She could recount their physical features to such a degree of accuracy that MacKenzie now felt able to use her description to try to find positive matches to missing persons in the area and see if Lawana recognised any of them.

If she did, they could begin to look for a pattern.

It was a sad truth, universally acknowledged by those in their profession that, when hunting serial killers, the bigger the number of deaths, the more information they could gather and the greater the probability of him eventually slipping up. In the case of Shadow Man, they had two known victims fifteen years apart, with no like characteristics other than the fact they were both women, both vulnerable in their own ways, both taken using a combination of planning and opportunity.

Now, with Lawana's help, they could name more of his victims and begin to build up a picture of his modus operandi, if there was one.

Besides, they knew one more thing about him now…

He had brown eyes.

CHAPTER 24

"I don't know what came over me."

"A sugar demon, by the looks of it," Ryan replied, surveying the pile of crumbs left over from the fruit scone, ham-and-egg pie and enormous slice of carrot cake Phillips had consumed during the time it had taken him to put a call through to his wife and enquire about their baby.

"You should never have left me alone—I can't be trusted with a menu like that."

Ryan chuckled. "I was barely gone for ten minutes," he said, laughing.

"That's all it takes," Phillips said, and his eyes followed a passing tray of French Fancies.

No, he told himself. Stay strong.

"The trouble is, I'm not built for cabbages and kale," he said. "I'm a man, not a bloody hamster. I need meat…I need protein…I need…"

"A muzzle?" Ryan suggested.

"This is no laughin' matter," Phillips said, as they left the tearoom, looking like a pair of down-and-outs stumbling out of a crack den. "I'm goin' to have to confess all to Denise, later."

"She'll never know."

"She will," Phillips argued. "The woman's got a nose like a bloodhound—for porky pies of both varieties."

"That's why we love her," Ryan said. "Doesn't help you, much."

Phillips let out a gusty sigh. "I'll deal with my punishment later, and hopefully it'll involve handcuffs," he said, with a lascivious rumble of laughter.

Ryan tried to block the image, to banish it from his mind, but…

Too late.

"Who's next on the list?" Phillips asked, and Ryan grasped the question like a lifeline.

"Angela's staff," he said. "She had three permanent members of staff who looked after the guest house and five other cottages in the village. There's her housekeeper-cum-lettings-manager, Pauline Whitton; her cleaner, Irina Pavlova—"

"Pavlova…" Phillips repeated.

"Keep your mind off meringue," Ryan warned him. "Then, there's the gardener, John Watson. Pauline and John both 'live in', with their own separate cottages on the Sandy Dunes estate. The cleaner has her own flat in Seahouses."

"Are they a couple—the housekeeper and the gardener?"

"Not that I'm aware of," Ryan said. "We can always ask."

Just then, his phone began to ring—Indiana Jones theme music blasting into the quiet village.

It was Detective Constable Reed calling.

"I'm at Sandy Dunes," she said. "I've been doing a standard search of the house, trying to find some information that could help us track down Angela's next of kin, and I found her will."

"Who gets the dough?" Ryan asked, coming straight to the point.

It was another universal truth that, for a certain breed of sociopath, money was and would always continue to be a strong motivator to kill.

"You won't believe this," she said. "Angela left everything to her gardener."

Ryan made a small sound of surprise. "Hang tight—we'll be along in a minute," he said, and ended the call.

"Been a while since you used that ringtone," Phillips remarked.

"They were filming the latest Indiana Jones movie at Bamburgh Castle recently, so it seemed fitting," Ryan said. "You'll never guess who's in line for a windfall."

"The butler," Phillips said. "It's always the butler."

"She didn't have a butler but, as it happens, you're not far off. It's the gardener," Ryan said.

"Well, that's a heck of a motive," Phillips said. "He did know how to access the house."

"It seems too obvious," Ryan said, as they reached the stone gates of the guest house. "Surely, if John Watson did away with Angela, he must have known we'd look at him hard, considering how much he stood to benefit."

"What have I told you, a million times?"

Ryan nodded and held up a hand. "I know, I know. Stop expecting crackpot killers to think like normal people."

"People would pay good money to hear that kind of wisdom," Phillips said.

"They'd pay more not to hear it," Ryan muttered, and they began making their way along the driveway towards the Sandy Dunes Guest House.

Doctor Gregory could only spare a day before he needed to return to London. After a productive session with Lawana and a quick pit-stop to re-fuel at a little café MacKenzie knew, she drove them both back to Newcastle post haste, where his next appointment awaited him in a small meeting room at Police Headquarters.

"It isn't the most convivial environment for hypnosis," MacKenzie worried, as she signed him into the guest log and offered him a visitor's badge.

"So long as there's a chair or a sofa, we can manage," he said.

They passed through the security turnstiles and into the office suite, where MacKenzie led the way upstairs and along a long corridor lined with identical grey-painted doors.

"I like what you've done with the place," he joked.

MacKenzie had grown so used to her surroundings, she no longer noticed its drab paintwork or homogenous features, but, looking through the lens of a stranger, she could understand that it didn't exactly scream 'homely'.

Then again, the work they did was far from that.

"It could stand a few plants, here and there," she agreed. "At least it doesn't carry a perpetual stench of drains, like the last place."

Give it time, Gregory thought, but was too polite to say anything.

"Here we are," she said, as they approached one such grey door that bore a sign indicating it was 'OCCUPIED'. "Mel's in here. Should I come in?"

"It's up to her," Gregory said.

MacKenzie gave a brief tap on the door and then entered, to find Yates standing beside the window.

"Doctor Gregory," she said, moving forward to shake his hand. "Thank you for finding the time."

Too much sadness, he thought. Sadness could curdle to anger, all too quickly.

The room was plain, with several two-seater tables arranged in a u-shape around a whiteboard affixed to one wall. On the opposite wall was a long, foam sofa, which obviously didn't belong.

"I borrowed the sofa from the break room," she explained, following his line of sight. "I hope it will do?"

He nodded, and slung his coat over the back of a chair. "Is Ryan about?"

Mel shook her head. "He and Phillips are up in Bamburgh, investigating the death of an old woman," she explained. "He says he'll see you later."

Gregory had originally planned to make the trip there and back to London in a single day, but after some gentle persuasion from his police friend, had accepted an offer to stay with Ryan and Anna at their home for the night. He was looking forward to relaxing with a glass of wine and good company, but, before then, there was work to do.

"MacKenzie tells me you'd like to try hypnosis to see if you're able to remember any more details about the night your sister went missing—is that correct?"

She nodded. "I was there, too," she said quietly. "I might have seen him—I probably did see him—without even realising it."

It was desperate ground, he thought, when you consider how many people had been in the club that night.

One face, among hundreds of others?

It was a tall order.

"We'll try," he said.

"Would you like me to stay?" MacKenzie asked, quietly.

Mel almost said 'yes', then shook her head. She wanted MacKenzie to be working on her sister's file at every available opportunity, not to be holding her hand while she lay on a coach trying to prod her own memory.

"I can manage," she said.

"If you change your mind, you know where I am," came the response, before MacKenzie let herself out and closed the door softly behind her.

"How does this work?" Mel asked, watching as Gregory rolled up his shirtsleeves and moved across to the water cooler.

"Drink?" he asked.

She nodded.

"We need to clear your mind so that it reaches a state of focused attention, with reduced awareness of everything going on in the periphery," he said. "When you reach this state, your mind is more able to focus solely on my suggestions—which will be based on the memory goals agreed between ourselves, before the process begins."

She told herself not to be frightened. Memories couldn't harm her, now.

"You can stop at any time," he said, reading her body language easily. "Likewise, if there's anything you'd rather we steer clear of, I'll do my best to make sure that happens."

She took a sip of water and swilled it around, thinking carefully.

"There isn't anything to avoid," she said, in the end. "I want to remember anything I can."

"All right," he said. "I also need to manage your expectations. This can work very well, with some people, but with others it doesn't work at all."

"We won't know unless we try."

"All right, then."

CHAPTER 25

MacKenzie made her way directly back to her computer and settled down to the process of entering a series of updated keyword search terms, based on the information Lawana had given them. It was always sobering to access the missing persons database and watch the number rising daily. More sobering yet was the knowledge that the true number was much higher, but some missing persons would never be reported to police because there was nobody who cared enough to pick up the phone, or they'd fallen through the cracks in the system.

She set aside any emotion she might have felt, and spent some time refining her search, focusing on the first description Lawana had given them:

…the woman looked like she was eighteen or nineteen… twenty, maybe. She had long, dark hair and tanned skin. She might have been of Middle-Eastern descent, or perhaps Greek…

The proportion of young women of that demographic in the North East was generally lower than in other parts of the country, many immigrant families having traditionally settled around London and its surrounds.

She entered the new terms, including potential ethnicities, and waited.

Searching...

MacKenzie reached for her coffee but hadn't yet taken a drink when her computer pinged out a notification that the search was complete.

Four potential matches.

She looked at each of them in turn, her sharp eye checking dates and inconsistencies, physical attributes and circumstances around their disappearance, until she whittled four down to two.

Farah Ahmad and Thalia Galanis.

The first was the daughter of a family who owned a well-known accountancy business in the North East, Ahmad Associates, while the second was the daughter of a restauranteur, who had owned a thriving Greek restaurant she'd frequented many times, over the years, until their daughter's disappearance had affected them too greatly and they'd lost heart.

The restaurant wasn't the same any more.

MacKenzie made a note of their names, and the dates they were reported missing: Farah around Christmas in 2007 and Thalia in the early part of 2008, only a few months after Gemma Yates was killed. She spent more time cross-checking Lawana's descriptions against the missing persons database, but came up with no more feasible matches for the time period in that region.

She moved on to the cold cases register, to compare the search against women who had already been found dead, but their killer never identified.

There, she found only one potential match with the characteristics Lawana had described, before she moved on to the next description Lawana had given:

…blonde, and she had a tattoo on her lower back, some sort of swirling pattern at the base of her spine…

Details like that were helpful to them, because it narrowed the search significantly—though it also told her that the woman's killer had photographed her body from all angles, and displayed them on his wall.

Sick, MacKenzie thought. Depraved.

She took a swig of coffee, sighed, and began again.

Sure enough, the search brought up only two possible matches for missing blonde women in their late teens or early twenties, with a tattoo listed on file. MacKenzie was in the process of looking at the forensic images of each woman to see if their ink matched Lawana's description, when she became aware that someone was standing behind her.

It was DCS Forbes.

MacKenzie felt a tremor of disquiet, and told herself she must have been miles away.

"Sorry, I didn't mean to startle you," he said, with one of his easy smiles, while his eyes strayed to the images on the screen, drinking them in. "I was coming to ask if you were free for our one-to-one chat, but I can see you're busy—"

MacKenzie wanted to continue with her search, but reasoned it was best to get the 'chat' out of the way so she could continue with the remainder of her day in peace.

"This can wait," she said, and clicked a button so the screen locked.

Forbes had looked at the same images, many times, when he'd felt the need, but it was worrying to see that MacKenzie was searching for them, too.

Their reasons were very different.

How close was she? What had Woman A told her?

He led the way to his office, and shut the door behind MacKenzie, intrigued by the shape of her neck, the curve of her skull.

She stepped further away, rubbing her arms for warmth.

"Have a seat," he said.

MacKenzie took one of the visitors' chairs and crossed one leg over the other. She wore smart black trousers and low, practical heels with a plain black silk shirt, but as he watched the flex of lean muscle she might as well have been half-naked, given the effect she had on him.

Forbes told himself to behave. It wasn't a free-for-all, and he'd already made his selection.

It was just a matter of time and opportunity.

"Well," he began, clasping his hands together. "I've heard many good things from the Chief Constable, and from your colleagues, Denise."

She said nothing.

"I also know that my job was once offered to you," he said. "I—ah, hope there won't be any awkwardness?"

She shook her head. "I can't imagine why there would be," she said. "Yours isn't a job I would relish, sir."

"May I ask, why?"

"I prefer to be on the ground, working actively on individual cases," she explained, and wished he'd hurry things along so she could get back to it.

"Yes, I miss those days," he lied. "All the same, I can't help but think that your skills aren't being used to their fullest."

"I'm happy with the balance I have between work and family life."

He nodded. "How do you find it, working for Ryan?"

"Actually, I'm sure that he would say we work together," she corrected him.

Another disciple, Forbes thought, with mounting irritation.

"Yes, but, surely you'd like to step up into the role of DCI and manage your own team," he said. "We need good leaders, like you."

MacKenzie had thought about it, of course she had. She'd also seen what the job entailed, having shadowed Ryan these many years.

"Not at the moment," she said, firmly. "I appreciate your concern."

It was a dismissal, he thought, but a very polite one, at that.

Dead end, here.

"All right," he said, spreading his hands. "If you need anything, want to discuss anything or run anything by me…"

She was already up and out of her chair.

"Thank you, sir."

A moment later, he was left looking at the empty spot where she'd been seated. MacKenzie was no fool, no vulnerable young woman he could mould or manipulate to his will, though he might have liked to try, all the same.

There were other ways to achieve the same result.

He picked up the phone.

"Lowerson? Yes, would you mind popping down to my office, for a moment? I have some good news for you, regarding that promotional pathway we were discussing yesterday."

Ego, he thought. It was a weakness, every time.

CHAPTER 26

"Mr Watson?"

John Watson was a burly man in his sixties, with leathery skin that was the product of many years spent in the Great Outdoors, and the most enormous hands they'd ever seen. They were encased in a pair of well-used gardening gloves and were presently being used to weed one of the borders lining Angela's beautiful formal gardens. The sun dipped low in the sky, and the light was an ethereal, misty shade as it touched the tips of the trees and warmed their skin.

"Aye," he said, glancing up at them from beneath the brim of an old baseball cap. "Who're you?"

"I'm DCI Ryan and this is my colleague, DS Phillips," Ryan said. "I believe you've already spoken to DC Reed?"

"Young lass?" he said. "Aye, she was askin' all about Angela, yesterday."

"Lovely gardens," Ryan said, lifting a hand to encompass their surroundings. "Is this your handiwork, Mr Watson?"

He gave a shrug.

"S'pose so," he said. "Angie liked certain flowers and wanted them plantin', but she took my advice on a lot of things. Soil's different, light's different, dependin' where you walk."

They nodded.

"It must have been a shock to find out what happened to her," Phillips remarked.

Watson brushed the soil from his knees and then heaved himself upward, to face them both.

"Aye, it was a bad business," he said, clapping his hands together to remove the worst of the dirt from his gloves. "Angie was gettin' older, though, and it wouldn't be the first time she'd fallen. Took a bad fall, a few months ago, down those stairs, over there."

He nodded towards the stone steps that led from the upper terrace down to where they now stood, in a patch of formal lawned gardens at the back of the house.

"Did she hurt herself?"

"Just a sprained wrist and a couple of grazed knees," he said. "Gave her a shock, mind. Said she felt light-headed, an' I think she went to the doctors after that."

"When was this?"

"'bout six months ago, I reckon."

They made a mental note to check Angela's medical records, if Reed hadn't already done so.

"Well, that's interesting to know," Ryan said. "However, I'm afraid we don't believe Angela's death was caused by an accidental fall. We're presently investigating her death as suspicious."

Watson looked sombre. "Who'd want to hurt her?" he asked, with what seemed like genuine confusion. "She was kind to all and sundry."

"That's very much what we'd like to find out," Ryan said. "We're trying to build up a picture of her life, and the people in it. Perhaps you could tell us how long you'd known Angela?"

"Forty years, at least," he said. "Her old Da' was still alive, when I moved up here with my missus—God rest her soul. I took a job with Tait's, back then, which was the gardening team that took care of this place and thereabouts. Old Fred Tait had the running of it until he retired, and I decided to start up on my own, after then. Angie kept me on, offered me a permanent position."

"Your wife passed away?" Ryan asked, as gently as he could.

Watson nodded, pressing his lips together. "Ten years ago," he said. "Cancer."

"Sorry to hear it," Phillips intoned, with real empathy. He knew what it was to care for a wife with terminal cancer, knew what it was to live with the aftermath and the grief that followed.

"Workin' with the land helped me get through it," Watson said. "Planting things, watching them grow, it all helps."

The three men paused by mutual assent to look around at the seeds Watson had planted, which now bloomed in a riot of colour.

"How would you describe your relationship with Angie?"

"Well, I s'pose she was more of a friend," he said, unpeeling his gloves to allow his skin to breathe. "She'd often have us over for dinners, and I'd run errands for her, here and there. We'd chew the fat, sometimes—all three of us, when Pauline came along."

"When did Pauline start working for Angie?"

"About six or seven months ago. She lost her husband, too, and needed a fresh start."

"You both live on site, here?"

"Aye, there's two cottages," he said, pointing his broad finger towards a cluster of stone buildings off a small courtyard by the side of the main house. "Pauline has one, I have the other."

It confirmed what they already knew.

"Would you say there was anything bothering Angie, before she died?"

Watson stuck his gloves in the back pocket of his khaki trousers.

"No," he said. "Oh, she had plenty to say about this and that—"

"What sort of things?" Phillips asked.

"Well, in a place like this, there's always somethin', isn't there? If it wasn't the Bansbury Trust she was managin', it was the Women's Institute or the Bamburgh Residents' Association. That was givin' her a right headache, with all the arguments over whether to put in a formal objection to Urwin's development."

"What development is that?"

They knew of George Urwin, of course. He was well-known in the region for being the owner of one of the larger estate agencies, and he'd branched out into property development with the benefit of a few well-placed contacts in the planning office. It seemed there were 'Urwin Estates' developments being thrown up all around the North-East, although they couldn't vouch for the quality of their building work.

"Well, he wants to cash in on Bamburgh, doesn't he?" Watson said. "Got his hands on a bit of farmland—he's been gobblin' it up over the past couple of years, hopin' to change its use from agricultural to residential. He bought the field bordering the garden here, just last year."

He nodded towards the western border, beyond which lay open farmland as it represented the very edge of the village.

"Angie and others kept puttin' in objections to the development, since it'd spoil the views and there's already another development on the other side of the village, for those who might need new housing. She wasn't against young families gettin' an affordable home, but she didn't appreciate blokes such as the likes of him tryin' to line his pockets."

"You'd say she was a woman of principle, then?" Phillips said.

"Oh, aye," Watson agreed. "She was a good woman and wouldn't stand for any monkey business."

"Turning back to yesterday, would you mind running us through your movements, once again?"

Watson scratched his chin with one muddied finger.

"Aye, well, let's see. I was up with the larks, in the mornin', because there was a bit o' fencin' to take care of, over at Cuddy's Rest, which is one of Angie's cottages in the village. Came down in high winds, the other night," he explained. "She wanted that taken care of, so I got onto that, first thing.

It only took an hour or so, then I came back to get on with some maintenance work here."

"Around what time, would you say?"

"I was back by nine-thirty," he said. "Angie wanted one of the holly bushes moving, so I was gettin' ready to do that, when I came across a woman and a little girl, up there on the terrace. Said she knew Angie and was payin' a visit."

Phillips smiled to himself, and exchanged a knowing glance with Ryan.

"Oh?"

"Aye, bit funny, if you ask me, that she was lurkin' round the back," Watson said. "Seemed nervy, n'all. Anyhow, she'd spotted Angie through the window, so I went inside to check. That's when we realised she was in a bad way."

That was one way of putting it, Ryan thought.

"What did you do, then?"

"Rang for the ambulance and the police," he said. "I came back out onto the terrace, but the woman was gone. She was sittin' in her car round the front while we waited for them to arrive—I s'pose the littleun was tired."

Ryan didn't bother to correct him.

"Did anybody else enter or leave the property, that you know of?"

"Well, that lassie stepped inside to see Angie for herself, but left again," he said. "I waited by the front door for the paramedics, and they came pretty quick from Alnwick."

He referred to the nearest hospital, south of Bamburgh.

"After that, a couple of bobbies arrived in a police car, and they looked things over," he said. "Not long after, Detective

Constable Reed joined them. She asked a few questions, then Pauline arrived and I took myself off, back to my cottage, to have a bit of a sit-down and a cuppa."

"It must have been a shock."

"Aye, it was."

Ryan nodded, and decided the time was ripe to gauge whether the man would be equally shocked by the news they were about to share with him.

"Do you know who's likely to inherit Angela's estate?"

Watson shrugged. "Some relative, or other, I expect," he said. "Though, she never mentioned anyone, so it may be that she left everything to the Trust. I couldn't say, but she must've been thinkin' about it, lately, because she asked me and Pauline to witness her will, the other week."

Ryan knew that already, having seen Watson's signature scrawled on the back page of the will Reed had found locked inside the old lady's writing desk.

"What if we were to tell you that Angie had left everything to you, John?"

Watson tipped up his hat to look between them with obvious disbelief. "I'd say that was a likely story," he laughed.

"It's true," Ryan said, simply. "Angela left everything to you, in her will."

Watson's face was a picture of comical surprise. "She—she never—?"

"She did, yes."

The man looked dumbfounded. "But—I'm not family," he argued. "I don't deserve it."

"She obviously felt that you did," Phillips said, watching him closely. "Didn't she tell you she was goin' to leave it to you? Didn't you see it, on the will you signed?"

Watson removed his cap to scrub the sweat from his balding head, and then replaced it.

"She never breathed a word," he said. "I didn't go readin' the will, either. She asked me in from the garden one day to sign and witness, but it was over in a few seconds, that was all it took. I didn't stop to ask about the details; it wasn't any of my business."

"How do you feel about it—knowing you stand to inherit all her money and property?"

Watson looked sickly. "To tell the truth, I wouldn't know what to do with it all," he said. "I don't need all of that. I'm happy with what I have."

"Then, you won't be disappointed to know that, while you were listed as a beneficiary, your claim will be invalid," Ryan said.

Watson merely raised his bushy eyebrows, then let them fall again into a relieved smile, which crinkled the skin around the edges of his eyes and softened his features.

"Easy-come, easy-go," he said, affably. "It's better this way, really. It's as I said—what would I do with all this, and more?"

He shook his head.

"A family should have this old place, and fill it with children," he said, squinting up at the house, whose windows glimmered in the late afternoon sun. "As for the rest, somebody else will enjoy managing it, I'm sure."

He fiddled with his hat again, and shifted his legs to ease the rheumatism in his joints.

"Is there anythin' else you need?" he asked.

"Not for now," Ryan murmured. "We'll let you get back to your garden."

Watson nodded politely, and made his way towards the shed, which was tucked behind some ornamental shrubbery. As they watched him lumbering off, Ryan turned to his friend.

"How did he strike you, Frank?"

"Straightforward, no frills, no nonsense," Phillips replied. "Didn't seem bothered, not one iota, about the money—or any of it."

Ryan nodded. "He's our most likely suspect, and I've never met a man less impressed to have been told he stood to inherit, nor more relieved to be told he wouldn't inherit, after all. He didn't even ask why the bequest to him was invalid."

Phillips had to agree. "Aye, I wouldn't have known that someone who witnesses a will can't legally benefit from it, if you hadn't told me. Still, unless somebody can vouch for him being at Cuddy's Rest, he doesn't have a firm alibi for that mornin', does he?"

Ryan shook his head.

Money was a strong motivator to kill, he reminded himself.

"He might not have known that you can't be both a witness to, and a beneficiary of, a will," he said. "He might have thought he stood to inherit everything, if Angela died."

Phillips pulled a face.

"If he did, then he's a bloody good actor," he said. "I'll tell you another thing…"

"What's that?"

"He wouldn't look good in any pink dress, that's for sure."

CHAPTER 27

"How do you feel?"

Melanie Yates shifted on the sofa. "I can't seem to relax."

"Your mind is too busy," Gregory said. "Why don't we try a different approach?"

"What kind of approach?"

"We could try a stream of consciousness," he said. "You say anything and everything that's on your mind, to try to clear out the clutter."

Yates shook her head. "I wouldn't want to frighten you, Doctor."

Gregory smiled, thinking of the many severely unwell patients he'd treated at Southmoor, the 'special hospital' for the criminally insane, where he worked as a Senior Clinician.

"Why don't you try me?" he offered.

Yates was tempted, but there were some things she couldn't risk her colleagues knowing. Some thoughts she daren't say aloud.

"Does our conversation have to be recorded?"

"Not without your permission," he said.

"Would you tell anyone about what we discuss?"

"Whatever you tell me is confidential, unless you consent to my disclosing the information to others—or unless the information you tell me would give rise to risk of serious harm to you, or others," he added.

That's what she was afraid of.

Reading her like a book, Gregory leaned back in his chair and linked his fingers comfortably.

"Mel, people often fantasise about killing," he said, and her eyes flew to his face, filled with guilt and surprise. "The difference is, very few people act on their fantasies."

She rubbed her forehead, which was beginning to throb.

"I can't seem to stop fantasising," she said. "I think of all the things I'll do to him, when we find him. I think about how I'll torture him, as he tortured my sister and others."

"We're all animals, when you strip away the trappings of society," he said. "Our natural reaction is to strike back when we're attacked or hurt, to defend ourselves or those we love."

"I'm worried it's more than that."

He studied her, reading the stress on her face, the shake to her hands, and wondered whether she was right to be worried.

"We may be animals, Mel, but we're highly evolved," he said. "We have the capacity to think and reason to an extremely high level. It's that reason and self-discipline that prevents our species from falling into anarchy or a state of nature. You have the ability to control your impulses; we all do."

Mel agreed, but thought again of the man they hunted.

"He didn't care about restraint," she said, bitterly.

"No, he didn't," Gregory agreed. "Which makes you better than him."

Mel took a couple of deep breaths and then nodded. "Yes. Yes, you're right."

He waited until she'd settled. "Would you like to try again?"

She nodded. "This time, I'm ready."

"Describe your safe place to me, Melanie."

The voice was distant, but not unwelcome. It made her feel secure.

"I'm in my room, at home."

"What does it look like?"

"There's a purple bedspread," she whispered. "There are posters on the walls, of programmes I like to watch."

"Which ones?"

"Buffy the Vampire Slayer," she said. "The OC, Gossip Girl…"

She described programmes that had typically run around the early noughties, then re-run in the years that followed.

"What else can you see?"

"There's a poster of Alanis Morrisette," she said, describing one of her musical idols at that time. "There are some photographs of me and my friends."

"Aside from the bed, what else is in the room?"

"A wardrobe," she said. "A long mirror on the wall. There's a small bookcase with a CD player on top, and a whole shelf of CDs. Next to the window, there's a desk and a chair."

"What's on the desk?"

"Notebooks, homework books," she muttered. "A lot of clutter…gel pens…a poster I haven't put up, yet."

"Which one is that?" Gregory asked, an innocuous question designed to continue putting her at ease.

"It's a self-defence poster. A collection of illustrations, showing a bunch of defensive actions women can take if they're attacked," she whispered, imagining herself unrolling the poster as she'd done fifteen years before, right before discarding it on the desk.

"Did you buy it?"

"No, I—"

No, it was a hand-out.

In that moment, Melanie's world came to a shuddering halt. She remembered exactly where the poster came from, and who had given it to her. She remembered two police officers, one male, one female, who had visited her school one afternoon to demonstrate self-defence. She remembered sitting on long benches in the gymnasium, listening to a lecture about personal safety. He'd stood in front of them, pretending to be normal. Pretending to care—and all the while, he was a predator.

It came flooding back, in terrible technicolour, a memory so clear she could still smell the body odour and pine cleaner that clung to the gymnasium walls.

She remembered him.

She remembered his face.

He'd called for a volunteer and, for a joke, she'd raised her hand. He'd crooked a finger and, like the fool she was, Melanie had strutted in front of her peers, ready to show them all how it was done. She remembered his arms coming around her, pretending to attack, pretending to grab her from behind. She'd hit out, employing the moves she'd been shown, and he'd smiled.

Any would-be attacker would have to watch out for you, wouldn't they? You're a fighter, aren't you?

Yes, she was a fighter.

"—Mel?"

Her eyes flew open, and she struggled upward, gasping for air.

Gregory hurried to her side, supporting her as she came out of the memory, speaking quietly and calmly, telling her to breathe in and out.

"Did you remember something?" he asked, urgently.

Melanie studied the floor at her feet, debating how to answer him. Gregory had said their conversation would remain confidential, unless she gave her consent for him to disclose it, but he'd also said he had a duty to break confidentiality if he considered she was a danger to herself… or others.

Yes, she thought, as the fire in her belly burned hotter than ever. She was a danger, now.

She knew his face.

She even knew his name.

"I think I'm going to be sick," she muttered.

Gregory watched her rush from the room, frowning as he tried to make sense of what had just happened. He could have sworn she'd remembered something and was unwilling to say what it was. On the other hand, she wouldn't be the first person to react badly to hypnosis, and, by the looks of her, she wasn't looking after herself properly.

When she returned, Melanie wore a smile that didn't reach her eyes.

"I don't think this is going to work, after all. I'm sorry to waste your time, Doctor."

"It's all right, Melanie. How are you feeling?"

"Oh, much better," she lied. "I had a funny turn, is all."

He wanted to believe that, but instinct was a powerful thing. "Is there anything you'd like to talk about—off the record?"

She swallowed, and avoided his eyes which, like Ryan's, saw far too much.

"Nothing especially," she said. "Although, I'm fascinated by the profiling work that you do. It gets a bad rap, but you apply a very scientific approach, don't you?"

Gregory was happy to accept a change of subject, if it helped her.

"Yes, I try to," he said. "A good profile can help a police team to narrow down a very wide pool of suspects, or decide in which direction an investigation should go. It isn't an exact science, by any means, and a profile should only ever be used as a guide, not as gospel."

She nodded. "If you were to profile the man we're looking for, what sort of characteristics would you think apply to him?"

Gregory ran a hand through his hair, and shook his head. "I haven't read all the files—"

"I mean, general pointers," she said, pressing him to answer.

He sighed. "Of course, there are general characteristics that tend to apply to organised serial killers," he said. "They tend to learn and develop, after each kill, which means they increase their level of sophistication."

"You mean, we're more likely to find mistakes with his earlier efforts?" she asked.

Gregory nodded. "It's not always the case—set against that, if they've been operating for a long period of time, they can also become complacent. It makes me think a little of the old statistic about most car accidents happening near to where people live, on roads they're very familiar with. Familiarity breeds contempt, and that works in the world of serial killing, too."

Melanie nodded. "What else?"

"Organised serial killers often take trophies from their crime scenes," he said. "I've met several who liked to slip these little trophies into everyday life, so they could see them out in the open, every day, and get a little thrill from it."

Melanie thought of her sister's clothing and the necklace she'd worn that night, and wondered where they were now.

"Organised offenders are, in general, socially competent and often friendly," he said. "They're the ones who hide very well in plain sight. They have a compulsive need to kill, like an addict has a compulsive need to get high, so they'll look for a fix again and again. They won't stop, because they can't."

Unless somebody stopped them, Melanie thought. For good.

"Of course, organised killers tend to premeditate their crimes, and leave very little evidence behind."

"He left one of his hair follicles on my sister—and DNA beneath Woman A's nails."

"I'd suggest that your sister is one of his earlier efforts, in that case," Gregory surmised. "As for the recent DNA trace, it seems his error was unplanned; he gave too low a dosage to his intended victim, which allowed her to take him by surprise and escape. Otherwise, he would likely have removed all traces."

"He's not crazy, then," Melanie muttered. "He functions."

Gregory nodded. "These kinds of criminal aren't insane," he said. "They know right from wrong, they're often psychopathic and show no remorse at all."

"Would they be able to hold down a job—say, a managerial or high-level position?" she asked, choosing her words with care.

Gregory nodded. "Organised killers are likely to be of average or above average intelligence, based on historic data," he said. "They're usually attractive, or averagely so, married or partnered with someone, employed or skilled… they often have what I'd call a 'specious' charm, and they know how to work a room. It's been known for killers of this kind to groom a victim very well, and talk them into walking into their own death trap of their own accord."

Melanie thought of the conversation she'd held with DCS Forbes about information sharing, and secret confidences, and felt sick to her core.

"They can be very savvy with police methodologies," Gregory was saying, and she almost laughed.

"Yes," she muttered. "I'm sure he covers his tracks very well."

"They tend to do this by keeping their workspaces very distinct," Gregory continued. "There's home, where they try not to bring their 'addiction', for want of a better way of describing it, and then there's where he finds his victims, where he takes them, and where he leaves their bodies or disposes of them. Each one is separate, and probably miles apart."

"There must be a way of narrowing the field," she said. "He can only travel so far, without arousing suspicion."

Gregory nodded.

"You tend to find that inexperienced killers go far from home, the first time," he said. "As they grow in confidence, they move closer to home, in reducing circles on a map. With an experienced killer, you tend to find he starts to get lazy, and hunts for his victims quite close to home."

He paused. "I'm happy to talk to you about this, Mel, but your colleagues are already investigating along these lines," he said. "Let them do their work."

She looked away, out of the window across the city, to where, in the ground beneath an old tree, her sister's ashes lay. Every year, she visited, and sat beside her sister's earth, talking to her and the tree she fed, as though she was still there.

Every year, she promised to avenge her death, and now she had her chance.

She wouldn't lose it.

With that, she turned on her heel and walked away, never stopping until she was well clear of the building and its inhabitants.

She needed to think, and to plan.

CHAPTER 28

Pauline Whitton hummed along to the radio as she scrubbed her cottage windows.

"Mrs Whitton?"

She spun around, cloth in hand.

"Oh, hello again, Chief Inspector," she said, and, for the first time he noticed a lilt to her accent that he couldn't quite place.

She turned to Phillips and became noticeably flustered, patting her hair back into place and brushing down the pink top she wore.

"I'm such a mess, today," she said, in a breathy little voice.

Ryan watched with amusement, while Phillips looked very much like a chicken who knew he was being eyed up for Sunday roast.

"This is my sergeant, Frank Phillips," Ryan said.

"Frank," she repeated, and gave him a coy smile. "What a lovely, solid sort of name."

Phillips mumbled something polite. "Aye, er, ta very much."

"We were hoping to ask you a few questions, Mrs Whitton," Ryan said. "Do you mind if we come in, for a moment?"

"By all means," she said, and ushered them inside a flagstoned hallway that was small but smart, coated in a shade of paint that was probably described as Mole's Eyelash or Pigeon's Breath. "Can I offer you boys a drink?"

"No, thank you very much, Mrs Whitton—we won't stay long," Ryan said, to Phillips' great relief.

Her face fell, but she was philosophical about it. "Well, we'll have to make the most of the time you have," she said, and put a firm hand on Phillips' arm to guide him towards her living room. "Ooh! My goodness, aren't you strong!"

Phillips was lost for words.

"It's all the cycling he does," Ryan said, with a devilish smile that wasn't lost on his friend.

"I do admire a man at your time of life who takes an interest in his physique," she said, eyeing up Frank's stocky build with a gleam in her eye. "A woman likes to feel there's a strong man to look after her."

"My wife certainly feels that way," Phillips took the opportunity to say, although it was a blatant untruth, for MacKenzie was one of the last women in the world who needed a man to 'look after her'.

Pauline's gaze fell to his ring finger, which sported a wide gold band she hadn't noticed before.

She tutted.

"Well," she said, briskly. "How can I help you gentlemen?"

They took a tentative seat on her sofa, which was pristine.

"As you know, we're now investigating Angela's death as 'suspicious,'" Ryan began.

"Yes, and what a dreadful, dreadful business," she said, in a hushed voice. "Why anyone would want to hurt that lovely lady is beyond me."

"She had no enemies, then?"

Pauline shook her head. "None that I can think of—well…"

There was always something, Ryan thought, and waited for the town gossip to come out.

"I suppose you know she was thinking of withdrawing her funding for the archaeology project."

Ryan and Phillips exchanged a glance.

"That's news to us," Ryan said, and thought that it might have been nice for Professor Soames, or any of his team, to mention it.

Perhaps they didn't know.

"Well, it was all very awkward," Pauline said, fiddling with the material of the jumper she wore. "Angela had supported their projects for years, but, as she told me only recently, she and Professor Soames didn't see eye-to-eye."

"How d'you mean?" Phillips asked, and then buttoned his mouth again, in case she took it as encouragement.

"Well, he's a bit puffed up, isn't he?" she said. "Angela was a very straightforward, honest woman. She didn't like any fiddling or funny business."

Which echoed what John Watson had already told them, and furthermore told them that Angela had been a good employer, if her staff were only too ready to tell them good things about her character.

"And Professor Soames had been doing some…funny business?" Ryan asked.

"Angela had her suspicions," Pauline said. "She'd asked her accountant to start auditing the funds he'd taken from the Bansbury Trust. Soames is one of the trustees, you know."

"Did her accountant find anything?"

"Well, that's just it, she never got a chance to find out," Pauline said, and her eyes filled with tears. "Poor dear. Anyhow, I'm sure the professor is breathing a sigh of relief about it."

"Surely, one of the other trustees would be suspicious, if there was anything untoward," Ryan pointed out.

"Well, you'd think so, but these big characters can be quite overpowering, can't they," she said. "I can vouch for that, myself, because Professor Soames can certainly be very demanding around the guest house. Fold the sheets, this way. Make my coffee, that way. Anyone would think he was the Queen of Sheba."

Phillips gave a snort of laughter, quickly stifled. "Er… that's very useful, thank you," he said. "Anyone else you can think of, who had a bone to pick?"

"Well, there was that dreadful Urwin man," she said. "Some folk call him 'Sir George', because he funnels a load of dirty cash through his charity and some daft civil servant recommended him for an MBE—but he's no knight, I can tell you."

"How so?"

"I heard him threatening Angela, clear as day," she said, pointing a finger at the pair of them, as if to stave off any argument to the contrary. "He'd come up the driveway in his great big silver Bentley—so crass, if you ask me, but then, money doesn't buy class, does it, dear? Anyway, he strutted inside the house as if he owned the place, running his eye over the paintings as well, I noticed. Well, I showed him into the library and Angela met him in there. Well, the door was ajar, you see—"

"We understand," Ryan said, and she gave a delicate little cough.

"I was dusting the clock, in the hallway outside," she said, with a wink for them both. "I happened to overhear their conversation and he was nothing but rude—and she, such a gentle lady."

She tutted again, and flicked away a bit of invisible dust.

"What were they arguing over?" Ryan asked.

"Why, this house, and her land, for one thing," she said. "Then, there's the matter of her objecting to his planning applications and speaking up about it, at the Residents' Association. She was popular with everyone, around the village, and they listened to her."

"He wanted to buy the guest house?"

"He's made several offers," she told them. "Angela told me about that, herself. Wouldn't take 'no' for an answer, that man. Well, he was hopping mad the other week, because his latest application had been thrown out, despite all his best efforts to wine and dine the planning officers. They know the village would raise holy hell, if they allowed him to build a hundred new houses on that land, over there."

"He must be quite frustrated," Ryan agreed. "But I hardly think someone would kill over it, do you?"

"Chief Inspector," she said, in the same hushed voice, as though frightened a ghost would overhear. "This house alone is worth almost two million. The other cottages she has are worth at least another four or five million, and there's plenty more I don't even know about, and wouldn't be indiscreet enough to ask. Angela always said, this house, this village, wasn't just home to her but a special place, full of history, and it should be protected."

Ryan might have agreed, but somebody obviously had other ideas.

"Well, we'll certainly be having a word with Mr Urwin," he said, and took down the details of his last visit, to the best of her recollection. "Coming back to more recent events, Mrs Whitton, would you mind telling us your movements, yesterday? When was the last time you saw Angela, alive?"

"Of course, dear. I saw Angie in the morning, at breakfast, with all the rest of them. They left around eight, or perhaps quarter-past, and I tidied up the kitchen after them. It was my day off, same as every Monday, but I like to help out where I can." She paused, thinking back. "After that, I took myself off to Alnwick to get my shopping in, and meet a few friends for a natter."

She named a couple of women in a book group she was part of.

"What time did you leave the guest house?"

"Ooh…well, it must have been around eight-thirty, perhaps slightly later but no later than eight forty-five, because I was in Alnwick by quarter-past-nine."

"Where did you meet your friends, and at what time?"

"Let's see. We met at the café in Barter Books—you know the place?"

It was one of the best bookshops in the world, in Ryan's humble opinion, as well as being one of the largest. Occupying an old railway station, it was filled to the rafters with second-hand books of all genres, rare books besides, and there were endless nooks and crannies with roaring open fires and squishy chairs where customers were invited to sit and enjoy their surroundings. A large café with cosy leather booths and more open fires was often full of bibliophiles enjoying a drink and a nibble while they enjoyed their purchases.

"We know the place," Ryan told her.

"Well, we met in the café around nine-thirty," she said. "We had a bit of breakfast and chatted over books—there's a local author who writes all about places in the North East, and her hero is this handsome police detective...you two might enjoy her stories, since you're with the police, yourselves."

Ryan and Phillips looked at one another.

"Frank prefers Jilly Cooper," Ryan said, with another of his wicked smiles.

Noting the return of the gleam in Pauline's eye, Phillips hurried to change the subject.

"Ah, what time did you get back to the guest house?"

"Oh, not until eleven, dear," she said. "I had a nice wander around the bookshop and made my way home, after. I was planning to have a walk on the beach, since it was such a nice day, but I never got a chance. By the time I came back, the place was crawling with police and ambulance staff."

She sighed.

"Did Angela ever mention The Pink Lady to you?"

"The ghost?" Pauline said, and nodded. "Yes, the past two weeks she went on about having seen her, around the guest house."

"What did you think about that?"

Pauline folded her arms across her chest. "Well, I mean to say, it's all a bit of fun, isn't it? Nobody really believes there's a ghost, do they? It's just one of those historical myths people like to tell, to add to the castle's lore."

"You don't believe she really saw a ghost, then?"

"To be honest, Chief Inspector, I wondered if Angela was starting to go a bit…" She paused to make a swirling motion with her finger next to her left temple. "You know, Alzheimer's and dementia are on the rise…I thought she might have been hallucinating, you know?" She tutted—for a third time, by Ryan's count. "Anyway, when I heard about her being at the bottom of the stairs…well, I thought, she's fallen. That's what she's done."

"And do you think that still?"

Pauline sighed. "It just doesn't ring true," she admitted. "Angie might have been knocking on the door of ninety, but she was all there in body and mind. She moved slowly, but she was sure-footed. She was still as sharp as a tack. I can't imagine her being taken in by anything."

Ryan considered this, and how much to tell her.

"Mrs Whitton, what if somebody dressed themselves up to look like The Pink Lady, and made it their business to frighten Mrs Bansbury—we understand she had a weak heart?"

Pauline put a hand to her own chest. "Who would be so cruel?"

"That's what we're going to find out," Ryan said simply.

Half an hour later, they extricated themselves from Pauline's living room and bade her farewell, Phillips having put personal integrity above his love for baked goods, when she'd offered them a homemade Bakewell tart.

"Well," Ryan said, stretching out his back as they began to walk into the village. "She certainly didn't hold anything back."

"I'll say," Phillips grumbled. "When you nipped off to the loo, she started tellin' me all about how lonely she was…"

Ryan grinned.

"Let me guess: she was hoping to meet a strong man, with a solid sort of name…like Frank?"

"You can shut yer pie-hole," Phillips told him. "I can't help it, if I'm irresistible to women. It's an affliction."

"I know, Frank. I know."

"I know somethin' else, n'all," Phillips said. "With Pauline fully alibied for the time Angela must have died, and the archaeological team fully alibied, that only leaves…"

"John Watson?" Ryan murmured. "Yes, I know."

"And the cleaner," Phillips put in. "They're the only ones who could have gained access to the house."

"Unless somebody thought outside the box, and paid someone else to dress up and do their dirty work," Ryan mused.

It was something to think about.

"Pavlova is next on our list," he said.

"I couldn't, mate, honestly. I'm still full after lunch."

Ryan stared at him, and then shook his head. "Being fatally attractive isn't the only thing you're afflicted with," he muttered, and left Phillips to trot after him as he made his way back towards the village.

CHAPTER 29

"You wanted to see me, sir?"

Lowerson stuck his head around DCS Forbes' office door, after a brief knock.

"Yes, come in, Jack."

Forbes locked one of the cupboards in his office and pocketed the key, before turning to face the young man who hovered in front of his desk.

"Have a seat," he offered.

"Thank you, sir."

"Regarding our discussion, yesterday, you'll be pleased to know I had a very productive chat with a former colleague of mine in South Tyneside Command, Detective Chief Superintendent Dodds," Forbes said. "He's actively looking to train up a couple of new DCIs, since a few have moved on or retired, in recent months. That means a couple of sergeant vacancies will become available. I recommended you, and he's keen to have a meeting with you, with a view to your making a transfer from the first of next month."

Lowerson was torn between gratitude and a general feeling that things were moving a bit too fast. He hadn't even had a chance to speak to Mel about the potential promotion, let alone speak to Ryan or the rest of his team.

"I'm grateful, sir, but—"

"But?"

"I'd like to speak to DCI Ryan about this, before I accept DCS Dodds' kind offer."

"Of course, I fully understand, but you should know there's been quite a lot of interest, already," Forbes said. "I wouldn't hang about for too long, if I were you."

"No, sir."

Forbes nodded, reached for a mint he kept in a little decorative bowl on his desk, then offered one to Lowerson.

"Incidentally," he said, as the young man unwrapped the little white capsule. "How's Operation Heartbeat progressing?"

Lowerson wasn't prepared to brief his senior officer, and was distracted by thoughts of whether to accept a move to another command unit.

"Ah, well, we had a breakthrough—of sorts—with Lawana," he said, blithely unaware that he'd given away the woman's first name without realising it. "She remembered a few details that have proven helpful in cross-checking for potential matches to missing persons or cold cases in the area. MacKenzie and I plan to pay the families a visit from tomorrow, to see if any of the victims could belong to the same man who killed Gemma Yates."

"That is good progress," Forbes muttered. Too good. "And the witness? Has she been able to describe her attacker, yet, with any reliability? It would be helpful, if she could."

"Well, to be honest, nothing more than we already knew—except that he has brown eyes. So, from what we gather, the perp is of average or slightly above average height, with brown hair and brown eyes, Caucasian, late-thirties to early fifties, without any memorable characteristics." Lowerson laughed, and made a joke in extremely poor taste. "She could have described half of the population in this city," he said, and then lifted a hand towards Forbes. "Even you, sir!"

Forbes forced his lips into a smile, stretching the skin over his teeth while his mind raced and his eyes scoured Lowerson's face for any sign that his comment had been more than an offhand remark.

Eventually, he gave a small laugh.

"Yes," he said. "Even me."

The sun was low in the sky by the time Ryan and Phillips collected the car and made the short journey to the nearby village of Seahouses. It was a place they knew well, having spent a few memorable days there investigating the murky world of shipwreck diving—and murder. But, more worrying than all that, as far as Ryan was concerned, was the possibility that their return to Seahouses would bring back a very specific memory that was best left in the past.

As he steered his car along the Links Road, he chattered about this and that, but, as they approached the outskirts of the village and eventually reached the High Street, he stole a glance across to where his sergeant was seated and hoped for the best.

"—Gregory is staying with us, this evening," he said, in a desperate, last-ditch attempt to distract Phillips from what was certain to come. "It'll be interesting to hear all about his time in New York—"

"There it is," Phillips whispered, and Ryan swore beneath his breath. "There's the bin, where it happened."

Ryan heaved a sigh. "Frank, how many times do I have to say, 'I'm sorry'? You do this every time we pass through."

Phillips clenched his fist and raised it to his lips, as if to stem a wave of emotion.

"It still feels like it happened only yesterday…"

"It was years ago, now," Ryan muttered, cursing the local authority for putting traffic lights so near to Trotters, where they'd once bought bacon stotties and where he'd once made the catastrophic error of throwing one away, half-eaten.

Phillips stared out of the window and raised his hand to the glass, as though reaching to grasp the stottie that was lost.

"You…can't have known what you were doin'," he said, and turned to Ryan with an air of kingly fortitude. "I forgive you."

Ryan could have laughed, for, to the outside world, it was ridiculous to mourn bread and meat, but such was his life in the North.

"Thank you," he said, working hard to keep a straight face. "Spoken like Good King Frankius of Bebbanburg. Now, let's put it all behind us, shall we?"

"There's only one way to do that," Phillips said, in the same faraway voice. "And that's to eat another—"

"Don't push it, Frank."

"Well, it was worth a try."

Once the traffic lights moved on, the two men followed the road until they came to a narrow turning, wide enough to fit a single car—just.

"I don't think I can get through there," Ryan said. "I'll park on the kerb."

He did just that, then they made their way down the alley towards a tarmacked courtyard, around which was arranged a collection of terraced cottages that had been divided into tiny apartments, each with their own front door.

"This is where Irina Pavlova lives," Ryan said. "Number Four, apparently."

They knocked on the door and waited, then knocked again when there was no sign of life.

They were about to leave, when Phillips pointed towards a curtain on the upper floor.

"I saw a twitch," he said. "She's at home, but avoiding us."

"Now, call me old-fashioned, but that always makes me suspicious," Ryan said, and crouched down to call through the letterbox. "Irina! This is DCI Ryan and DS Phillips, from Northumbria CID. We only want to talk to you—you're not in trouble. Answer the door, please, or we'll have to keep coming back."

They waited and, after a moment, there came the sound of footsteps on the stairwell in the hallway beyond, a short pause, and then the door opened.

"I was in the bathroom," she lied.

"Of course," Ryan said. "May we?"

She shrugged a skinny shoulder and stepped aside, so they could enter.

"Please be quiet," she snapped, in heavily accented English. "My mother is sleeping."

Ryan and Phillips nodded, toed off their shoes, and followed the staircase upward to the little flat Irina shared with her mother. Upon reaching the first floor, they were met by a strong stench of bleach and some other chemical, which didn't quite cover the more pungent odour of dried urine that had evidently soaked through the carpet and clung to the floorboards.

"She isn't well," Irina explained, pushing past them to move along the narrow landing towards a door at the end, which opened into a small living room.

They followed, and Ryan was forced to duck his head as the eaves almost took it off his shoulders.

"Why are you here?"

The woman couldn't have been more than twenty-one, Ryan thought, but she spoke as though she'd lived a much longer life, with the weariness of a much older person.

"We're investigating the death of your employer, Angela Bansbury," he said, and watched her eyes skip away, focusing somewhere over his right shoulder. "We'd like to ask a few standard questions."

"Do I need a lawyer?" she asked.

Ryan raised an eyebrow. "Do you feel that you need one?"

She looked between them, wondering if they were setting a trap, and he shifted his feet.

"Look," Ryan said, holding up his hands in mute appeal. "We're all tired, and I'm sure you are too. If you have something you think we should know, it's best that you tell the truth. It will be much worse, if we find out later."

She paled, but stood firm.

"I don't know anything," she said. "Angela was old, she fell down the stairs. It could have happened to any old person."

"But it didn't," Ryan said, and his voice grew hard. "It happened to her, and we'd like to know how and why."

The tone of his voice shocked her, and they could see she was on the cusp of telling them something.

Ryan took a risk.

"Irina, if there's anything you want to tell us, we'll listen," he said quietly. "If you want a lawyer, we can call for one, now."

"I can't afford a lawyer," she mumbled.

There was legal aid, but that only applied when someone was charged. As far as they knew, she'd committed no crime.

"Okay, look, why don't we start again?" Phillips suggested, adopting a fatherly tone to put her at ease. "Sorry to be a bother, pet, but d'you think I could have a glass o' water? My throat's parched, after all the sun, today."

Natural kindness won out, and she nodded, moving off to the kitchen somewhere down the hall. A moment later, they heard a tap running.

"Let me try," Phillips murmured, and Ryan nodded.

Frank had a way, sometimes.

She came back in with a glass of water, and he thanked her profusely, taking a long drink to prove he'd been thirsty.

"That's better," he said, and gave her one of his best smiles, which elicited a reluctant one in response.

"It's okay," she whispered.

"How about we have a sit down, love?"

She didn't like it, but she allowed it, and they seated themselves around a tiny circular table which held two chairs. Ryan remained standing and removed himself to the window so that she could believe he wasn't there at all.

"Now, why don't you start by tellin' us how long you've been workin' for Angela?" Phillips asked.

"A year," she replied, keeping her answers short. "I put signs up in the newsagents and the pubs, and she answered one of them."

"Was she a fair employer?"

Irina's eyes welled with tears, which she blinked away. "Yes," she said, almost inaudibly. "She was."

"Do you know anyone who'd want to hurt her? Anyone at all?"

Again, tears welled, and slipped over, running in two silent tracks down her face. Irina scrubbed them away with the back of her hand.

"I don't know."

Phillips gave her another one of his fatherly smiles. "Are you sure about that?"

"I've just said so."

All right, he thought. Softly, softly.

"Where're you from originally?"

Her face became shuttered again. "Russia," she admitted.

"I've never been," Phillips said, keeping his voice light. "I'm sure it's a lovely country. Incredible culture—ballet, literature…"

She let out a harsh laugh. "If you have money, yes," she muttered. "Not if you are poor."

He could say the same of anywhere, Phillips thought, but there was poverty…and then, there was poverty.

"So, you decided to make your way over here?" he guessed. "Well, I'm sure Angela was very grateful for all your hard work. She was certainly too old to try to do it, herself, wasn't she?"

Irina looked across to where the tall, handsome man stood by the window, and felt that his eyes could read her soul.

Her soul that was now black.

"I—I need to look after my mother," she said, in a rush. "I don't know anything about what happened to Angela. I didn't work at the guest house, yesterday—I was here, with my mother, all day. You can ask her."

But, as they would learn, Irina's mother was bedbound and unable to speak.

"All right," Phillips said, coming to his feet. "Why don't we come back tomorrow?"

She looked as though she'd rather tell them both to go to hell, but instead she folded her arms across her chest, defensively, and stood aside for them to leave.

As they passed along the hallway, Ryan happened to glance inside one of the two bedrooms they passed, and imagined he saw a flash of pink hanging in an open wardrobe.

They'd find out, tomorrow.

CHAPTER 30

MacKenzie and Lowerson had spent much of the afternoon contacting the families of those missing persons and cold case victims they'd identified as potential matches to their unknown killer. For the most part, it had entailed a series of harrowing conversations, speaking to families who, at first, thought they were calling with news and were then disappointed to learn they were merely calling for information. Now, as the afternoon drew to a close and before she needed to leave the office to collect her daughter, MacKenzie decided to make one last call.

It couldn't be any harder than the last ten.

She dialled the number, and a woman's voice answered.

"Hello—Mrs Galanis?"

"Yes, who's this?"

"My name is Detective Inspector MacKenzie," she said. "I have a few questions regarding your daughter's disappearance, but if it's a bad time to talk…"

There was a quiet sigh at the end of the line.

"When is it ever a good time to talk?" Thalia's mother said, and her voice held a sleepy quality to it, which MacKenzie recognised as a side effect of hard, sedative drugs or long-term antidepressant use.

"Thank you," she murmured. "I was hoping you could fill in some blanks for me, about what happened back in 2008?"

"What do you need to know? I thought they'd stopped looking for her."

MacKenzie caught her breath, moved by the immeasurable sadness conveyed in that one, single sentence.

"No, we never stop," she said quietly. "But, sometimes, we run out of leads. It so happens that we might—might—have something to investigate, so we're looking at like crimes. Your daughter's case popped up as a possible match."

"They never found a body," Gina Galanis said suddenly. "My daughter could still be alive."

MacKenzie didn't argue with her, she simply listened. "I understand, Mrs Galanis," she said.

"You couldn't possibly understand."

MacKenzie thought of Samantha, and of how she'd feel if anybody ever took her from them. She'd rip whoever did it to pieces, limb from miserable limb. She'd hunt them down, like a dog, and put them down so their rabid toxin didn't harm anyone else.

But, still, she didn't understand, for she'd never been put in that position.

"I'm sorry," she said simply. "You're right, Mrs Galanis. I don't understand, but I would like to try. I care about what happened, and about finding the truth."

Gina let out another sigh, and there came the soft sound of a cigarette being puffed at the other end of the line.

"All right," she said. "What do you want to know?"

"In the first place, I don't have an address on file for you," MacKenzie said. "Can you tell me where you were living, at the time of Thalia's disappearance? I presume it was near your restaurant, in town?"

"No," Gina said. "Back then, we had a big house in Darras Hall. We sold it, after the restaurant...well, we just sold it."

MacKenzie took down the address, and thought that Darras Hall was only a couple of miles from Ponteland, where Melanie Yates' family had lived, and near to where their old police headquarters was based. It must have been a daily insult for her colleagues to know that a killer had taken lives—in one sense, or another—right beneath their very noses.

It was the height of arrogance.

"How did it happen, Mrs Galanis?"

She took another long drag on her cigarette, before speaking.

"Thalia was young, Inspector—only just eighteen. She was looking forward to starting university in the autumn," she said softly. "My daughter is smart, you see. She's very smart."

Gina flipped back into the present tense, determined to think of her as alive, and not dead, rotting in the ground somewhere—or worse.

"We brought her up to be independent," she said. "But, now...I wonder, I worry...we gave her too much freedom."

"Why do you say that?"

Gina cried softly, almost inaudibly, but MacKenzie heard it nonetheless.

"I can call back," she offered. "I don't want to upset you, Mrs Galanis."

"It isn't you," she mumbled. "It makes no difference when you call…I cry every time I think of it."

MacKenzie said nothing, and waited until the woman was able to speak again.

"Thalia was her own girl," she said, after a long pause. "But we trusted her. She wasn't a fool; she knew how to take care of herself, Inspector. She even did one of those self-defence courses, with real police, so she could learn some moves."

"That's good," MacKenzie said. "She was aware of the dangers."

"Not aware enough," her mother said wretchedly. "She went out with her friends, one Friday night, after school. She was over eighteen, Inspector, and we thought… we thought she knew how to be safe. But then we got the call from her friends. They said she was gone, they couldn't find her anywhere. She'd disappeared into the night."

MacKenzie heard an alarm bell ringing in the back of her mind, louder and louder; so loud, she knew this one was one of his.

"Where was she last seen?" she asked.

"At a club called Underground Headquarters," Gina said, bitterly. "They had no CCTV footage, no proper security. They said the cameras were defective. We tried to sue them for negligence, but the case collapsed...we tried everything we could think of, Inspector, until there was nothing more we could do."

"It wasn't your fault," MacKenzie said. "We shouldn't have to lock up our daughters, Gina. They should be free to go out, to dance with their friends and live their lives without fear. It's every person's right."

Later, when MacKenzie ended the call, explaining she had her own daughter to collect, Gina left her with a parting message.

"Hold her close, Inspector. Never let her go."

MacKenzie stared at the monitor, at Thalia Galanis' smiling face, and then collected her things.

Not before noticing one, last, interesting fact.

The last person to access the file had been Andrew Forbes, but the login was dated three years ago, not anytime during the past couple of days, as she might have expected. Even then, it would have been strange.

MacKenzie eyed the time, and made a swift call to Frank, who would need to collect Samantha.

She had a little more work to do, it seemed.

CHAPTER 31

Melanie Yates walked until exhaustion halted her progress, then she found a bench and sat down.

It turned out to be next to Wallsend Library.

She stayed there for a while, as the light faded and people came and went, while her mind tried to make sense of what it knew to be true.

DCS Forbes.

Andrew Forbes, the decorated police officer and detective.

Husband and father.

Killer.

She thought of his face, as he'd spoken of his understanding for her loss, her grief, her frustration and, all the while, he'd been the author of their misfortunes. How he must have been revelling in her pain, in her family's pain, all these years. How he must have laughed to himself, in the dark hours of the night, as he remembered his crimes…as he made love with his wife.

He deserved to die.

No more families should suffer as hers had suffered. No more young women should be taken and used like objects without hearts or souls, mere vessels for his sickness.

She would not allow it to continue.

Unaccountably, Ryan's face materialised in her mind's eye, and she smiled sadly as she thought of his last words to her, the previous day. He was a good man, an honourable man, and he'd made the correct decision for himself and his family, when the time came to deal with his own monster.

But then, that monster had died, in any case.

If Keir Edwards had lived, would Ryan be so philosophical about things? Would he be so certain of 'right' and 'wrong' if the man languished in prison, or escaped again, to harm other innocents? More likely, the anger would fester and eat away at his resolve, as it had done to hers.

Perhaps, when the time came, Ryan would understand why her choice was different. He would recognise her pain and forgive her for taking the revenge that was owed to her, but honour and duty would still win out; he would still bring her in.

She wouldn't blame him, either.

Were she in the same position, she would do the same thing.

Unless…

If she could find a way to make it look like an accident, or self-defence, it would solve all their problems. Of course, Ryan would know, he'd always know, but to the outside world he could say it was something other than premeditated murder.

He could tell himself that, if he wanted to. They all could.

Melanie the murderer, her mind whispered.

She let out a small cry, and hugged herself for warmth.

"Is there anything you need, flower?"

A kind-looking face appeared by her side, and Melanie guessed she was one of the librarians from the building at her back, leaving work for the day to return to hearth and home.

There was only one thing she needed.

"I'm fine, now," she said, and meant it.

The woman remained concerned, but nodded, taking in her smart clothing and generally neat appearance. She didn't look like somebody in need of help.

Perhaps not the kind of help she was able to offer.

"Well, take care, won't you?" the lady murmured, before moving away, casting a final glance over her shoulder.

Melanie watched her go, glad to be alone with her thoughts once again.

She had no evidence.

That was the biggest stumbling block. She didn't know how he had evaded the DNA matching, but he had, and she could only assume he'd substituted his own DNA record for some anonymous person, for the purposes of the police record. No wonder they'd never found a match, for the one who was a perfect match had ensured his data would never be discovered.

Her fingers curled into claws, as she imagined raking them down his face, as Lawana had done.

Lawana.

If she could only take a picture of him to show Lawana, the woman was sure to confirm he was her unknown attacker. But, to do that, she'd need to find Lawana's address, and the only way to access that information was to hack into MacKenzie's or Ryan's account. In her feverish state, she was tempted, but ultimately discarded the idea as being too risky, and too much of a betrayal of trust.

She already knew it was him. Lawana would only confirm the fact.

How to get him alone?

Then, it came to her, the crushing knowledge she hadn't quite fathomed before.

She had been the one he'd seen, at the school gymnasium. She, with her long hair, before she'd cut it, a month later. Her blue dress, which Gemma borrowed; her usual Friday night haunt.

Oh, God, she could see it all, now.

She'd always wondered why Gemma had left, without a 'goodbye', and without attracting attention or making a fuss. She'd wondered why nobody noticed them leaving, nobody questioned it at all.

It was because he was a police officer.

A trusted man of the law, with gravitas and authority, who'd probably frightened her sister with talk of trouble and cautionary tales. He'd probably seen her long hair, her blue dress, and thought it was the same girl he'd seen all the previous Fridays; the one who piqued his interest at the self-defence lecture, at her high school.

Instead, he'd taken the one who knew nothing about it; a girl who'd planned to become a mathematician, who'd wanted to use her brain to help others. A young woman whose worst crime had been her wish for acceptance, and to be loved by a sister who'd never understood her, had always been ever-so-slightly embarrassed by her dowdy twin.

The tears fell, but Melanie didn't notice.

She saw what he saw, in the club that night. A girl lost in the crowds, confused and tipsy, ready to go home. He saw his chance.

And now, she saw hers.

The reckoning was coming.

Shortly before five o'clock, Melanie took a taxi back to Police Headquarters.

She made her way directly upstairs and along the corridor, not stopping to say 'hello' to her team, but continuing to the very end, where he occupied a corner office. His PA had left for the evening, so she chanced a knock on the door.

"Come in!"

His voice rubbed along the nerves of her spine like acid and she shuddered, controlling her bowels with a strength she scarcely knew she had.

She arranged her features into something that passed for 'normal', and grasped the handle.

"Ah, Mel," he said, dropping whatever he'd been doing to drink in the sight of her. "Come in and shut the door.

I'm glad you stopped by; I have a bit of news for you, as it happens."

She lifted her eyes to look at him and, for the first time, saw what she hadn't seen before. What she'd been too blind to see.

A demon, in human form.

Now that the veil had lifted, she saw the way his eyes studied her, as she was studying him. He was probably thinking of all the ways he would kill her...but, that was all right, because she was doing the very same thing.

"Good afternoon, sir," she said, in a tone she barely recognised as her own. "What news might that be?"

If he sensed a change in her, he put it down to stress, or something equally mundane.

Not once did he consider that she might know him, and what he was.

"I understand Woman A has had a breakthrough, of sorts," he said, coming around to the front of the desk to lean back against it.

She watched his every move, a part of her willing him to try it.

Come on, she thought. Make your move.

Show yourself.

But he continued to smile at her, looking like every other Average Joe she'd ever seen walking the streets of the city. Nobody would pick him out of a crowd, and it was that invisibility cloak that had shielded him from sight, and protected him.

"That's very good news," she said. "Has she been able to describe her attacker, then?"

"Apparently, he has brown eyes," Forbes said.

She looked into those eyes now, and saw nothing but darkness. All the evil of the world lay hidden in those brown eyes, Melanie thought, and she'd watch them die before the week was out.

"It doesn't help much," she said. "Is there anything else?"

"She was able to describe some of the victims she saw in photographs on the wall of the grain room," he said, using his personal reference for his last special place.

None of the police team had ever referred to it as a 'grain room'.

Melanie smiled. "That's very good news," she said. "It won't be long before Jack and Denise will make some connections to missing persons and cold case crimes."

"You have a lot of faith in them," he said. "It would be so much easier to expedite the process. There must be hundreds of potential matches, but it'll take them weeks and weeks to work their way through a list like that. If only there was some way of finding out about Lawana's descriptions…"

He clucked his tongue, as if he was thinking of a way around the problem, but Melanie saw what he was doing. He hoped to plant an idea in her mind, to manipulate her poor, desperate heart into accessing her boyfriend's work computer, using his password to find out sensitive information from the file.

And, when she skipped back to him with the information, he'd find some way of suggesting they meet with Lawana and extract even more details. He'd ask her to hack into Jack's computer again, this time to find the address of Lawana's safe house.

Then, he'd kill her.

"Yes, it's a pity," she said, affecting an air of disappointment. "I suppose…no, I couldn't do that."

"Do what?" he queried.

Both play-acting, she thought. Two hunters, searching for the same kill, but only one of them would win.

"I could see if Jack has anything on his laptop," she mused. "I know it's wrong, but, if it's for the greater good of the investigation…"

"Leaders have to take executive decisions, Mel."

Oh, how much poison he poured, she thought. As though it was honey.

"I'd only use the information to try to help," she said aloud.

"Of course," he soothed her. "I know that, and I'm giving you my express permission. We can iron out any hiccups, later."

"Thank you, sir," she breathed, keeping her eyes lowered in case he should see the truth of what lay behind them.

"Perhaps you can update me, in the morning?"

"Yes, sir," she muttered. "Good evening."

"Sleep well," he said, after she'd gone, running down the corridor to the ladies' room, where she threw up the meagre contents of her stomach.

CHAPTER 32

By the time Ryan returned home, darkness had fallen over the village of Elsdon and the house he shared with his wife and child stood out like a beacon, perched on its small hill overlooking the valley. He'd fallen in love with the land and the views, which he'd gifted to his wife as a wedding present, and they'd built a home he thought they'd live in forever.

That was before men had come for Anna, the previous year, breaking into their sanctuary and stealing away their peace and sense of security.

Now, more cameras had been fitted and more locks put on the door, but it didn't remove the niggling fear he still felt as he drove up the hill and swung into their driveway; a part of him still expected to find her gone, taken from him, as she had been once before.

He saw her car in the driveway, alone now that his parents had returned home to Devon, and turned off his engine.

Everything was fine.

Still, he could see through some of the windows where the curtains hadn't yet been drawn, which meant that somebody else could see into their home and their lives, if they wanted to.

"Get a grip," he whispered, and scrubbed his hands over his face, shaking off the day.

But when he stepped through the front door and was met with silence—absolute silence, but for the whirring sound of the extractor fan above their oven—the worries swarmed back again, and he stood absolutely still, listening for his daughter's cry or his wife's laughter.

Nothing.

Then, there came the sound of a man's voice and, to Ryan's ears, it sounded angry.

He scoured the hallway for a weapon and grabbed an umbrella from the stand beside the door, which he gripped in one hand like a spear. Moving slowly, he peeked inside open doorways as he made his way along the hallway, towards the kitchen and family room.

As he approached, he began to make out the occasional word.

"…and I'll HUFF and I'll PUFF…"

Ryan stood outside the kitchen door and rested his forehead on the panel, laughing at himself. He set the umbrella aside then stepped inside to find Alex Gregory sitting at the kitchen table. Emma was sitting on his lap, obviously enthralled while he read her the story of the Three Little Pigs.

Anna stood by the oven stirring a saucepan, which she set aside when she spotted him.

"Hello, stranger," she smiled, and crossed the room to wrap her arms around him.

He returned the embrace, and then turned to the other man who was now blowing raspberries on his daughter's hand.

"Alex, it's good to see you, again."

Gregory stood up with Emma in his arms, and flipped her so she 'flew' through the air towards her daddy.

Ryan smiled, and caught her up in his arms, overjoyed to hear her laughter.

"Good to see you, too," Gregory said, watching how easily Ryan handled his child, thinking how well he'd taken to fatherhood. "You have a beautiful little girl, there. She was trying to read along, too."

Ryan nodded, pride shining in his clear grey eyes.

"She's talking already—only simple words, but apparently that's unusual for her age."

"Daddy," she said, and squished his cheeks in between her chubby hands, so his lips formed an 'o' like a blowfish.

She giggled again.

"She had a good day at nursery," Anna said, from across the room.

"That's great," Ryan said. "And how was your day?"

That was equally as important, considering Anna had been at home with Emma for months. It had become her world, but he knew his wife was ready to reclaim a bit of her own identity, and Emma was ready for the next stage of development.

"I'm fine," she said, with a gentle smile for his thoughtfulness. "The first hour or so, I didn't know what to do with myself, so I went for a run and felt better for it. Then, I wrote a chapter or two of my book."

"Anna was telling me about the new venture," Gregory said, reaching across to take the plates from Anna's hands. "It sounds great."

Ryan nodded.

"She can do anything she puts her mind to," he said, with absolute conviction.

With her back turned, one hand stirring the soup she'd made, Anna felt emotion well in her throat. It meant so much to have someone believe in her, as Ryan did.

"Thank you both for having me to stay," Gregory said, as they settled themselves at the table and Ryan slotted Emma into her highchair. "Your home is lovely, and the views are spectacular."

Anna smiled, but it didn't quite reach her eyes, and Ryan noticed.

Perhaps she felt the same way he did, which was that their special place had been sullied.

"Thank you," he said. "But then, it's hard to find a bad view in these parts."

"Do you ever miss the South?" Gregory asked, as they settled down to eat. "You grew up in Devon, didn't you?"

Ryan nodded, and thought back to the days of his childhood.

"Devonshire is lovely, too," he admitted. "The terrain is different, though; softer, somehow, whereas I'm…"

"Tough as old boots?" Anna put in, with a wink.

"I was going to say, 'rugged', like the landscape around here," Ryan said, in a dignified tone he'd heard Phillips use many times before.

Gregory chuckled.

"Life up here seems to suit you," he said, watching Emma munch her way through pieces of bread she dipped into a small bowl of the soup her mother had made.

"Boots," she said, pointing at her father, and made them laugh again.

"That's me told," Ryan grinned, and kissed the top of her downy head. "How about you, Alex? Any chance of you settling down with a good woman?"

Gregory smiled, but his eyes grew shadowed.

"If I found one like yours, perhaps I would," he said, raising a glass towards Anna, who clinked the edge of it with her own.

"There's only one Anna," Ryan said, his eyes shining at the woman seated beside him. "But there might be someone perfect for you, out there. Perhaps you haven't met them, yet."

"Perhaps," Gregory said, and thought of a woman he'd met in America, one with dark eyes and a warm heart. "The question is whether I'll be smart enough to know it, when I do meet them."

"That's the trick," Ryan agreed, and then turned to his daughter. "Almost bedtime for you, little one."

"I'll take her upstairs, so you two can catch up," Anna offered. "You probably have things to discuss."

They thanked her, both men made a fuss of the baby, then waved her off.

Ryan turned to Gregory in the quiet that followed their departure, and read concern on his friend's face.

"Coffee, first, then you can tell me what's on your mind."

Ryan and Gregory settled themselves in the living room, where Anna had set a small fire. The night air had turned chilly and, whilst Anna had been born and bred a hardy northerner, she felt a modicum of pity for those who were accustomed to balmier climes. Additionally, she'd set out a joke book on 'Translating Geordie Phrases' upon which she'd stuck a post-it note that read, 'Refer to this, if in doubt'.

Gregory picked it up and chuckled.

"I'll say it again, Ryan: you're a lucky man."

"I know," Ryan replied, and handed his friend a dram of whisky, now they were technically 'off the clock'. "She's far too good for the likes of me, but I thank my lucky stars she doesn't seem to mind."

Gregory smiled, took a sip of his drink and felt warmer from the inside-out.

"You met with Lawana, today?"

Gregory nodded. "It went well, but I'm sure MacKenzie will bring you up to speed with the details," he said. "She hasn't remembered everything, yet; she isn't ready to. But it seems her mind has unlocked another door, because she was able to recall new information—particularly about the women she'd seen on his 'trophy wall' inside the kill room."

"That's great news," Ryan said, thinking of next steps and never doubting that MacKenzie and Lowerson would have taken them already.

He took a sip of his own drink to fortify himself before turning to what was really troubling them both.

"You met with Melanie, as well?"

Gregory nodded, and read Ryan's unspoken question. "You know I can't tell you confidential details," he said. "Not as a clinician."

"I know that."

Gregory chose his next words with care. "I can, however, tell you my observations about her demeanour—not taken from anything she told me, but rather as one person might note in another, from their body language."

Ryan nodded. "And?"

"I'm worried," Gregory said, not sugar-coating the message he needed to impart. "She's in a bad place—a dark place, I think—and she isn't choosing to share it with anyone."

Reading between the lines, Ryan understood that to mean she hadn't confided in Gregory, who was usually able to draw out even the most closed personalities.

That alone was worrying, without the rest.

He had one question uppermost in his mind, and he was almost afraid of the answer.

"I don't need to be a psychiatrist to take an educated guess as to what she's thinking about," Ryan said. "She's told me some of it, though I'm aware she's holding back the worst parts. I tell myself, we're all entitled to secrets—and who am I to judge? I harboured some dark thoughts myself, back in the day."

He paused, and knocked back the rest of his whisky.

"Will she act on her thoughts, Alex? That's what I need to know."

Gregory leaned forward in his chair, thinking of the young woman he'd spoken to earlier in the day, and the lies she'd told him.

"If I wanted to cover myself or play it safe, I'd say something like, 'Anybody is capable of aggression, in the right circumstances'. To a large extent, that's true, but it would be a cowardly reply, so I'll tell you what my gut is telling me right now, as someone who's worked with a hell of a lot of people who've acted on their worst thoughts," he said. "Yes, Ryan, I think that, if she finds this man, Melanie will kill him."

They fell silent, each man processing the import of those words, while the fire crackled in the grate.

"You could be wrong," Ryan said eventually. "We could be wrong. Nothing is ever set in stone."

Gregory nodded. "I hope we're both wrong," he said.

They fell into a companionable silence, each man caught up in his own thoughts about Melanie Yates, each hoping she wouldn't stray onto the wrong path, along which neither of them could follow.

Anger was a lonely road.

CHAPTER 33

"Mel? Can I have a word?"

Lowerson decided he couldn't put off the discussion any longer, and cornered her while she was making a cup of tea.

She looked up, without much interest.

"What is it?"

He stuck his hands in his pockets, and decided to say it quickly.

"I've been offered a promotion by the new DCS," he said. "It would mean transferring to South Tyneside, but there's the promise of a sergeant's post, by the finish."

Melanie's hand froze, and it didn't take long for her to realise what Forbes was trying to do.

He wanted her alone, and lonely besides. He thought she needed a man by her side, to feel safe, and therefore, if he siphoned Jack away to another command area, she'd feel defenceless and come to trust and rely on him, even more.

Perhaps that plan might have worked, if she hadn't remembered who he was.

"Mel? Say something."

She began stirring her tea again, wondering what to say to Jack.

Of course, she wanted to tell him everything, to cry on his shoulder and hatch a plan together to entrap the man who'd killed her sister. But Jack would want to do things the 'right' way, the lawful way, rather than in accordance with natural justice.

She couldn't have that.

Nor could she tell Jack that his promotion was really a means to use him, rather than a genuine reflection of his capabilities. That would cut all the deeper, since it would be the second time he'd fallen foul of a false promise of advancement.

Though she loved him, in that moment, she knew Jack's ambition was his greatest weakness, for it blinded him to all else.

"Are you going to take it?" she asked.

He was hoping she might have congratulated him, but he supposed that was too much to expect.

"I was thinking of it," he said. "Is there any reason I shouldn't?"

She swallowed, knowing that by omitting to tell him what she knew, that was tantamount to another lie. When he found out, he'd be devastated.

There were always casualties in war, and hers had been fought for more than fifteen years.

"I'm happy for you," she said, pinning a bright smile on her face. "Not before time!"

Later, he would ask himself whether he'd known it was a lie, and had simply chosen to believe what he wanted to believe, but, in that moment, he took her words at face value.

"Thanks," he said. "I know it'll be strange, at first, me being in a different office…"

He wasn't ready to think about that, so he pushed it from his mind and tried to focus on the benefits.

"On the other hand, it's a better pay bracket, more responsibility…I just need to let Ryan know."

"How do you think he'll take it?"

"I hope he'll be happy for me."

"Ryan isn't the kind of man to hold anyone back," she said.

Except if their goal was to exact revenge.

"This calls for a celebration," she declared. "Why don't you get some glasses, and hunt out that bottle of champagne we never got around to drinking on Valentine's?"

He busied himself and she watched him, hoping he would forgive the betrayal, hoping he would understand.

At that moment, he happened to look across and caught the expression of sadness on her face.

"Hey, are you okay?" He set the bottle aside and moved back to take her in his arms. "Are you worried things will change between us, or something like that? I know we won't be working together, directly, but we'll see each other at home. We'll just have to make a bit more effort to spend quality time together, that's all. Especially when Operation Heartbeat is over."

Her cheek rested against his chest, and she listened to his heartbeat, steady and strong.

"It'll be over soon enough," she whispered, and he smiled above her head, thinking of the progress they'd made that day in finding some potential matches.

He only wished he could tell her all about it, but he was a man of his word.

Melanie waited until Jack had taken himself off for a bath, and then retrieved his work laptop from its leather sleeve, where he'd left it on the hallway table. She listened for the sound of a bathroom door opening, but all she heard was the tinkle of water running into the tub, followed by the indistinct sound of a podcast playing and she knew Jack would be occupied for at least half an hour.

She took her chance.

It was a small matter to access the computer files, considering she guessed his password immediately—Jack was often guilty of keeping old ones running long past their sell-by date, and it seemed he hadn't changed it in a very long time. Melanie didn't allow feelings of guilt to factor into her decision-making, because her actions were for the greater good and that was the only consideration as far as she was concerned.

Quickly, she located the relevant files and brought up the most recent summary document.

There, Jack had listed the names and case numbers of potential victims based in the North-East. Her eyes soaked up the information greedily, and she made quick copies of the names, dates and any other pertinent information that might help when she was doing her own research.

Then, she brought up MacKenzie's shorthand transcript of Gregory's session with Lawana, hurrying to find the details she needed about the women she had seen, then making her own scribbled copy.

In the bathroom, she heard the podcast finish, and the swish of water as Jack pulled the plug.

She needed to hurry.

There was little time for much else, but she noted one final thing of interest: a scanned image of a death certificate relating to a man by the name of Stuart Mallen, a name she recognised instantly from her own in-depth knowledge of every individual involved in her sister's case. Mallen had been one of the bouncers manning The Boat on the night her sister disappeared; not one of the men she'd spoken to, on the door, but one of the security men who circled the interior, keeping the peace.

Mallen had been murdered in an assumed gangland killing, back in 2009.

Case closed.

She shut down the file, then logged out and turned off the computer, slipping it back into its sleeve before returning it to the hallway table.

When Lowerson came out of the bathroom, pink and smelling of lavender bath salts, he found Melanie curled up on the sofa, channel-surfing for a movie they could watch together. For the first time in weeks, his heart lifted, and he felt they had turned a corner.

Life was looking rosy, again.

Melanie waited until Jack had fallen asleep, then set to work.

She settled herself at the kitchen table with her own laptop, this time, and retrieved the notes she'd made earlier. So far, it seemed her colleagues had found three possible victims—two missing persons, and one cold case murder. Each was based in the North East, which they assumed was the killer's hunting ground, and each went missing after her sister's death in summer of 2003 but no later than spring of 2008. It was likely that Jack and Denise would soon grind to a halt in their cross-checking of Lawana's descriptions, and they would come to realise the likely matches for victims in the North East dried up after 2008. They would consider various reasons for this: perhaps, they might think, the killer sated himself, and took a hiatus from killing after indulging himself in a spree. It was true that some killers could last for years, satisfied with their memories for long stretches of time, before feeling the urge to kill again. Then again, they might think he'd become adept at hiding his crimes, more sophisticated in his methodologies, which made it harder for them to detect 'like' crimes; or, they might think he'd given up the game, altogether, or died himself. The final likely possibility was that he was nomadic, or had moved away from the area, which was the truth of the matter, if they only knew it. If Jack and Denise came to this last conclusion, they would be faced with the monumental task of trying to find potential victim matches to missing persons or cold case murders in the whole of the United Kingdom—assuming their quarry had remained in the country. It was an impossible task, and without any idea of his identity they would be stabbing in the dark.

They didn't know what she knew.

They didn't know his name and, therefore, didn't know his personal history, as she did.

Andrew Thomas Forbes was forty-three. He had a wife, Jenna, who was forty, and two children, a boy and a girl aged thirteen and fifteen, respectively, which meant that his wife had been pregnant or had just given birth around the same time he'd been killing her sister, amongst others. He held a degree in Business Studies, a Master's degree in Philosophy of Law, and several other postgraduate diplomas relating to policing and governance, as well as numerous other certificates in forensic science.

All the better to hide himself with, she thought.

Forbes had a solid police record, an unblemished reputation as a murder detective, and countless high-profile collars that had elevated him to the rank he now held. With every new certificate, every new commendation, he cushioned himself against any possible whisper of doubt that he was the man he said he was. The higher he climbed the social ladder, the less believable it was, at least to the outside world, that Andrew Forbes could be the monster she knew him to be.

He hid within the folds of his own middle-class respectability, but it wouldn't save him.

Not from her.

Andrew Forbes had moved around the country. After Ponteland, he and his family had lived in the small, upmarket town of Woodstock, on the outskirts of Oxford, while he'd worked for Thames Valley Police Constabulary. After that, he'd returned north, but had lived and worked south of the River Tyne, which is where he'd decided to try to kill Lawana.

What she wanted to know was, who else had he hurt, when, and where?

Melanie decided to expand her research to Oxfordshire, and logged onto the Register of Cold Cases to begin a painstaking search that would take her through the night and into the early hours of the morning.

By the end, she knew she was right, and had gathered a further eleven names she strongly suspected to have been his handiwork. However, this was only the product of a couple of hours' research, and Melanie knew there could, and would, be many more.

He'd been operating for years.

CHAPTER 34

Andrew Forbes was seated on the sofa in his living room, one arm resting comfortably on the arm rest with a bottle of Italian beer in hand, the other arm draped around his teenage daughter, who was snuggled against him. They watched an old, black-and-white movie version of *The Thirty-Nine Steps*, which happened to be one of his favourites, and she didn't seem to mind that it didn't feature any muscular men in superhero costumes, or weedy-looking young men who happened to be five-hundred-year-old vampires, or some such nonsense.

"Dad?"

"Yes, poppet?"

"Did you hear about the woman who died, down in London?"

"Lots of people die," he said, in a flat voice. "Which one do you mean?"

"I mean, the woman who was walking home and got into a stranger's car because she thought he was a police officer," his daughter said, and felt his heart begin to hammer against her ear, where she rested her head on his chest.

Forbes stared straight ahead, focusing his attention on the movie.

"You shouldn't worry yourself about things like that," he said, in a tone she hadn't heard before.

"We're all a bit worried," she said. "Me and my friends."

He found himself in No Man's Land; an odd place he'd never visited before, where he was suddenly uncomfortable in his own skin, and wished she would stop talking. He kept his home life and his hobby very separate and didn't like to be reminded of one when he was fully immersed in the other.

"Let's watch the movie," he suggested, and turned up the volume to give her the hint.

She settled for a moment or two, then tried again.

"Mum told me that you used to give talks to teenagers about self-defence," she said softly. "Can you show me some moves, Dad?"

Forbes' skin crawled, his head ached, and he itched to be far, far away.

But his daughter awaited a response.

"Sure," he said eventually. "Why not?"

He paused the movie, and turned up the lights, just in time to see his wife enter the room with a cup of tea for them both.

"What's this?" Jenna asked.

"Dad's going to show me some self-defence," his daughter said.

"Careful, now, don't hit any of my photo frames," his wife said, hurrying to move them out of the way as they cleared an area in the centre of the living room.

Forbes faced his own flesh and blood, but remembered a time when it had been Melanie Yates standing before him, and experienced something like a computer crash as his brain struggled to make sense of two competing impulses. On the one hand, he felt protective towards his daughter; not for her own sake, but as a mark of pride. On the other, he felt far more complex and desirable emotions when he thought of Melanie, and of how she'd fight him, one day.

"—Dad?"

"Yep. Right, now, the key thing to remember is always to focus on the vulnerable areas," he said. "These are the eyes, the throat, the nose, the solar plexus, the groin and the knees. When you're old enough to have your own car, make sure to use your keys as a weapon but, until then, there are lots of things you can do to evade a surprise attack. Most women haven't the slightest idea how to even try."

"What sort of things?" his daughter asked.

"Obviously, you can kick your attacker in the groin, if you get a clear shot," he said, remembering Lawana's bullseye, and how it had left him rolling in pain on the floor of the grain store. "You can use the heel of your palm to cut upward—like this."

He showed her the action.

"Excellent," he said. "Now, one of the simplest moves is to grab an attacker's wrist—take their little finger and ring finger in one hand, and their middle and index finger in your other hand, and bend the wrist back."

"What if I can't grab their hand?"

"Hit him with a fist or shove a finger between his collarbones, or into his Adam's apple," Forbes replied. "But, by far the best, is to attack the groin."

He showed her several more moves and, for twenty minutes or more, was able to entirely forget himself.

By the end, he was so moved by their bonding experience, he decided to do something extraordinary and gift her one of his most prized possessions.

"Wait there," he said, as his daughter was preparing to leave for bed. "I have something for you."

He moved into his study and shut the door behind him, then made directly for the sideboard and the cavity where he kept the key to some of his special things. He'd also risked keeping one or two 'emergency' items, for occasions when he couldn't wait and needed to touch, or to see, that which had belonged to one of his girls.

He reached inside the box and brought out a long, silver pendant in the shape of a feather. He held it carefully, fondling it between his fingers, and closed his eyes to remember how it had looked against her skin, that last time.

So long ago, now, the memory was beginning to fade.

Perhaps a new owner would help to improve his recollection.

When he returned, he held out the necklace to his daughter with a tender smile.

"I was going to wait to give this to you on your birthday," he said. "Nearly sixteen—where has the time gone, eh, Jenna?"

His wife smiled, delighted to see him so engaged with his children and with her.

It made a change.

"Here you are, poppet."

His daughter took the necklace from him and held it up, her face creasing into a smile.

"Thanks, Dad! I love it. Can I try it on, now?"

"Let me help you," he said, eager now to see the necklace against her young skin. "Lift up your hair."

When she spun around, it was no longer his daughter he saw. It was a girl, long dead, dancing in a blue dress that now lay in a room of his creation, bearing the bloodstains that were also his creation. He'd discarded her body long ago, and that had been a mistake; something he put down to inexperience. Now, he was never so feckless, and their bodies were never found, nor indeed any trace of the women he took. It had taken some years to come around to his preferred method but, now he'd found it, he stuck to it.

"Night, Dad. Thanks, again."

His daughter leaned up to give him a hug, then gave her mother the same treatment, leaving them both in the living room.

Jenna was about to excuse herself to go to bed, when she caught a look in her husband's eye.

"Andy?"

"Why don't we stay up a bit later?" he suggested. "Just you and me?"

She could never have known that she was a vessel for his need, nothing more, but Jenna Forbes was a kind-hearted woman who'd been worn down by life, and a loveless relationship. She jumped at the scraps of affection he showed her, even when her heart whispered that something was wrong.

"Somethin' on your mind, love?"

In a house several miles away from where Andrew and Jenna Forbes assumed the missionary position, Frank Phillips got into bed with his wife, who seemed unusually quiet.

"Hmm? Oh, nothing, really," she said, leaning across to turn off her bedside lamp. "I sometimes think I've been in the job for too long, that's all. I'm seeing suspects around every corner."

"Oh? Who've you got your beady eye on, this time?"

Phillips had taken extra care to brush his teeth twice, after his exploits at the tearoom, earlier in the day, but he knew his wife's superior nose for sugar and sin was a force not to be reckoned with.

"You'll probably laugh at this," she said. "But, when I was looking into some potential matches for victims in the area, I happened to check their old case files. I don't know why I decided to check the log, as well, but I did. Just one of those things, I suppose. Anyway, I clicked on it and…there it was. The last person to look at Thalia Galanis's file was DCS Forbes, three years ago."

Phillips scratched the end of his nose, while he thought about it.

"Could be lots of reasons why he was looking at those files," he said. "There's plenty of times when we check old case files or missing persons, while we're looking for 'like' crimes. Maybe he was doing the same thing and her name cropped up, but didn't end up being a match. That's a simple enough explanation."

MacKenzie remained troubled.

"I thought that myself, until I decided to check the logs for each and every 'like' crime we're looking into," she said. "Guess who comes up on the list of previous users? One or two, I could understand, but…every one?"

"Aye, it does seem like a bit of a coincidence," he said.

"I'll mention it to Ryan, in the morning."

"I'll be seein' him tomorrow, anyhow," Phillips yawned. "We're goin' up to Bamburgh again, to interview someone."

"How's it goin' up there?"

"Gettin' closer," he said. "I can feel it. Another chat with this lass and I think we'll be another step closer."

MacKenzie snuggled down beneath the covers and leaned across to kiss him goodnight.

"Mind you don't get lost, while you're up there, and wind up in The Copper Kettle again."

Phillips' eyes flew open and he turned to her in the darkness.

"How did you know—?"

She reached across and patted his cheek, as she might have done a simpleton.

"It's like a moth to a flame, Frank. Just don't let it happen too often, or else it won't just be your Lycra shorts that'll rip along the arse crack."

CHAPTER 35

Wednesday

When the call came through, Ryan awoke immediately.

There was never any groggy, stumbling transition from sleep, only an instant return to consciousness and the knowledge that whoever was calling him didn't bring glad tidings.

"DCI Ryan," he said, keeping his voice low as he slipped out of bed.

"Sir? It's DC Reed. I'm very sorry to trouble you at home, at this hour."

He glanced at the clock, which read five-thirty.

"What's the problem?"

"A body has been found on the beach in Bamburgh, sir. I thought you'd want to be the first to know."

"Who?" he asked.

"It's Angela's cleaner, Irina Pavlova."

Ryan closed his eyes, thinking of the young woman they'd spoken to in Seahouses.

"You're sure?"

"Yes, sir. I recognise her."

"All right," he said. "She has an invalid mother. Make sure someone goes to take care of her, if need be. I don't think there's any other family in the country, and we don't know how long she's been left alone."

He rattled off the address.

"Yes, sir. I'll take care of that straight away."

"When was the body discovered?" he asked, coming back to the matter in hand. "Has the scene been secured?"

"Control Room had a call from a dog-walker less than half an hour ago," she said. "They referred the matter to me, since they know I'm already investigating a suspicious death in the area. I hope I did the right thing, calling you so early, but I wasn't sure how you'd want to run this, sir, given that more people will be heading down to the beach soon."

Ryan snuck past his daughter's open doorway, where she still slept soundly, and moved swiftly downstairs towards the kitchen, where coffee awaited, and he could speak freely.

"Where was she found, exactly?"

"Amongst the dunes, not far from the base of the castle on its northern elevation," she said. "I've posted two officers to guard the site, and cordoned off any access to the public, for now, but I need permission to close off the beach."

"You have it."

"Thank you, sir. I've taken the liberty of contacting the forensics team—"

"Good," he said. "I'll meet you on the beach in half an hour."

"Thank you," she said, obviously relieved.

"Oh, and Reed?"

"Yes, sir?"

"Two more things. Firstly, you don't need to keep calling me, 'sir.'"

"All right, s—thank you."

"Secondly, why the hell didn't you tell me you had a kid waiting for you, at home? I'd never have kept you so long, yesterday, if I'd known that was the case. How are you placed for childcare this morning?"

At the other end of the line, Charlie smiled, and could understand why his team spoke so highly of him.

"I appreciate that," she said. "My mother stays with us three nights per week, so I'm covered today—thank you for asking."

"It's hard, juggling parenthood and a job like ours," he said. "Let's not make it any harder than it needs to be, eh? Tell me if you need to change shifts, or anything like that."

"I will," she promised.

He nodded, turning on the coffee machine with one hand while he held his mobile phone in the other.

"All right. Stay put, Phillips and I will join you soon. What kind of coffee do you like?"

"I—" she was taken aback, never having had a senior officer bring her coffee before. "Just milk, one sugar please."

"Right. Thirty minutes, Reed."

Ryan was true to his word, for, on the dot of six o'clock, he appeared on the crest of the dunes with Phillips by his side, both men dressed for the cool morning wind that swept in from the sea and whipped up the sand at their feet. Alongside a small field kit of nitrile gloves and other protective coverings, he carried a cardboard tray of hot drinks in one hand, and Reed thought she'd never seen a more welcome sight.

"White, one sugar," he said briskly, handing a cup to her, which she accepted gratefully. "Frank? Tea, for you."

"Ta," the other man said, taking a slurp. "Looks like the forensics team are here already."

He jutted his chin towards the tent being erected nearby, its tarpaulin billowing on the breeze as the CSIs grappled to stake each corner into the ground.

"They arrived about ten minutes ago," Reed told them. "It's a different Senior CSI this time—Tom Faulkner?"

Ryan and Phillips both smiled.

"Must be back from his holidays," Phillips remarked.

"We'll let him get set up, then have a word with him," Ryan said.

"I'm still having trouble locating any next of kin for Angela," Reed said, while they waited. "Her solicitor is out of the country, at the moment, but he was due back in the UK last night, so if I don't hear from him this morning I'll chase him up."

"Good," Ryan said. "We need to know who inherits, now that Watson's claim is invalid."

"I had an update from the pathologist, too," Reed told them. "I'll send through his report but, as expected, he's confirmed the cause of death as acute myocardial infarction—otherwise known as a heart attack."

"What about post-mortem interval?" Ryan asked, while his eyes watched the tide roll back and forth along the sand, leaving arcs of shadow in its wake.

"He thinks Angela had been dead less than an hour when your wife and John Watson found her," Reed told them.

"Fresh, then," Phillips said, and Ryan pulled a face at him. "Well, I'm just sayin', she was probably still warm."

"There's more," Reed said. "According to her medical records, Angela was on blood-thinning tablets to help regulate arrhythmia of the heart, and try to prevent a heart attack. However, the toxicology report doesn't show any sign of them in her bloodstream. It did report abnormally high levels of caffeine."

Ryan took a thoughtful sip of his coffee and tried not to worry about how much caffeine might be swimming around his system, on any given day.

"Was she in the habit of taking her blood thinners?" he wondered. "Plenty of people are prescribed medicines, but whether they take them is another matter."

"I found a pill tray on her dressing table," Reed said. "You know, the ones labelled with each day of the week? It was empty. Individual medicines and bottles have been bagged and tagged, but I can tell you I remember seeing a couple of them with pharmacist stickers on the front, which would suggest a specific prescription rather than something she'd bought over the counter. Perhaps they were the blood thinners."

"Check it out," Ryan advised. "On the face of it, despite evidence to the contrary, Angela hadn't been taking her tablets. My next question is: did she drink too many caffeine-heavy drinks? Even a layman like me knows that would be against any doctor's advice, given her condition."

Reed nodded. "I can ask Pauline, or the archaeological team," she said. "They'd have known her habits, especially over the past two weeks."

"You're thinkin' someone could have replaced her pills with somethin' else?" Phillips wondered aloud. "Aye, I'm thinkin' the same."

"Any one of them could have done it," Ryan said. "They all had opportunity."

"Watson did say Angela had fallen, before," Phillips reminded him. "Maybe that was to do with the arrhythmia? It tends to make folk light-headed. If she wasn't taking her tablets, maybe that's how she ended up at the bottom of the stairs—"

"It doesn't explain the pink material," Ryan muttered.

"Aye, but that could be somethin' or nothin'," Phillips said.

"If it hadn't been removed, deliberately, then I'd agree with you. As it is, Angela had spoken of seeing a ghost for two weeks prior to her death. Factoring in what we now know about her medication, and this is starting to look a lot like a carefully planned programme of abuse."

"Where does Irina fit into it all?" Phillips wondered.

"She was the Pink Lady," Reed suggested, and Ryan nodded.

"Yes, I think we may very well find a pink costume hanging in her wardrobe," he said.

"Why would she do a thing like that?"

"Most likely, because she was threatened, paid, or maybe both," Ryan replied, draining the last of his coffee before facing the inevitable. "We may find her immigration papers aren't as full and complete as they should be, which is something that could have made her vulnerable."

"Poor lass," Phillips said, rubbing a hand over his eyes. "Maybe I should have tried a bit harder, yesterday. If we'd stayed a bit longer, worked on her…"

"You can't second-guess these things, Frank. She had the opportunity to tell us and she didn't. Perhaps she planned to speak to her accomplice before doing anything; we just don't know."

"Her accomplice?" Reed queried.

"Make no mistake, Irina was an accomplice to murder," Ryan said, flatly. "Vulnerable or coerced, she still made a choice, and she chose to help terrify an old woman to death. My sympathy doesn't extend that far."

He began pulling on his gloves.

"Come on, let's see if she can give us a clue about who was the mastermind."

CHAPTER 36

Melanie Yates was up long before Jack awakened, but she'd pressed a soft kiss to his cheek before leaving him and asked his sleeping form to forgive her, and to understand the reasons for her deception. Then, she'd driven directly to Andrew Forbes' house, in the Great Park area of Gosforth, which was a nice, family-oriented suburb of Newcastle upon Tyne. She'd parked on a neighbouring road with shared access to the cul-de-sac where he lived, and waited for him and his wife to leave; he, to drive to the office, and she, to drive their children to school.

Only then did Melanie exit her own car and walk around to his front door.

The house was at the end of a row of detached properties, but the nearest neighbour was close by and could look out at any moment to see her approaching Forbes' front door. That being the case, she kept her head low and held the brown packing box in front of her, playing the part of a delivery person, should anyone ask questions later.

When she reached the door, she set the packing box down, looked around for signs of any CCTV cameras, and was surprised to find there were none.

Either Forbes believed he had nothing to hide, or there was nothing to find.

Either way, she was going in.

Melanie retrieved a small, metal implement from her pocket and, with another look over her shoulder, set to work on the locks. She was no expert, and never claimed to be, but she knew as much as she ever cared to and had enough rudimentary skill to jimmy a standard lock.

Still, as the minutes ticked by, she began to worry, until there came a comforting click and the door opened.

Without hesitation, she stepped inside, shutting it behind her.

The alarm was on—she could hear it beeping—and Melanie took another chance, flipping up the keypad to try one of three number combinations she'd given herself permission to try, before abandoning the attempt.

1, 2, 3, 4

The first of two 'standard' combinations a manufacturer often used as a factory default.

The beeping continued, so she moved onto her second attempt.

0000

The second 'standard' combination she knew a manufacturer often used.

Again, the beeping continued.

Now, she tried her wild card.

2007.

The beeping stopped.

Of course, she thought. He'd used the year of her sister's death as a memorable number.

Not stopping to think about it, she turned to survey the monster's home and found it alarmingly normal. The floors were carpeted beige to match the walls, where a series of photographs hung in frames depicting a smiling Andrew with his family. Her eyes stung as she looked at each of their faces, even those of the children, whose father had destroyed so many other families while they enjoyed the cushion of a stable family life—albeit living with a psychopath.

Not their fault, she reminded herself.

She turned away, blinded by tears, which she scrubbed away with the heel of her gloved hand before investigating each of the downstairs rooms, moving silently from living room to dining room, to kitchen and cloakroom until, finally, she reached a door that was locked.

His study?

Why would a man need to lock a door inside his own house? she might have asked, if she'd been his wife. But he would've told her he was protecting the children from the disturbing content of his work files, no doubt.

The man had an answer for everything.

Melanie took out her toolkit again and worked on the lock, her fingers growing sweaty inside their plastic sheath.

Tick, tock, tick, tock, her mind whispered.

She focused herself on the task, swearing as she lost her grip once or twice, until the door finally gave way.

Forbes' study was another example of plain décor, with cream walls and very little clutter on the desk. There were a few frames of his certificates, pictures of him in dress uniform accepting some commendation or another from the Chief Constable or the Mayor, and even one of him smiling with a foppish-looking Boris Johnson, at some police function or another.

She turned to the only other major piece of furniture in the room, which was a large sideboard set against one wall. It was heavy, made of oak or something similar, and its doors were firmly locked, as were the drawers at his desk.

He must keep the keys on his person, she thought.

She checked her watch and knew there was no time to work on the locks on the sideboard, nor the locks at his desk.

It was time to leave.

Rushing now, she shut the door to his study and tried desperately to lock the door behind her.

"Come on," she muttered, fiddling with the metal, this way and that. "Lock, for God's sake…"

Finally, she heard the click, and rose unsteadily to her feet, feeling faint.

Keep it together, she told herself.

Melanie stumbled towards the front door, just in time to see Jenna Forbes making her way along the path, door key in hand.

Thinking fast, she spun around and set the alarm again, then pelted upstairs, two-at-a-time, to find a place to hide, until it was safe to leave. Heart racing, she made for what must have been his daughter's bedroom and rushed inside, dropping to the floor to crawl beneath the girl's bed and wait until the coast was clear.

Downstairs, she heard the front door open and close again, then the beep of an alarm before it was deactivated.

It never got any easier, looking upon the bodies of the dead.

Ryan could remember every one of them; their names, how they'd died—and how they'd lived. They occupied a room in the back of his mind, a permanent space where, at first, they'd squatted. At first, he'd tried to expel them from his memory, to cast them out for somebody else to mourn. When that hadn't worked, he'd learned to live with them, or else go mad.

Now, as he looked down into the shallow channel of sand where Irina Pavlova lay, he resigned himself to adding her name and face to the growing number and gave thanks that it wasn't half so bad as some he'd seen.

Then again, these things were relative.

Her thin body lay upright and, even beneath the stark illumination of several large, freestanding camera lights within the confines of the forensics tent, her skin was a translucent grey and waxy in texture, so she resembled a mannequin, all the blood in her system having collected on the underside of her body, where the skin would be purplish-brown by comparison. The exception to this was the skin around her neck, which displayed several contusion marks that would be consistent with manual strangulation.

Her eyes were wide open and staring, filmed white and coated with a layer of sand.

"I'll—y'nah, I best see if they've found anything in the vicinity..." Phillips said, feeling the contents of his stomach begin to roll.

For once, Ryan didn't joke, and merely nodded.

"Ask Reed if Irina's mother can talk to us," he said. "We need to know her last movements."

Phillips nodded, and bade a hasty retreat.

"Good to see you again," Faulkner said, coming to his feet from where he'd been kneeling on some plastic sheeting beside the body. "Been a little while, hasn't it?"

"Which is good news, I suppose," Ryan said, with a smile. "Good to see you, too, Tom. How was your holiday?"

"No dead bodies and about fifteen degrees warmer, so, I have to say, better than here," Faulkner joked.

Ryan laughed.

"No place like home," he said, and then turned to the girl lying a few feet away. "What can you tell me about her, so far?"

Faulkner lifted the goggles he wore, so he could see his friend more easily.

"As you've probably guessed, we're looking at a case of manual strangulation, I'd say," he replied. "I'll wait for the pathologist to confirm, but I'd bet that her larynx is crushed."

"Male or female perp?"

Sometimes, it was possible to estimate a handspan based on the position of each contusion and, from there, they could use a cross-section of average handspans to guess whether they were looking for a male or female killer.

"Well, put simply, if you pair up the position of each bruise, I'd estimate the person who strangled her has a handspan not too far off mine," Faulkner said, and held up his hand for Ryan to see. "I happen to know I have a handspan that's slightly below average for a male of my height and age, which means it could also be slightly above average in size, were I a woman."

"Very helpful," Ryan drawled.

"Well, you did ask," Faulkner joked.

"You wouldn't say the person who did this has overly small or large hands, then?"

Faulkner shook his head. "Not based on my past experience but, as you know, that's Pinter's department."

He referred to the Senior Police Pathologist attached to Northumbria CID, Doctor Jeffrey Pinter, who had a permanent office at the Royal Victoria Infirmary, in Newcastle. Although there were many good pathologists and Ryan had nothing especially against the one based down the road, at the nearer hospital, he'd requested that Pinter be the one to look at Angela's body and he'd be doing the same with Irina for, despite the man's foibles, he was the very best at what he did.

"Any prints?" Ryan asked.

Faulkner nodded. "For once, I'm pleased to say we have a sloppy killer," he replied. "No prints, but lots of good material from around the girl's throat—fabric traces, other bits and bobs. When d'you need the analysis?"

At another time, if their department had been busier, Ryan might have had to make a more ruthless decision when it came to conservation of resources. However, at that time, he could afford to ask for an expedited turnaround.

"Give me the twenty-four-hour service, Tom. Let's see if we can have this case put to bed by the end of the week."

With one final, compassionate glance at the shell of what had once been a person, he nodded to his colleague and dipped back outside, glad to leave the cloying atmosphere of death behind him.

CHAPTER 37

Mel stayed beneath the bed for more than two hours, in a state of constant anxiety and fear of discovery, which was heightened when Jenna Forbes had taken a turn around the room with a hoover, and tidied the bedclothes only inches above where she lay, frozen in place. Eventually, she heard the sound of the front door opening and closing again, then the dim sound of Jenna starting her car's engine.

Only when the house had been silent for more than five minutes did Melanie risk rolling out of her hiding place and rising to her feet once more. Her limbs were stiff and her neck aching from the uncomfortable position where she'd lain, and she took a moment to stretch, casting her eye around the teenager's room as she did so.

It wasn't dissimilar to her own room, at the age of fifteen.

A pink and turquoise striped duvet covered the bed, which was laden with fluffy scatter cushions of different sizes and shapes. Two small bedside tables rested on either side, topped by shaded lamps. Above the bed, a poster of Dua Lipa dominated, though there were other musical acts scattered on the walls around the room. Dream-catchers hung from the windows and caught the light, which blinded her for a second as a shaft of sunlight beamed through the crystal shards. Blinking away the spots, Melanie re-focused and saw there were various trinkets on the window-ledge, ranging from small porcelain animals and a stack of postcards propped inside a letter-holder to a wire-work jewellery stand in the shape of a tree, which held a number of ear-rings and necklaces.

She looked away, preparing to leave the room now the coast was clear, when her heart lurched violently against her chest.

Slowly, she looked back at the jewellery stand, taking one step forward, then another.

Melanie stopped in front of the window, eyes blazing, breath coming in shallow gasps as she reached out to touch one necklace, in particular. It was a silver pendant, long and delicate, its drop shaped like a delicate feather.

It belonged to her sister.

Nobody could tell her it was a copy, or a coincidence. She knew, with every fibre of her being, that Andrew Forbes had taken this from her sister when he'd killed her, and had now given it to his daughter, who was only a year younger than Gemma had been, to wear around her neck. He'd given his child a dead girl's necklace, a girl he'd murdered in cold blood, and titillated himself by looking at it, out in the open.

She wanted to scream, to break things, to burn his stinking house to the ground.

But she had a better plan, one that she meant to see through.

Logic told her to leave the necklace where it was, whilst a stronger desire to reclaim what had been her sister's overcame all else.

She snatched up the necklace and hung it around her neck, tucking it safely beneath her shirt where it couldn't be seen. Then, she left, uncaring that the alarm went off as she ran from the house, and that the CCTV camera on the streetlamp at the end of his road would likely pick up her flight.

It didn't matter.

By the time any footage came back, Forbes would already be dead.

Towards lunchtime, Ryan met Phillips and Reed outside Irina Pavlova's apartment building, which had already been secured by a couple of Reed's local constables. They were now tasked with obtaining preliminary statements from her neighbours and anyone else who might feasibly have known her comings and goings, while they prepared to search her former home for evidence that, aside from being Angela's regular cleaner, she had also moonlighted as The Pink Lady of Bamburgh.

It didn't take them very long to find damning evidence in the affirmative.

"This what we're lookin' for?" Phillips asked, holding up a bundle of candy pink chiffon.

They would need to check its consistency against the scrap of material Reed had photographed, and they'd need to check it bore the evidence of Pavlova having handled and worn it, but, on the face of it, they'd found their ghostly spirit, who'd been little more than flesh and blood.

"How's the mother doing?" Ryan enquired, after they'd bagged the dress.

"Not great," Reed told him. "She'd had an epileptic fit, when social services attended earlier this morning. Apparently, she has a host of illnesses, ranging from epilepsy to narcolepsy and advanced multiple sclerosis. To top it off, she's largely non-verbal following a massive stroke, six months ago."

"Lordy," Phillips said. "Narf makes you feel lucky, doesn't it? I may be a fat bastard but, if that's all I've got to worry about—"

"C'mon Frank, that's not true," Ryan cooed. "You know you're a fat, baldie bastard, if anything."

That earned him a none-too-gentle punch on the arm, and Reed rolled her eyes at the pair of them.

"I heard from Angela's solicitor," she said, and they grew serious again. "He got in touch to say that—"

At that moment, Ryan's phone interrupted them.

"Tom? That was quick."

At the other end of the line, Faulker cupped his phone to shield it from the wind that continued to pummel from all sides.

"I heard from my team, back at the lab," he said. "They made a start with the first lot of samples we sent back, and there's been an immediate match with some of the trace DNA we picked up from the girl's neck area."

Ryan held his breath.

"And? Who is it?"

"The DNA matches a sample taken previously from the person who found the body of Angela Bansbury—it belongs to a man by the name of John Watson," Faulkner said. "Does it mean anything to you?"

Ryan frowned, his intuition entirely at odds with what the evidence appeared to suggest.

"Yes, it does. Anything else?"

"The technicians say there looks to be quite a bit of natural residue—soil, maybe—that was caked on the skin. They've found a couple of tiny fibres, so they'll push on with those and see what they can tell us."

Unbidden, an image of John Watson peeling off his gardener's gloves the previous day popped into his mind.

"Okay," he said. "Thanks for such a speedy response."

"There may be more," Faulkner said. "I'll let you know as soon as anything else comes back."

Ryan ended the call and looked across to where Phillips and Reed waited, with bated breath.

"Well, howay, man! The suspense is killin' us here!" Phillips bellowed.

"Sorry," Ryan said, rubbing an agitated hand over the back of his neck. "Faulkner says they've found a match. The trace DNA they extracted from Irina's neck area belongs to John Watson, Angela's gardener."

"He's the only one without an alibi for the time Angela died," Reed pointed out, after a momentary silence. "We shouldn't be surprised."

"If Irina was the one to frighten Angela into a heart attack on the stairs, then it may not be relevant who was or wasn't around at that time," Ryan pointed out. "In fact, I'd have thought they'd be at pains to cover themselves with a solid alibi, if they knew they'd hired Irina to give the old woman a shock at a time when nobody else would be with her."

Reed fell silent again, considered what he said and then nodded.

"No gettin' away from the evidence, is there, lad?" Phillips said, though he was as troubled as Ryan. "I know he didn't strike any of us as the killin' kind, but it takes all sorts. We've been wrong in the past."

"When?" Ryan challenged him.

Phillips opened his mouth, then shut it again.

"Well, there's always a first time," he amended. "When do we think Irina died?"

"Pathologist hasn't had a chance to do a post-mortem yet, but from the state of her body and bearing in mind that Irina had lain outside exposed to the elements, he thinks she died in the early hours of this morning. Maybe one or two o'clock?"

"The village would have been sleeping," Reed murmured. "Nobody would be around at that time—although, any earlier and you'd chance running into someone having a late-night picnic on the beach."

Phillips shivered at the thought of it.

"Most people won't have an alibi for that time," he said. "They'll be tucked up in bed, at home with family or whoever."

"Unless they happen to live alone," Ryan said, thinking of Watson in his stone cottage.

Phillips blew out a long breath and folded his arms across his paunch.

"Y'nah what we've got to do," he said.

Ryan nodded.

"I do, and we will."

They needed to arrest John Watson, like it or not.

CHAPTER 38

MacKenzie looked across to where Jack Lowerson toyed with a vegan sausage roll.

Normally, she'd have made a joke about it not being the 'real' thing, though she knew he was a lifelong vegetarian and respected his choice. They enjoyed plenty of friendly back-and-forth, usually, but theirs had been a quiet office, lately, and they both knew why.

"No Mel, today?"

He looked up, and shook his head.

"I assumed she'd come in early," he said, after making sure they couldn't be overheard. "She left before I woke up, this morning."

He didn't bother to tell her that he wasn't sure Melanie had been to bed.

"Maybe she's in the field," MacKenzie said, holding on to optimism with both hands. "She has her own cases to attend to, after all. It could be that she decided to get out and about."

Lowerson thought back to the previous evening, replaying their conversation with eyes no longer shielded by rose-tinted glasses.

"She wasn't herself, last night," he murmured, turning to face Denise fully now. "I know she hasn't been herself for a while, but this was different. I can't describe it."

"Melanie met with Doctor Gregory, yesterday," MacKenzie said. "Perhaps it gave her a new perspective, and she needs some time to think it over."

Lowerson looked away, to hide the hurt he felt at knowing now that Melanie hadn't so much as mentioned her session with Doctor Gregory to him, let alone whether it had given her a new perspective.

But, he had his pride, and he was a loyal man, so he said none of that aloud.

"She seemed…I don't know, Denise. She seemed harder, somehow. Like she'd closed off a part of herself."

MacKenzie was about to respond, when she caught sight of DCS Forbes passing by the open doorway, presumably en route to his office.

She had a question she needed to ask him.

"Jack, I'm sorry to interrupt our conversation, but there's something I need to speak to Forbes about—I'll be back, soon."

"DCI Ryan and DS Phillips, entering Interview Room A at Alnwick Police Station. Also present is John Watson, of Gardener's Cottage, Sandy Dunes Guest House, Bamburgh, for the purpose of questioning under caution. The time is thirteen-thirty-seven."

Ryan seated himself beside Phillips at a small rectangular table bolted to the floor of one of a couple of interview rooms at the nearest police station to Bamburgh. They sat opposite John Watson, who looked between them both much like a puppy who'd just received a vicious kick to the belly.

"Mr Watson, I understand you've waived your right to have a solicitor present—is that correct?"

"Yes," he said. "I don't need any solicitor to tell you that I don't know what any of this is about."

"We'll come to that," Ryan said, crisply. "Although you haven't been charged with any crime, you are being questioned under caution regarding the murders of Irina Pavlova and Angela Bansbury."

Ryan repeated the standard caution, for the benefit of the tape.

"Mr Watson, when was the last time you saw Irina Pavlova?"

Watson ran a hand over his hair, which stuck out at odd angles.

"Must've been last Saturday," he said, obviously trying to remember. "She doesn't work on a Sunday or Monday and I didn't see her around the guest house yesterday, so yes, it must've been on Saturday. She worked a full day at the guest house, then popped into my cottage for an hour to give me a hand with the laundry. That's somethin' I've never been any good at."

He started to give them an easy smile, then seemed to remember where he was, and his face fell again into sad, tired lines.

"You didn't see her at any time, last night?" Ryan asked again.

Watson shook his head.

"No, not at all."

"Where were you last night, between the hours of ten o'clock and four in the morning?"

Watson smiled, presumably thinking it was a silly question.

"I was at home, in my bed," he said, with relief. "I had the telly on, watchin' a bit of mindless drivel to switch my brain off. All this stuff about Angela's been upsettin', hasn't it?"

Ryan and Phillips looked at one another, but remained steadfast.

"Can anybody vouch for that, John?"

Phillips used his first name, a classic device to create a feeling of trust.

"Well, no, o' course they can't," Watson said, with the first sign of panic. "I don't live with anyone, anymore—"

He paused, collecting himself.

"Look, Pauline only lives next door," he said. "She probably heard the telly on, or maybe saw my lights on… you could check wi' her."

Seeing lights in a window wasn't the same as seeing someone in the flesh, and Ryan knew that any prosecution team would certainly point out the difference to a jury.

He braced himself to ask the question uppermost in his mind.

"Did you kill Irina Pavlova, John?"

Watson looked thoroughly horrified.

"Well o' course I didn't! Why would I want to hurt the lass—or anyone? She was just tryin' to make her way…why don't you look for some sex maniac, or someone? They're the ones you should be lookin' for, not some old duffer like me."

Ryan wanted to believe him, but the DNA evidence was compelling and that was ultimately what convicted a person at trial.

"Can you explain how our forensics team came to find your DNA on Irina's throat, John? She was brutally strangled, by someone's hands. We believe those hands might have been yours."

And yet, as they looked across the table at Watson's enormous hands, they knew his handspan didn't match the estimate Faulkner had given.

Something didn't fit, and they needed to know which part.

Watson paled, his face draining entirely of colour so that he appeared much older than his years beneath the harsh strip lighting.

"I—I don't understand how that can be. There must have been some mistake."

Phillips shook his head. "We've checked," he said. "The traces we found are a positive match to the DNA sample you gave us on Monday, as part of our routine investigation."

Watson held his head in his hands, but looked up at that.

"Well, hang on a minute, now. Just hang on a minute," he said, pointing a finger between the pair of them. "Ask yourself, if I was plannin' on doing away with the poor lass, why would I give you my DNA sample, for goodness' sake? Surely, I'd have made some excuse?"

"Perhaps you thought it would look more suspicious to refuse to give a sample?" Ryan replied.

Watson fell silent again, but not for long.

"Wh—what about this sample, you say you've found. Now, there's something else. If I was going to—to do somethin' like that, don't you think I'd have worn gloves? Why would I leave my DNA for the police to find?"

Ryan smiled slightly, because it echoed his own private doubt. John Watson was an outdoorsy man, someone without frills, airs or graces, but he was no fool, and it was only fools who left a trail behind for the police to follow.

Fools, or people with a specific agenda.

"Perhaps you did wear gloves," Phillips suggested, thinking of the soil residue the forensics team had also found around Irina's neck area. "Perhaps you wore your gardening gloves, and didn't think about the trace DNA until it was too late."

"I lost my gloves," Watson muttered, half to himself.

"What's that?" Ryan leaned forward, urgently. "What did you say?"

"I said—I said I lost them," Watson repeated, with wide, fearful eyes. "Why do you ask?"

Ryan didn't reply directly, but called a break.

"Ten minutes," he said. "I'll have some refreshment brought in for you."

He stopped the tape, read out the time, and walked swiftly from the room with Phillips at his heels.

"What was that about?"

Phillips' legs worked double time to keep up with Ryan, as they made their way along to Reed's office.

"Think about it, Frank," Ryan said, without breaking stride. "Somebody could have taken Watson's gloves and used them to kill Irina—all they'd need to do is turn them inside out. I couldn't figure out why the handspan doesn't match his, but that would explain it. The contusion points on Irina's neck match another person's hands, but they used Watson's gloves to do the deed and try to set him up."

Phillips didn't disagree, but there was one problem…

"We haven't any evidence to support that theory," he said. "What we do have is a man who has no alibi at the time of either murder, plenty of motive as the beneficiary of a will—it doesn't matter that the will is invalid, it matters that he believed at the time of Angela's murder that the will would be valid—and a shedload of quality DNA evidence against him."

"I know, it looks bad," Ryan agreed. "But, Frank, let me ask you this: do you believe that the man sitting in there killed either of those women?"

Phillips set aside all he had just said, and consulted his gut, which had never failed him before.

"No," he answered. "I don't think he did."

"Neither do I," Ryan said. "We aren't usually in the business of disproving guilt, Frank, but, as you said before, there's a first time for everything and I don't fancy having an innocent man on my conscience."

They turned into Reed's office, as she was on the telephone. Spotting them, she held up a finger to indicate she'd be done in a minute.

"That was Angela's solicitor," she said, once she'd replaced the receiver. "I told you, he's just returned from a business trip to find a tonne of messages from me."

"What can he tell us?"

"Well," she said, ticking the messages off on her fingers. "Firstly, he agrees that the will we found that was signed by John Watson would indeed be invalidated, by virtue of him being a witness. However, it turns out that will's the wrong one—Angela made a more recent will, which was properly witnessed, in the presence of her solicitor."

Ryan and Phillips wore varying expressions of surprise.

"Who benefits from the new will?" Ryan asked.

"Same person," Reed said. "John Watson."

They digested that nugget of information, and then Ryan spoke again.

"There's a chance John doesn't know about the new will," he said. "We can tell him, and try to gauge his reaction, like before. But, more importantly, what we need to ask ourselves is: who would want to kill Angela, using Irina to achieve that goal, and then make sure John didn't inherit Angela's money?"

He looked between them.

"The next of kin," he said, and turned to Reed. "Get the solicitor back on the phone, and tell him to redouble his efforts to find the next beneficiary, if John doesn't inherit."

"But being in prison wouldn't prevent him from inheriting, would it?" Reed argued.

"I'm not sure about that, but being the signatory on a will for which he's also a beneficiary would prevent him from inheriting, remember?" Ryan said. "We're assuming this person doesn't know anything about the new will that Angela made with her solicitor, so they're working on the basis that Watson won't get a penny, regardless."

"They're in for a shock, then," Phillips said. "Another one."

Ryan smiled fiercely.

"Somebody has tried to be very clever," he said. "Let's make sure we're even more so."

"I've got an idea," Phillips said.

"Is it a…cunning plan?" Ryan wondered.

"Watch it."

CHAPTER 39

Andrew Forbes opened his front door and scented the air.

Lasagne, or some meaty Italian dish, for dinner.

"Is that you, Andy?"

He ground his teeth, elbowing the door closed behind him.

He hated to be called, 'Andy'.

"Yes," he called out, in return. "Dinner smells good."

"It'll be on the table, soon," Jenna said, coming out from the kitchen to meet him.

He braced himself for her kiss, tried not to let his repulsion show, and then hung his jacket over the newel post.

"Before I forget, could you give the burglar alarm company a call for me, tomorrow?" she asked him.

"Why?" he asked.

"It was playing up, earlier today," she said. "First, it was beeping even before I opened the front door after dropping the kids at school, and I only just got to the keypad before the siren was due to go off. Then, when I came back from the supermarket, it was going off, full pelt, for all the estate to hear. I had Derek on about it, from next door."

Forbes counted to five beneath his breath, and reminded himself that mundane matters such as these were the price that he paid for enjoying an otherwise extraordinary existence.

"I'll call them," he said, walking through to the dining room, where he found his son and daughter already seated.

His daughter looked tearful.

"Something the matter, poppet?"

She lifted her eyes, then looked away. "It's the necklace you gave me," she whispered. "I can't find it."

He thought his heart might have stopped, for a moment, and when it restarted the blood that rushed around his body was white hot with rage.

"You—lost it?" He could barely get the words out, and his daughter looked up at him with genuine fear, something she'd never experienced before.

"N—no, Dad, I promise, I didn't lose it," she stammered, trying to stem the flow of tears. "I put it on my special jewellery tree, on my window ledge, last night. It was there when I left for school, this morning, I know it was."

"Well, the fairies didn't take it," he ground out, and then stopped himself as a far more worrying thought entered his mind.

The alarm going off. The necklace missing.

"I'll be back in a moment," he said, and hurried down the hall to his study door.

When he tried the handle, it was locked, as he'd left it.

Initial relief gave way to doubt, and he bent down to peer at the lock, reaching for his phone to shine a torch beam into the small cavity. At first, he saw nothing untoward, but then…

Then, he spotted the tiny scratches on the inside of the lock.

Someone had tampered with it.

He moved away from the door and sat down on the stairs nearby, calling to his family that he'd join them in a minute. He stared at the wall, unseeing and unblinking, thinking of all the possibilities.

Ryan, most likely.

Lawana must have identified him.

MacKenzie? She'd been asking questions about those cold cases, and he'd been forced to tell her some cock and bull story about having looked at them in connection with some case, back in South Tyneside.

But, had she believed him?

These thoughts, and many more, swirled through his mind, but it was only when his phone began to ring that he knew for certain.

"Hello, Melanie."

"DCS Forbes," she said, in a cheerful tone. "I'm sorry to bother you after work, but I had to tell you the good news, since you've been so supportive, these last few days."

"What good news is that?"

"Well, I have to confess, I did what you suggested and logged onto Jack's computer last night," she said. "I'm so glad that I did, because I found out some wonderful news.

The team got a tip-off about where he keeps his kill room, some lock-up or other, according to the notes. Anyway, they've planned a raid, first thing tomorrow morning."

"That is good news," he said.

"We're one step closer to finding the bastard—excuse my language, sir. I knew you'd be as pleased as I am to hear this."

Forbes smiled like a shark.

"More pleased than you know, Melanie. Let's celebrate together, at the first opportunity."

"Thank you, sir."

She rang off, and he held the phone in the palm of his hand, before pocketing it again. Then, very calmly, he walked back into the dining room and sat down to dinner with his wife and children.

He would need his strength, for what was to come.

From the interior of her car, which was parked in the neighbouring street, Melanie looked down at her mobile phone and thought about calling her boyfriend, her friends and colleagues, or even her family, and telling them everything.

Then, she looked across to the footwell on the passenger side, where a small firearm lay in its holster.

They would try to stop her, she thought.

She didn't need their help with this. She had the advantage, and the element of surprise. She was leaving nothing to chance—she had fitted an AirTag tracking device to Forbes's vehicle earlier in the day, just in case she was unable to follow him without being seen.

Andrew Forbes wouldn't know what had hit him, until it connected with the centre of his heart, if he had one at all.

"Angela's left all her money to you, John."

Ryan and Phillips had returned to the interview room, where John Watson was polishing off a cup of sugary tea.

"Aye, you said this the other day, but you also said that I couldn't inherit after all, because I'd been a witness—remember?"

Ryan smiled to himself. "Yes, we remember. You'll still inherit, because it turns out that Angela made another will, one that was properly executed," he said, and watched surprise flit over Watson's face for the second time in as many days.

"I—I'm gettin' too old, for all o' this," he said. "I never wanted the blasted money, nor the houses. I don't know why Angela left it all to me, nor why she'd want to, but I'll gladly give it away if it'll stop the pair o' you thinkin' o' me as some murdering maniac."

He sat back in his chair and folded his arms, clearly having reached the end of his tether.

"Perhaps she thought you were a man who could be trusted," Ryan said, and happened to agree with Angela's judgment. "Maybe she wanted to thank you for all the small kindnesses you paid her—we know you helped her with all sorts of odd jobs, John. We know you drove her anywhere she needed to go, and kept her company on her hospital visits. The doctor's surgery told us about the 'gentle giant' who held her hand while she had to have some tests."

Watson looked down at his workman's hands, and clasped them together.

"Aye, well. I felt sorry about her not havin' any family to keep her company," he said. "She was a nice lady, Angie was. She deserved to have friends about her."

"We think she had someone close to her who pretended to be a friend, but was anything but," Phillips chimed in.

"Now, listen here, I've already told you, I thought a lot of Angie—"

"We don't mean you, lad," Phillips said, and Ryan smiled privately at his sergeant's indiscriminate use of the word, 'lad'. For Frank, it applied as a descriptor to all men aged between five and ninety-five.

"Oh," Watson said.

"The thing is, there's still the problem of your DNA being on Irina's body," Ryan said. "That's a very serious problem and, until we can provide some reasonable explanation for it, you're our prime suspect."

Watson looked dumbfounded. "Well, I never."

"However," Ryan said, at length. "Phillips and I have a theory about what might have happened here, and why. The problem is, we have no proof."

"That's a pity," Watson said, with glorious understatement. "What are you going to do about it?"

"It's more a question of what we might do about it," Phillips said, leaning in to speak man-to-man. "Do you want to let this person rob you of your freedom? Your inheritance?"

"I'm not bothered about the inheritance," Watson said again. "But, aye, I'd rather not spend the last of my days behind bars, if it's all the same to you."

"We thought that might be the case. We've got a bit of a plan, but it's risky."

Watson was suspicious. "What d'you mean, 'risky'?"

"Well, I'll be straight with you, lad," Phillips said, looking him squarely in the eye. "We think somebody wants to do you in."

Watson's eyes rounded like saucers. "Me? What the heck for?"

"The money, o' course," Phillips said, and Ryan nodded in agreement. "We reckon Angie has some relative, one she doesn't even know about or is estranged from, who's the next in line to inherit, if something happens to you. It's the only reason why someone would want to kill Angela and scupper things for you. Even someone like Soames, who stood to have his funding withdrawn, wouldn't care who inherits so long as the Bansbury Charitable Trust continued to provide funding—which is something outside of his control."

"So, we think the person we're looking for has been acting as a friend," Ryan said. "They could be one of the archaeology staff, like Gwen or JJ…or even Pauline. They've all had access to the house these past few weeks; any one of them could have found Angela's will, looked at the contents and put two-and-two together. Any one of them could have tampered with her tablets, and then paid a vulnerable young woman, or coerced her, into becoming an accomplice, before killing her too."

"Don't forget tryin' to pin it on muggins, here," Watson grumbled.

Ryan inclined his head.

"So, the question is, do you want to help us to uncover this person, John?"

Watson nodded. "What'll it take?"

"A bit of courage, but we'll be there waiting in the wings," Ryan assured him.

Watson held out his broad, scarred hand and each man shook it, but Ryan held on for a moment longer to issue a mild warning.

"Of course, you understand, if we're wrong about you, John—"

"Aye, you'll nick me, good 'n' proper, and chuck away the key."

"Exactly."

"Seems fair."

CHAPTER 40

Following a brief, interesting phone call with her husband, Anna set Emma down on her play mat and made another call, this time to Gwen Meakings, of the Bamburgh archaeological team.

"Hello, Anna, how are you?"

"I'm well, Gwen, thank you. Listen, I'm just calling to say I'm hoping to pop back for another visit, next week, but I wanted to ask how you're all getting on?"

At the other end of the line, Gwen made herself more comfortable in the armchair she occupied in the sitting room at Sandy Dunes Guest House, oblivious to those who might be listening to her conversation.

"Oh, we're all getting by," she said. "I'm sure you already know there's been another murder up here, so that's put the wind up everyone."

"Mm, yes, I'd heard," Anna said, and handed Emma her favourite picture book to look at. "Do you have any theory about who's responsible?"

"No, not at all," Gwen said, worriedly. "First, Angela, and now, this? It's dreadful. I can't think why—?"

"Well," Anna said, very deliberately. "I probably shouldn't be repeating this…"

"Oh, I won't tell anyone," Gwen said, and meant it, at the time. "What is it? Have you heard something?"

"Well, you know that Angela's gardener was going to inherit all her wealth?" Anna said.

"Yes, I was very happy for him—until I heard he wouldn't be, after all," Gwen said. "Something about an invalid will?"

"Mm," Anna said. "Well, this is the good part. There was a second will, which also names him as the main beneficiary, and that one was properly executed by Angela's solicitor, which means he's still going to inherit after all."

"That's marvellous," Gwen gushed. "I'm so happy for him—"

"There's the usual legal fine print," Anna said, as an aside. "If John were to pass away within thirty days, then everything reverts to Angela's next of kin, whoever they may be."

"Oh, but I'm sure nothing will happen to him, so he'll get to enjoy it all," Gwen said. "Only, didn't I hear that he was arrested, or taken in for questioning?"

"I couldn't say," Anna lied. "I heard he wasn't very well, the last time Ryan saw him. I'm sure he said John had gone home, to rest up—something about the flu, maybe?"

"Poor thing," Gwen tutted. "I should head over with a bowl of soup, especially as he's all on his own."

"That would be kind," Anna said. "Well, I must be off—see you next week."

Having done her civic duty for the day, Anna sent a quick text message to her husband and then lifted Emma into her arms.

"Time for a bath," she said. "Now, just so you know, we're not supposed to tell fibs—but, in this instance, it was all in a good cause."

At the Sandy Dunes Guest House, Gwen Meakings thought about what Anna had told her, and stood up from her chair, intending to get that bowl of soup for John Watson.

"Can I get you anything, Gwen?"

"No, thank you, Pauline," she replied. "I can help myself."

"Something sounded serious, on the phone. I hope everything's all right?"

Gwen looked at Pauline's friendly, round-faced expression and thought that it couldn't do any harm to tell one person.

"Oh, fine, fine," she said. "It's only that I've just heard John isn't feeling very well, and he's laid up in his cottage on his own. I thought I'd take him some soup, to keep his strength up."

"You're a kind soul," Pauline said, and patted the woman's shoulder.

"Well, not that anything will happen, of course, but we can't let anything happen to him in the next thirty days," Gwen said, keeping her voice low. "You know how John was going to inherit all this?"

"Mm hmm," Pauline said, leaning in to listen. "But, then, he wasn't."

"Well, now he is again," Gwen said, excitedly. "Angie made another will, and did it properly, apparently. He'll get everything, unless he dies in the next thirty days." She laughed it off. "There's no reason that should happen."

"No," Pauline agreed. "But then, he can be reckless. I've lost count of the times I've told him to turn his gas burner off, or remember to have his chimney cleaned, for carbon monoxide." She tutted. "Still, as you say, there's no reason any of that should happen."

Gwen shook her head. "I'll get that soup," she said, and moved off towards the kitchen.

Pauline watched her go, a frown marring her face. When she looked up, it was to find JJ watching her from the other side of the room, and she almost jumped.

"JJ," she said, with a nervous laugh. "I didn't see you, there."

"People seldom do," the other woman said, and left the room.

The housekeeper shivered as a sudden gust of wind howled through the cracks in the old house and rubbed her arms for warmth. There were malevolent spirits at work, she thought, and not those of the dead.

Those of the living.

By eight o'clock, Melanie still hadn't returned home.

Jack left another message on her phone and then prowled the walls of their home, stopping occasionally to pet the cat, who trailed after him like a shadow.

"Are you worried?" he muttered, giving the animal a good scratch. "Yeah, me too."

When another half an hour slipped by and she still hadn't answered her phone or returned his messages, concern tipped over into active panic and he did the only thing he would ever do, in times of true emergency.

He rang his best friend.

"Jack? Is everything okay?" Ryan picked up the call immediately, from his position in the back room of John Watson's tiny cottage in Bamburgh.

"Ah, no, not really," Lowerson replied. "It's Mel. She still hasn't come home—in fact, I haven't seen her since last night. I think I heard her leaving the house, very early this morning, and I assumed she was getting a head start on the day, but—"

"When was the last communication you had with her?"

Lowerson rubbed his forehead, trying to think clearly.

"Ah—I had a strange sort of text message from her, at around eleven this morning. She said she was sorry and hoped I'd forgive her. I thought she was apologising for being…well, for being a bit difficult the past few weeks. I wrote back that there was nothing to forgive."

Ryan thought of what Gregory had told him the previous evening, and interpreted her message very differently.

"Has she spoken of anything to do with Operation Heartbeat—today, or yesterday?" Ryan asked him. "Think carefully, Jack."

"No," he said. "In fact, she's been unusually quiet about it, the past couple of days. I thought—well, I thought she'd calmed down a bit, after her chat with you and with Doctor Gregory. I said some things to her, which I now regret—"

Emotion clogged his throat, and he could no longer speak.

"It's nothing you've said, I'm sure of it," Ryan told him. "Jack, I think there's a chance she might have found the man we've been looking for. I think she might have found him and wants to kill him."

"Unless he kills her, first," Jack said, brokenly. "Why—if she'd found him, why wouldn't she tell me? Tell us?"

Ryan knew precisely why. He'd felt the same emotions when his own sister died.

"She thinks we'll stop her," he said. "Which we will."

"But, how?" Jack demanded. "We have no way of knowing where she is or who this man is."

Phillips, who'd been listening with half an ear to the snatched pieces of conversation, suddenly began waving his arms about.

"Hold on a sec, Jack. Frank, what's the matter? Did a bee sting you?"

"It's Denise," he said quickly. "She was going to speak to you about it today, but I said I'd see you in person—I'm sorry, I plum forgot to mention it, in all the excitement."

"Mention what?"

"Denise was looking into 'like' crimes, and she happened to notice something peculiar on the digital logs," he said quickly. "DCS Forbes was the last to access several of the same case files, at different times over the past few years—some he looked at more than once. She was going to ask him about it."

Ryan smelled a rat. Often, killers returned to the scenes of their crimes or tried to relive the memory of their actions in some other way. It was usually the reason they kept trophies, so they could gain some sort of pleasure or release by remembering what they'd done. They already knew from Lawana's testimony that the man they sought was a collector of photographs, amongst other things, so it was not outside the realms of possibility to imagine he'd feel the urge to look at his handiwork, now and then, and remember what they looked like before he'd killed them.

"Did MacKenzie seem troubled about it?" he asked.

"Aye, she did."

That was all Ryan needed to know.

"There's something else," Lowerson said, when Ryan came back on the phone. "Another strange pattern. It concerns the death of a bouncer, who worked on The Boat on the night Gemma Yates went missing. He turned up dead, not long afterwards, and it was chalked up as another gangland murder. There was quite a spate of them, back then, because Jimmy 'The Manc' was still fresh on the scene and tensions were high."

He referred to a notorious gangland criminal, once feared and revered, now dead and gone.

"What pattern?" Ryan asked.

"Forbes was the one to work the case," Lowerson said. "Just as he seems to have had a hand in all the files we've been looking at, in some capacity or another. What's stranger still is that his name doesn't appear on all the records; sometimes, we only know he was involved because the victims' families happened to mention it."

"What a coincidence," Ryan said, in a tone that was deadly calm.

He thought of all the times Forbes had enquired about Operation Heartbeat, and the times he'd been forced to intercept his subtle attempt to draw out members of his team, particularly in respect of Lawana. It sent a chill up his spine even to imagine her place of refuge being divulged to the very man whose attentions she'd managed to survive; it would be a betrayal far too deep to fathom.

Ryan told himself it was too fantastic; too bold to imagine a man of Forbes' standing in the community, all the while being little more than a base killer.

All the same, he could believe it. Oh, yes, he could.

"Does Melanie have her phone?" Ryan asked.

"Yes," Lowerson replied. "It isn't switched on, though."

"Doesn't matter, we'll try to trace it," Ryan said, and looked across to Phillips, who gave him the 'thumbs-up' motion and put a call through to the Digital Forensics team to put the wheels in motion. "It'll take time, though, Jack. Is there anything else you can tell us?"

Jack tried desperately to think of something—anything.

"If I were her, I'd have checked out Forbes's family home," he said. "He lives somewhere in Gosforth, I think."

"I'm on my way, Jack. Stay where you are, in case she comes home, but call me if you hear anything in the meantime," Ryan said.

When he turned to Phillips, the other man gave him the 'shooing' motion.

"Go, as quick as you can," he said, without hesitation. "I've got things well in hand, here, and there's a couple of plain-clothed constables waiting by the gate. Howay and help young Jack."

Ryan put a hand on his friend's shoulder, and then left without another word.

CHAPTER 41

While Ryan slipped out of John Watson's cottage and skirted around the perimeter of the guest house towards his car, Pauline Whitton slipped a selection of crushed Warfarin tablets into a paper sachet that bore the name of a well-known cold and flu remedy. Then, with a very careful line of superglue, which she kept in the 'odds and ends' cupboard in the guest house kitchen, she re-sealed the edge of the sachet and waited a couple of minutes for it to dry.

"Ready?"

Pauline reached for the packet that held the flu sachets and made a show of selecting one to take across for John.

"I thought he could use one of these," she said, shaking out a fresh sachet. "Could you pass me the honey from the cupboard to your right, over there?"

While Gwen turned away, Pauline substituted the fresh sachet for the one she'd prepared earlier and was all smiles when the woman turned back again.

"Right, I think we've got everything," Pauline said. "Let's go and see how he's getting along."

It had been a simple matter to convince Gwen that they should both go and visit John, and she made a point of stopping by the living room, one last time, to check whether its occupants needed the fire stoking, with the express intention that they should see them together, in case any questions arose after John was found dead, most likely the following day.

But, detective, I was with Gwen all the time—wasn't I, Gwen?

I couldn't possibly have done anything, or Gwen would have seen me…

Perhaps John took an overdose of the blood thinners he'd been stealing from Angela's pill tray? Maybe he realised it was the end of the road and, rather than go to prison, he'd take his own life?

That's what she'd be telling the police, and anybody else who'd listen.

The two women left the house via the patio doors and then followed the pathway, nattering about the archaeological finds the team had uncovered in the past week—which was mostly old pots and pans, if Pauline understood Gwen correctly—until they reached the courtyard, which was overlooked by two cottages. The one on the left with the freshly-painted door and the ornamental trees either side of it was hers, while the grubby one on the right with the boot scraper and the old horse trough was John's.

Pauline let out a short, angry sigh that was pure frustration.

It was a source of constant irritation that he made absolutely no effort with his front door presentation, despite being a dab hand with all things horticultural. No wreath at Christmas, no ornamental borders and certainly no hanging baskets, either.

Well, she wouldn't have to worry about that for much longer.

Soon, the only flowers John Watson need worry about were the ones that would decorate his grave.

"Knock, knock!"

Pauline trilled out the saccharine greeting as John opened the door to the two women, dressed in checked pyjamas, a thick fisherman's jumper and a blanket around his shoulders, for good measure. Phillips had applied a liberal sprinkling of vinegar to John's eyes, so that they watered profusely and were now an angry shade of pink, which gave the overall impression of a man suffering from a fever.

"Oh, you poor thing," she continued, barging into the cottage without waiting to be invited. "When Gwen and I heard you were laid up in here, we knew we had to come with some provisions."

"I don't—" John began.

"Now, there's no need to thank us," Pauline said, waggling her finger at him. "What are you doing out of bed?"

"I—you knocked at the door—"

"Straight back into bed with you," she said. "Shoo! We'll bring you a nice tray of things to tempt you. Gwen? Why don't you make sure he does as he's told, and let me know if he needs any more blankets."

"It's just a cold," John tried to say. "I'll be fine, after a good night's sleep."

Gwen took his arm and began guiding him back to his bed.

"You heard the woman," she said. "You best do as your told, or we'll both be in for it."

They shared a smile, and, for a moment, John almost forgot he was supposed to be playing a part.

He coughed a few times, belatedly, for effect.

"Heavens," Gwen muttered. "That does sound chesty. Don't you worry, Pauline's got a cold and flu remedy she'll make up for you, with a nice dollop of honey inside."

As he climbed beneath his bedclothes, he allowed Gwen to fuss over him—which was not strictly necessary, but he enjoyed nonetheless—and waited for Nurse Ratched to arrive with her dose of 'special' medicine.

"Here you go," Pauline said, a couple of minutes later. "Lentil soup and a nice hot toddy, to ease your throat. Drink it all up."

She plonked herself on the end of the bed, waiting for him to take the first mouthful while Gwen left the room to tidy up his kitchen and plump the pillows in his living room.

"Come on, before it gets cold," Pauline said, to chivvy him along.

"I'll have it later," he replied. "I'm really very tired."

She tried to conceal her frustration but couldn't quite manage it.

"It won't be the same, later. Come now, drink up."

"I'm grateful to you, Pauline, but I'm really not in the mood."

"You don't know what's good for you," she said, between gritted teeth. "I'll have to help you."

"No, I really don't want anyth—"

She held the mug to his lips, and made to tip the warm liquid down his throat.

John grabbed her wrist with a hand that was no longer weak, but strong. When she looked into his eyes, they were remarkably clear, no longer red and weeping but sharp and watchful.

Pauline sensed the trap, even before it was revealed.

"No—" she began.

"Yes," Phillips said, stepping into the room from where he'd concealed himself, in the guest bedroom. "Put the mug down."

Pauline looked between them, and decided to bluff her way out.

"DS Phillips?" she said, in the same, simpering voice she'd used before. "This is a lovely surprise…"

"Put that mug down," he repeated, in a tone that brooked no argument. "Step away from the bed."

Pauline let out an awkward laugh.

"What's going on here?" she said. "I was just trying to be kind."

"We'll know if that's the case, once we have that liquid tested," he said.

She let it spill onto the carpeted floor.

"Silly me," she said. "Butter-fingers."

"It makes no difference," Phillips said. "Forensics can test the carpet fibres, just as easily, or the inside of that mug."

She lifted her chin.

"What are you implying? That the cold and flu remedy is poisoned? It came from a fresh sachet, as Gwen can attest."

"Did you call for me?"

Gwen wandered back through, tea towel in hand, and was shocked to find another visitor to their small party.

"Detective…Peters, was it?"

"Phillips."

"How nice to see you, again. What's going on?"

"Oh, I'm just about to arrest your friend here on charges of murder and attempted murder."

"John?" she whispered, turning to him in accusation.

"No, the other one. She put something nasty in that cup she just tipped onto the floor."

"Pauline?" she squeaked.

"Oh, for God's sake, I can't put up with this any longer," Pauline burst out. "Yes, it was me. And, no, my name isn't Pauline, it's Kerry. My father was Angela's brother, but I never knew him. My mother was just one of his conquests, you see, and he wasn't too keen on having anything to do with a kid. I ran one of those Ancestry DNA searches, a few years ago, and, lo and behold, his name popped up—"

"No offence," Phillips said, cutting into her monologue. "But nobody asked to hear your life story, pet. Save it for your solicitor and the jury, eh? Some of us have got bigger fish to fry."

With that, he reminded her of her rights.

"Pauline Whitton, or Kerry Whateverherface, I'm arresting you on suspicion of the murders of Angela Bansbury and

Irina Pavlova, and of the attempted murder of John Watson. You do not have to say anything, but anything you do say…"

The woman they knew as Pauline turned to the big man on the bed with eyes full of venom.

"This—all this—should have been mine," she spat.

"Aye, well, it's funny how the world turns, isn't it?" John said, cheerfully. "Mind your arse, on the way out."

CHAPTER 42

It was almost ten o'clock, by the time Forbes was able to leave his house.

He made an excuse to his wife about having forgotten something at the office and promised to be back home soon. From her position inside her car, which was parked in the same place she'd chosen earlier in the day, Melanie waited for his SUV to pass on its way to the main road, which would be her signal to move.

It must have come as a shock to him, she thought idly, when he'd heard that the police had uncovered his hideaway; how she would have liked to have seen his face, but it had been satisfying enough to hear his surprise at the other end of a telephone line. It may not be true that the police were going to raid his lock-up, or whichever miserable hole he'd chosen for himself, but all that mattered was that he believed it to be true and was motivated to hurry back there and move his entire operation, to evade discovery.

And when he made his move, she'd be right there waiting. It was the only way to find out where he'd hidden his surviving trophies—all that remained of the women he'd killed.

Her hand strayed to the necklace she wore beneath her shirt, and thought of her sister.

Soon afterwards, Melanie ducked down in her seat as his car crawled by the side street where she was stationed. She started the engine with fumbling hands, conscious that she mustn't lose him and her only chance to avenge her sister.

If she could remove him from the world, it was one less monster to worry about, and she'd have kept the promise she made to herself and her parents, all those years ago.

Perhaps, they might find it in their hearts to forgive her.

To love her, again.

Melanie kept a safe distance, leaving several cars between them so that he wouldn't spot her in his rearview mirror and become suspicious. He made for the A19 northbound, following the road along past Annitsford to the north of the city of Newcastle, then headed north-east towards the coast, and eventually on to the small town of Blyth, thirteen miles from Newcastle.

Blyth had a long history, with its port dating all the way back to the twelfth century, but it was the coal mining and ship building of the eighteenth and nineteenth centuries that really helped the town to flourish. However, when those industries began to decline, the people of the town declined with it, and some fell prey to the drugs trade that seemed able to smell vulnerability from a long way away. Despite this, the town had seen some major regeneration efforts and was, once again, on the up; indeed, a row of pretty, pastel-painted beach huts lined the dunes overlooking its long, windswept beach and it was here that Andrew Forbes had decided to settle himself, having only recently moved his possessions from the lock-up in Westerhope where, eventually, the stench of vermin had driven him to more salubrious surroundings in which to enjoy himself.

It had taken extensive planning to secure one of the beach huts, especially as they were in great demand and short supply. He'd been forced to use his connections in the town to bump his application up the waiting list, and his decision to use his real name and credentials was made with the strategic knowledge that the beach hut would, indeed, be used by his family and friends.

It was the bunker he had dug out beneath its floorboards, deep into the heart of the dunes, that required a special key to enter.

It had taken months to excavate, ever since the unfortunate incident at the grain store. He hadn't planned to use his family's beach hut as the new setting for his hobby room, but, necessity compelled him and, after all, it was the perfect way to hide in plain sight.

Nobody would ever think to look there and, as for anybody hoping to escape, they'd be buried ten feet beneath the ground in a metal-sheeted room of his own design, without windows and with ventilation provided only by an oxygen tank he replenished from time to time.

Everything was meticulously planned.

There would be no more mistakes.

"There's still no answer."

Lowerson was almost beside himself with worry, by now, and Ryan took his shoulders in a firm grip, to steady his nerves.

"Keep it together, Jack," he said. "We'll find her."

"How?"

"Digital Forensics are already running a trace on Melanie's phone," he replied. "She's one of us, so they'll work flat out until they have her last transmitted location."

"That could still take hours," Jack said. "I can't wait around here for the phone to ring."

Ryan said nothing for a moment, and then picked up his own phone to place a call to the Chief Constable.

They needed a full-scale effort, and they needed it now. He wanted every bobby on the beat to be looking for her; he wanted every ANPR camera in the city precincts to be checked against her car registration plate, as well as that of DCS Andrew Forbes, and he wanted it done immediately.

Morrison answered after several rings.

"Ryan," she said, irritably. "I'm in the bath."

"I don't care," he snapped, taking her breath away with his outright insolence.

"I've a good mind to—"

"Save it for tomorrow, ma'am," he said. "We have an emergency."

He outlined the problem, told her what needed to happen and asked for her approval.

Then, he waited while she processed the shock.

"You're absolutely sure it's him?" she asked, eventually.

"Honestly? No, ma'am, I'm not, but I'm as sure as I can be in all the circumstances. If I'm wrong, I'll issue our new DCS a very public, very grovelling apology. But, if I'm not, and he's hurt a single hair on Melanie's head, I'll kick his arse from here to kingdom come."

"You're getting more northern by the day," she remarked, while she thought of the best course of action and tried to manage her own overriding fear that Melanie was now lost to them.

"You have my authority to act," she said simply. "Whatever you need, get it done."

"Thank you, ma'am. I'll do my best."

"You know what this means, don't you?" she said.

He waited.

"It means that's the third DCS who's turned out to be a raving psychopath," she grumbled. "I swear, the position is cursed."

"We'll worry about it, later," he promised. "For now, just keep the line clear."

Once he'd rung off, Morrison gave up on any dream she'd had of a soothing, oil-scented bath and pulled the plug, thinking it was perhaps time she pulled the plug on trying to fill the position of Detective Chief Superintendent altogether.

CHAPTER 43

Melanie held back as she watched Forbes enter the beach car park, which was completely empty at that time of night, and deliberately drove further along the coast road to park on the kerb so that she wouldn't be seen. From her vantage point, she watched him sling what appeared to be an empty sports bag over his shoulder, and then make his way towards the beach huts on the dunes overlooking the beach.

She looked down at the firearm and reached for it, feeling the weight of it in her hand before checking the safety catch was on, and tucking it inside her jacket. Then, with a careful glance in either direction, she exited the car and jogged across the road to the car park and, from there, followed his footsteps towards the beach huts.

Melanie moved swiftly, the weight of the firearm pressing against her chest while the night air whistled all around, howling between the wooden frames so they creaked and moaned like souls in torment, obliterating all else—including the sound of anybody's approach.

As she reached the end of the row, she slowed, moving softly now against the wooden decking at her feet. Her heart raced, her hands shook, but she reminded herself of why she was there and for whom.

For Gemma.

Quickly, she snuck a glance around the edge of the hut, and spotted his shadowed figure illuminated beneath the greenish-white light of a lamp. He was further along the row, perhaps seven or eight huts along, and he was in the process of unlocking its door.

She whipped her head back again, out of sight.

Now, she knew where he went.

What happened next would be up to her.

Morrison had barely managed to dry herself off, when her phone rang again.

"Ryan—?"

"Sorry to bother you at home, ma'am," her PA began.

"Sorry, Debra," Morrison said. "I was expecting someone else."

"I've just received a communication from DCS Forbes's wife," Debra said. "Something alarming has happened at home, and she wondered if we'd be good enough to check it out, for her?"

Morrison was surprised. "What's happened?" she asked, and found herself wondering what would become of Jenna Forbes, when all was said and done.

"It's a bit of an odd one," Debra began. "Apparently, one of their children was using a tablet device at home this evening, and an alert popped up to say that their position had been tagged by an AirTag device—"

"A what?"

"It's a device that's supposed to help people find their phones, keys and things," Debra explained. "We have one at home, actually, and it's quite handy…anyway, it works off Bluetooth technology, so you pair the AirTag—which looks like a little round-headed key—with whichever device you don't want to lose, and you can track its location at any time using a different device. It's all part of Apple, so if you're logged into your ID, you get the alerts on all your devices."

"I see," Morrison said slowly. "So, what was so alarming about that?"

"Well, you receive alerts when there's suspicious behaviour, too," Debra said. "It's a feature to prevent stalking, and things like that."

Morrison joined the dots quickly.

"So, you're saying there was an alert on the tablet in the Forbes family home, but that alert related to DCS Forbes's car or some other device having been tagged? I'm presuming it caused alarm because they don't own an AirTag, themselves?"

"Exactly, ma'am," Debra said. "Mrs Forbes is worried somebody undesirable has fitted an AirTag tracker device to her husband's car, and intends to do him harm. She's been unable to contact him, you see."

Morrison wisely chose neither to confirm nor deny the last part.

"Tell Mrs Forbes we'll look into it," Morrison said, and put an immediate call through to Ryan.

Lowerson recognised the device immediately, and hurried through to the living room, where he'd last seen her laptop.

"Mel uses an AirTag for her computer, normally," he explained. "If she's used the AirTag to track Forbes's location, then we can log onto her computer and find out where she is—that's assuming she's with him."

He told himself not to think about what could be happening, right then, and to focus on what was within his power.

He snatched up the computer and tried the last-known password, which was declined.

"She's changed her password," he said, running a shaking hand over his face. "I've tried all the ones I know about."

"Is that her work computer?" Ryan asked. Police-issued devices came with 'master' codes, which allowed managerial staff to access their contents in emergency scenarios, such as this.

"Hand it over."

He tapped a few keys to unlock it, then handed it back to Lowerson, who went to work finding the information they needed.

Hurry, Ryan thought. Hurry.

"Here," Lowerson said. "Last known location is Blyth beach."

He rattled off the coordinates, which they could enter into a GPS navigation device to find the exact spot, when they were on the road.

"Let's go," Lowerson said, already grabbing his coat. "There isn't a minute to lose."

There certainly wasn't, Ryan thought, because there was something else to consider.

If Melanie's AirTag had paired itself with Forbes' Apple ID devices, in her effort to track his car, and his family had received the alert on their tablet at home, he was sure to have received an alert on his own mobile device.

Andrew Forbes let himself into the beach hut, taking his time to open the locks in order to give Melanie a chance to follow him to the correct hut.

He liked to give them a sporting chance.

As he stepped inside the wooden interior, with its nautical-themed benches and towels, his phone jingled to let him know he had a notification.

He tugged the phone from his pocket and read the message from Apple to say that his device had been tagged by an AirTag.

Clever girl, he thought.

It really added to the spice and thrill of it all, to know that she was a worthy conquest. He'd known it, all those years ago, in the gym hall. He'd known it just by looking into her eyes, and reading the rebellion there, the intelligence.

It made the end all the sweeter.

He slipped the phone back into his pocket and wished he could peek outside again, to watch her approach, but that would spoil her fun. She believed she had him, and it was uncharitable to take away her victory too soon.

Reality would come crashing down, soon enough.

Ryan called for full reinforcements, with instructions to approach the location from all sides.

His only concern was that they'd be too late.

Meanwhile, he and Lowerson made their way to Blyth at full speed, blues and twos flashing, using every means available to cover the ground in half the time it would have taken an ordinary driver to go from one side of the river to the other, and from there, on to Blyth.

Luckily for them, Ryan drove as though the hounds of hell were yapping at his wheels.

He wound through the city streets and steamed along the A19, with traffic parting like the Red Sea to make way for the unmarked car. Civilians probably passed comment about power having gone to their heads, but, on this occasion, Ryan didn't care to defend it.

Lowerson spoke barely a word throughout the journey, except to act as navigator, which he performed in a calm, exemplary manner.

"She's all right, Jack," Ryan said, as they flew past a white van. "I feel it."

Lowerson might have sneered at 'feelings' in the face of the terrifying prospect that lay before him, but he didn't.

"Thank you," he said instead. "I hope you're right."

He had to be right.

CHAPTER 44

Melanie kept to the back of the huts, creeping forward with extreme caution until she drew near to the one belonging to Andrew Forbes. It was pastel blue, and, in other circumstances, she might have said it was charming but, for the task she had in mind, any place would have done.

She reached inside her jacket and grasped the firearm, which was something she tried never to deploy. Though she worked in law enforcement, Melanie preferred always to use negotiation skills, diplomacy or other talking strategies in the first instance, moving to proportionate force only when it was necessary. As for weaponry such as the one she held in her hand, all of Ryan's inner circle were qualified as specialist firearms officers, but that didn't mean they liked using them.

She'd hoped to remain that way, but life threw up its little moral dilemmas, such as the one she now faced.

Beyond the wooden walls of the hut, there was a spider; one who chose human women for its prey, feasting upon them, drawing out the eventual kill so that the process would sustain them for months, sometimes years at a time.

This monster, this spider they called 'Shadow Man', did just that: he kept himself hidden, managing his ego better than many of his cohort, so that he could remain operative for much longer, never giving in to the weakness of peacocking in the press, or drawing attention to himself in any other way. His strength was in his anonymity; his ability to be an 'everyman' who blended in with the world around him to such a degree that people didn't see the danger until it was far too late.

Melanie looked down at the firearm again, and hesitated.

From this moment on, she would be a different woman to the one she'd been yesterday, and the day before that. If she entered the web and killed the spider, it was only a hollow victory, and she knew it. She'd need to stage things as a killing in self-defence, and that part, she could do. It was the killing itself that gave her most cause for concern.

A spider was still a sentient creature.

She held back while a battle waged in her mind between all the ideals she'd held dear regarding 'right' actions and all those she'd ever considered 'wrong'.

It was funny how the line blurred, depending on the circumstances.

She reached up to clasp her sister's necklace, hoping to draw strength from it, in her moment of greatest need for, as she huddled against the beach hut in the darkness, Melanie no longer recognised the woman she'd become. She didn't know the woman who'd planned and plotted to take a life; who'd lied to all those she loved and who'd put revenge above all else.

She didn't know her at all.

Melanie began to cry, and the tears rolled down her cheeks unchecked.

"Ten more minutes," Lowerson said.

Ryan glanced across at his friend, whose face was a mask of utter desolation.

"It isn't over," he reminded him. "This isn't over, yet."

Jack nodded dumbly, and stared out at the landscape which passed him by in a blur.

"I wanted to marry her," he said softly.

"You still can," Ryan shot back.

"You don't understand," Jack said, with a little shake of his head. "Even if she's alive and well, something has changed, now. She isn't the person I thought she was."

"Because she has it in her to be violent?" Ryan wondered.

"No." Jack gave a sad smile. "Because she lied to me, again and again, without so much as blinking. I can't trust her."

"Don't do anything rash," Ryan warned him. "This is not the moment to be taking decisions that affect your life, and your future, believe me. Concentrate on getting her back, whole, and work on re-building trust, later."

"Can it be re-built?"

It was true that, in their relationship, he and Anna hadn't been tested in that way, thank God, but that didn't mean he couldn't see and hear the tales of those all around him.

"Of course it can, if you really want to," he said. "You love her, don't you?"

Jack nodded. "Of course I do."

"Then cut her some slack," he advised. "Besides, you'd be an absolute nightmare to live with, if the tables were reversed."

Jack wanted to argue, but it was only the truth. "Five minutes," he said quietly, as they entered the outer limits of the town of Blyth.

Melanie hesitated for so long, she almost missed her chance.

Behind her, the door to the hut opened again, and Forbes stepped outside. She jumped to her feet, her footsteps soft against the sand and protected by the wind, which continued to wail like a banshee. She watched him walk along the promenade towards his car and, this time, his sports bag appeared to be full.

She watched him through the narrow gaps in the beach huts, shadowing him from ten paces behind, shielded by the underside of the huts which provided natural cover.

When he stepped out into the open again and crossed the short stretch of sandy grass leading to the car park, she knew she had her shot. There'd never be another one like it, never another possibility to shoot him like a fish in a barrel.

But, she didn't raise the firearm.

It remained by her side, hanging limply from her fingers while she watched him leave.

This time, she cried for herself, and for all she had almost thrown away.

Ryan had done his best to teach his staff the lessons he'd learned from his own mistakes, and one of those lessons was never to turn your back on a monster, a spider, or whatever you wished to call the people who looked like human beings but lacked the fundamental personality traits that constituted 'humanity'—such as empathy, compassion and an ability to love and be loved in return.

These were things that Andrew Forbes knew nothing about, and would never know.

They were things that Melanie Yates knew a great deal about, and could go on sharing with all the friends she had and those she had yet to make; with her chosen partner in life and with her family, if they would only let her.

But she forgot Ryan's lesson, out there on the beach.

She turned her back on the spider.

It was for a good reason, which was her fear he may be holding a woman captive, one she was duty-bound to try to rescue, but it was a risky strategy whichever way you looked at it.

Melanie watched Forbes walk all the way to his car before she turned and crept towards the entrance to the beach hut, which was padlocked. She still had her little set of tools and she hurried to open the padlock, pausing to draw on a pair of nitrile gloves before she stepped inside.

What she found inside was very ordinary, much like his house. This was no dungeon, filled with macabre devices of torture, nor were there any signs that anybody had been hurt.

She experienced a wave of frustration and anger.

This had to be the place.

Perhaps he'd already taken everything suspicious and loaded it into his sports bag. That would explain the spartan feel to the place.

On the other hand…

Melanie spotted a polyester rug beneath her feet, one designed for use indoors and outdoors, and when she crossed the room, there was a change in the sound her footsteps made against the wooden floorboards

The ground beneath the rug was hollow.

With a glance back towards the main door, she tucked the firearm into the back of her jeans and then sank to her knees. She pulled a corner of the rug back to reveal bare floorboards, then ran her fingertips along the edges until she found one that moved. When she did, she realised it lifted a whole section of floorboards and, beneath the floorboards, there was a trap door.

She lifted it up, hesitant at first, frightened of what she might find, and all the while moving closer and closer to the centre of Andrew Forbes' web.

The problem with a spider's web was that, once caught, you seldom broke free.

CHAPTER 45

Forbes waited until he could be sure that she'd gone inside, and then doubled back around, keeping to the shadows. The beach was deserted at that time, especially since the winds had picked up, heralding the coming of a storm. He heard the waves crashing somewhere out to sea, but they held no interest for him, now.

He only had eyes for one person, and his mind sought only one outcome.

His feet moved silently against the sandy floor until he reached the beach hut, whose door swung back and forth in the wind, creaking on its hinges.

She didn't hear him until he was almost upon her.

He watched her for a moment, enjoying himself, relishing the anticipation until the moment he would take what he wanted, and then take some more. He stood there, a dark shadow framed in the doorway while she grappled with the trap door, struggling to lift its heavy weight that was part-wood and part-metal.

"Let me give you a hand with that."

Melanie gave a strangled cry which became a breathless wheeze as he lunged at her from behind, grasping her arms so that she couldn't reach for her gun. She tried rearing back, using her head to butt against his jaw and buy herself some time, but he anticipated the move and dodged her efforts easily.

In fact, he laughed.

"I always said you'd be a fighter, didn't I?"

"Go to hell," she snarled, and came back harder, kicking out with her feet, thrusting back against him so they crashed to the floor. All the while, his arms remained like steel bands around her chest and the zip on her jacket tore during the struggle, along with a few buttons on her shirt beneath.

She hardly noticed, because every ounce of energy was given to survival.

He used his superior weight to pin her down, rolling back and forth to dodge her efforts to attack his groin area.

"I hoped you'd be like this," he purred, and she felt his breath against her ear, panting not with the exertion but with something else…something worse. "It was…you…I wanted that night."

He carried on talking to her, waiting for her to stop trying to escape, to go limp in his arms, as they all did, eventually.

"It was a simple case of mistaken identity," he said. "I think you should consider thanking your sister, for that. Without her to entice me, your life might have been very different, don't you agree?"

Melanie screamed, wriggling like a cat, trying to bite him, claw him, but finding only air.

He was too practised.

"That's it," he growled. "Let it all out, so we can get to the fun part."

With that, he took a fistful of her hair, wrapped it tightly around his hand, and slammed her head against the wooden floor.

She came around, just as he was lowering her into the metal box he'd built beneath the ground, the last place she would ever see, if he had his wish.

As she was dragged across the wooden floor by her feet, her sister's necklace became undone and loosened from her neck. Through the haze of concussion, Melanie grasped it with her fingers, clinging to the silver thread while she ordered her body to respond to her mind, which was screaming for it to wake up and fight.

But, her legs were already bound, and her hands would soon be pinned by her sides, on the bed he'd made especially for her.

She cried out, a long, keening sound as the trap door slammed shut overhead.

She thought of Jack, and of how she'd never told him, one last time, just how much she loved him.

Then, she thought of her mother, and of how she would have lost both of her daughters to the same man, whose greed and sickness overcame all else.

"Where?" Lowerson shouted. "*Where?*"

"The huts!" Ryan shouted, pointing towards the row of beach huts lining the shore.

They'd spotted Melanie's car parked further along the road, and then Forbes's vehicle in the car park nearest the huts.

They must be close.

Both men sprinted through the darkness, legs pumping hard as they covered the ground at speed.

"Which one?" Lowerson cried out, and didn't think but began shaking the door of each one, working his way down the line.

Ryan ran ahead, eyes checking every doorway until he came to one without a padlock.

"Jack!"

Lowerson turned and pelted towards him, and together they booted down the door, which was held only by an internal latch.

Inside, they found nothing but a plain space, furnished simply with a table and four chairs, some beach towels and rugs, a couple of folded deckchairs.

"Let's try the next—"

Lowerson made as if to leave, but Ryan's hand stopped him.

His friend pointed to the floor, where a rug had been rolled back and a framed print that had once hung from a tack on the wall now lay on the floor, its glass broken into shards.

Ryan raised a finger to his lips, and moved quietly to inspect the flooring more closely.

Lowerson braced himself, keeping his eye on the doorway behind them, until Ryan found what he was looking for.

"On three," Ryan murmured, taking a firm grip of the trap door.

One...

Two...

He must have dosed her with something, as he'd done with the other women.

That was Melanie's abiding thought as he manipulated her body out of the clothing she wore and dressed her up, as he'd wanted to do for so long. The blue dress fit her body more snugly than he remembered, now that she was a woman rather than a sixteen-year-old girl, but he found he didn't mind her added curves.

If anything, he preferred them.

He tied her legs to the bed and then found the CD he'd made, years ago, which held all the music that had been playing on The Boat that night. He slipped it into a battery-operated player—it was hard to come by retro items like that, these days, but it was amazing what you could find on eBay.

The thumping beat of Voodoo Child encircled them, and he smoothed his hair back with hands that shook.

"Can you believe, I actually feel a little nervous," he admitted, stalking around the bed he'd placed in the centre of his bunker, beneath a string of spotlights.

He liked to see his handiwork.

In the corner of the room, there was a camera set up on a tripod, and against one wall he'd fashioned a workspace with every tool his heart could ever desire. In the cupboards beneath, he kept more practical items, such as plastic sheeting and bleach.

Against another wall, there was a stockpile of acid.

"I've missed you," he breathed, and his face loomed above her, eyes almost black. "It'll be even better than the first time. I know it."

In her hands, Melanie clutched the sharp end of the pendant from her sister's necklace, the jagged edge of a silver leaf.

She moved her lips, as though she was trying to speak to him.

"What are you trying to tell me?" he wondered, and curiosity demanded he find out. "Hmm? What is it?"

He leaned closer, and she saw the bulge of the carotid artery pulsing in his neck.

"This…is…from…Gemma," she whispered.

He saw only the glint of silver as she thrust upward in a stabbing motion, scoring the skin so deeply it severed the artery. He cried out, a gurgling sound, and clutched a hand to the wound in a futile effort to stem the blood flow, which pumped out in a constant stream, pouring over his fingers in a river of red.

"What—what have you done?"

She would never forget the look of confusion he wore, for as long as she lived.

As his body drained of its lifeblood, he tried to remain upright but instead lurched forward, blood gushing as he fell, arms flailing to the plastic-coated floor. The room was built for heavy blood loss, but he had no idea it would be his own.

As his sight began to fade and the line between reality and unreality merged, he looked up to see Melanie one final time and fancied he saw another girl instead—a young girl of sixteen, with dark hair and kind eyes, who loved animals and had hoped to have a family of her own, one day.

Three!

Ryan put his back into it and pulled back the trapdoor with a grunt, muscles contracting with the effort, while Lowerson surged forward, practically diving into the bunker with a roar of anger and grief, terror lodged deeply in his chest at the thought of what he would find.

He found death, but not in the way he had imagined.

His feet skidded on the plastic, which was now covered in pints of wasted blood that had begun to coagulate in rivulets around a single bed in the centre of the space, upon which Melanie lay motionless.

He saw the blood, and his heart shattered.

"Mel! No!"

He rushed forward, while Ryan hurried to join him. "It isn't her," he said, taking in the scene. "Jack, it isn't her blood!"

Lowerson fought to see through the tears he shed openly, then noticed what Ryan had seen lying in a heap on the other side of the bed.

Forbes.

He pressed shaking fingers to Melanie's throat, searching for a heartbeat, and wept again when he found one, thin and thready, but there all the same.

"She's alive," he managed. "Ryan, please. Please help me get her out of this—"

His friend was already working silently to free her legs, scoring at the plastic cable ties with the edge of an army knife his father had once gifted him.

One leg worked free, leaving deep red grooves against her skin, followed by another.

"I'll lift her," Ryan said, and it made good sense given he was taller and, likely, stronger. "I'll hand her up to you, okay?"

Lowerson agreed, and was ready to take her when Ryan climbed the short metal ladder with Melanie balanced carefully over his shoulder.

"I've got her," he whispered, rocking her against him while Ryan headed out to meet the police teams who were descending upon the scene.

"I've got you, now, Mel. It's over."

EPILOGUE

Two memorial services were held for the sixty-four women the serial killer Andrew Forbes was suspected to have murdered; the first was held in the centre of Oxford, where the majority of his victims had been taken, and the streets flooded with students from many of the surrounding colleges, and from both universities in that town, all of whom wanted to show their support and respect for the women who had passed, whilst also showing their disdain for the man who had misused his position and his power to ensnare those whom he had been tasked to protect.

The second memorial was held at Bolam Lake, in Northumberland, at the site where Gemma Yates's family had chosen to bury their daughter's ashes in the ground at the foot of her favourite tree, so that she might be a part of it, forever. Hers was one of only a handful of bodies that were ever recovered, so the families of Forbes's assumed victims gathered in that place alongside her parents and imagined that their lost children also lay peacefully amongst the roots of a beautiful oak tree.

The Chief Constable spoke on behalf of her constabulary and was forced to stop, just once, to lean her hand against the bark of the tree and draw strength from the girl she would always feel she had failed, whilst meeting the eyes of another she was glad to still have with them, one she was very proud to call one of hers.

Melanie had been able to save herself, in more ways than one, and it had taken courage.

When it came time to leave, she walked alongside her parents in peaceful silence, their hearts a little lighter than before. It would take time to heal all that had gone before, but it was a new beginning, and the prospect of losing both of her children had crumbled the walls Caroline Yates had built for herself, over the years, sent them tumbling around her head as she'd run along the hospital corridors to be with her child—the child she had never stopped loving.

Ryan and the rest of his team followed behind the Yates family and Lowerson, in full dress uniform. Amongst the crowd that had gathered from all around the North East were Ryan's parents, who'd travelled from Devon to pay their respects, as well as Anna, who walked alongside his mother with their arms linked, in silent support.

It was a good day, filled with good people, and it made everything worthwhile.

AUTHOR'S NOTE

'Bamburgh' is really a tale of two stories: one, set in the village, which is truly as picturesque as I have described, with a castle so magical it calls to mind every make-believe game of knights and princesses ever played, and evokes every myth, legend, historical drama or ghostly tale you might imagine. I have loved the place since childhood, when I can remember sitting up tall in my booster seat, to catch the first glimpse of that wondrous castle appearing through my mother's windshield, much like Emma might have done in the backseat of Anna's car.

With such love of a place comes a great sense of responsibility. In my book, I have barely scratched the surface of what could be written about Bamburgh; in fact, it was hard to focus on just one, workable storyline, when so many ideas present themselves! I think it's important for me to say that, obviously, there are no nefarious archaeologist characters roaming around (that I know of). There is, however, a fantastic archaeological project ongoing since the 1960s and you can read all about it, if you'd like to learn more. The 'Sandy Dunes Guest House' was, in fact, inspired by a grand old house on the outskirts of the village which had fallen into some disrepair but was otherwise as I have described: characterful, Georgian, trailing with foliage and brimming with trees—the perfect spot for a bit of murder…

The slightly 'cosier' killings in Bamburgh (if one can call killing 'cosy'!) were intended to offset the darker elements to Melanie Yates' storyline, and the natural empathy you, the reader, may feel for her sister and her family. I always feel it's important for a story to hold a bit of lightness and darkness, so that we can enjoy a range of emotions when reading, without coming away feeling too downcast.

I hope some of you may have the opportunity to visit the real-life Bamburgh Castle, some day, and walk along its astonishing sandy beach but, if that isn't possible, I hope you can imagine what it is like from some of my descriptions.

My grateful thanks go out to everyone who has contributed to the writing of this book, and chiefly to my friends and family for their ongoing love and support. Finally, enormous thanks go to you, Dear Reader, for your kindness in helping to make 'Bamburgh' my twenty-second UK #1 bestseller. I can hardly believe it.

Until the next time…

LJ ROSS
MARCH 2022

DCI Ryan will return in

LADY'S WELL

A DCI RYAN MYSTERY

Turn the page for an exclusive sneak peek . . .

LADY'S WELL – PROLOGUE

Holystone village, Northumberland

Twenty years ago

The woman lay on a bed of autumn leaves, her spine shattered beyond repair.

"This was your fault."

She heard their voice as if through water; dim and distorted, the words garbled. They continued to talk, muttering as they paced around her body, and the physical pain began to recede. Her conscious mind went with it, floating from her body to enter that 'Otherworld' she'd heard people speak of.

Was this it? she wondered. *Was this death?*

"Look at me while I'm talking to you."

The blow to her head had caused an enormous clot to form at the base of her skull, so she couldn't have moved nor controlled the direction of her gaze, even if she'd wanted to. All she could do was emit a long, guttural moan.

"You never had any respect for me. Well, look where you are now! Nothing but dirt at my feet."

She thought she saw stars through the branches overhead. When another brutal kick was administered to her ribcage, she felt nothing at all.

"You've always been *selfish*, and *self-centred*."

More kicks, more harsh panting from the exertion.

"Nobody will miss you. D'you know that? *Nobody*."

Through the fog, a vision of her son materialised, though she knew it couldn't be real—merely a trick of the mind. She smiled at the image of the boy he'd once been, with eyes the same as her own. Tears began to fall down her cheeks as she lay in the fold of the earth, where once she'd played as a child and walked with her love, hand in hand. Her fingertips brushed the soil and, as the last vestiges of life drained from her body, she thought of Nick again, kicking up the leaves in his blue wellie boots many years before.

I love you, Mummy.

I love you, too, sweetheart.

It was only ten minutes later, once the mindless, visceral anger was spent, that they realised she was dead.

CHAPTER 1

Lady's Well, near Holystone village

Hallowe'en—twenty years later

Day moved swiftly towards night, and the leaves that once burned golden brown began to wither. No longer a warm canopy, but a menacing cloak in the gathering darkness, at the centre of which was an ancient pool. Its waters were perfectly still as the shadows crept closer, long fingers reaching towards the people gathered beside it.

"Blessed Samhain to all," Sabrina said, as she moved around her small congregation. "We are the sum of all that has come before us. The fires of our ancestors burn brightly within us."

Blessed be, came the chorus.

She held a torch aloft and walked around the circumference of a circle, lighting four smaller torches staked into the ground and positioned at the cardinal points for north, south, east and west, each one separated by a scattering of pine branches and flowers.

"We will carry the memories of loved ones who've passed from this world into the Otherworld through the long months of darkness. For, in the darkness, the world will replenish," she murmured. "Be not afraid of death, for it heralds new life."

All the same, she lit several pumpkins, their shells carved into ghoulish effigies to ward off unwelcome spirits of the dead, who could more easily cross back into the world of the living on that special night of the year.

Sabrina blessed the circle just as the last rays of sunlight burnished her head with a bright halo of light, then reached for a bowl filled with water from the well. She held it in one hand, drawing out a small ornamental dagger with the other, the tip of which she touched to the surface of the water.

"I consecrate and cleanse this water that it may be purified and fit to dwell within the sacred circle," she said. "In the name of the Mother Goddess and the Father God, I consecrate this water."

She touched the dagger tip to some salt she'd brought in a Tupperware dish.

"I bless this salt that it may be fit to dwell within the sacred circle," she said. "In the name of the Mother Goddess and the Father God, I consecrate this salt."

She turned to face north, then walked around the circle once again, visualising her energy stretching across it like a forcefield.

"Here is the boundary of the circle," she declared. "Naught but love shall enter in. Naught but love shall emerge from within. Charge this by your powers, Old Ones!"

By the time the circle was sealed, and the brave were seated comfortably within its hallowed ground, the temperature in the clearing had dropped and the sun was little more than a thin, fiery line just visible through the surrounding trees.

"For centuries, these waters have healed the sick," she began again. "The spring was named 'Lady's Well' after the Virgin Mary, from the Christian faith, but we of the Old Ways know that the powerful source of this water was gifted by the Mother Goddess herself, to quench the thirst of every living thing in these parts and heal that which may need healing. For the Mother sees everything through the water—including all that we *cannot* see."

She gestured for a young woman from the village to step forward. "Helen, of Holystone village," she said. "What do you seek, on this Samhain night?"

A woman of around thirty moved forward and tried to find her voice. "I seek to heal my heart," she managed. "My husband has left me for another woman and now she's pregnant. I was never…never able to have a baby. I am broken in heart and in mind."

The older woman felt a small stab of pity. The secular part of herself was already aware of what had happened—it was the talk of the village that young Grant Newman had been carrying on with some fancy woman from the city and had upped and left his wife of two years to start again. He'd found Helen's country ways too parochial for his newfound tastes and had shattered her modest dreams of a home and family.

"That is indeed hard to bear," she said, and took the woman's hand. "But you have *much* living yet to do, and whatever has happened is for the best. It is the wish of the Mother and the Father—"

Helen began shaking her head from side to side, unwilling and unable to stomach any more well-intentioned advice. "I can't *sleep*," she said, and set down a bag of coins as an offering on the alter with a heavy hand. "I can't *eat*. All I think about is the two of them together, while I'm sure they don't think of *me* at all." Her lip wobbled, and she tried to stem the flow of bitter tears. "I can't live this way," she said, half to herself. "I don't want him to be happy with *her*. I want him to remember he was happy with *me*. I want him to *suffer*. I beg the Mother and Father to help me."

Frowning, Sabrina held her hand a little tighter. "That is the path of darkness," she cautioned. "And it is not the path we follow."

Something inside her shivered.

"We must not look outwardly, but inwardly," she said. "We must look to ourselves, Helen. Do not sully your mind with thoughts of revenge; cast out his betrayal and make space for better things."

She held up the bowl of water.

"Look into the water and see yourself through the Mother's eyes," she murmured. "You are perfect, just as you are, for you are built by Her creation and form part of the wondrous blessings that surround us. Let the lightness of your soul shine through the darkness and be whole again. Blessed be, Helen."

Blessed be, the chorus of voices said.

She dipped her hand into the water and blessed the woman, murmuring words of healing. Then, she rose to her feet and turned north, drawing herself in, feeling the cosmic energy course through her body once more.

"On this night, when we bid farewell to the light and welcome in the darkness until Yuletide, the veil between this world and the next is at its thinnest."

She paused, allowing her words to echo on the quiet air, accompanied only by the soft crackle of burning wood and the distant call of a night bird.

"All around us, the spirits walk," she said, with a smile. "In this world and in the Otherworld, there are forces of Good and Evil."

A sudden gust of wind charged the air, whipping up the leaves from the ground as if to punctuate her words. The torchlight flickered, and those within the circle looked all around, unnerved and curious in equal part.

"Let us look into the mirror, through the eye of the Goddess, and see what she can tell us."

Sabrina believed she'd been blessed with Second Sight and stepped outside the protective circle to walk to the very edge of the well, where she knelt and watched her own flickering reflection against the inky black water.

"I see love," she called out to Helen. "There is *love* in your future, a far greater and more powerful love than before."

Helen wanted to believe it.

She wanted to believe it so badly.

"What else?" she dared ask. "What's his name?"

"That will never be known, unless your heart is healed and open to finding and discovering the new love the Mother will create," came the reply. "Remember, from decay comes renewal and rebirth. Old wounds and hurts must be healed."

Helen found herself nodding. "Can you—can you see my grandmother? What does she say?"

"Edith is with you always, not just on this night," the woman replied, and raised her hands high. "Let us see if her spirit will join us."

She cast her hands aloft, then sank them into the cold water of the well. "Edith! We are—"

Her voice trailed off as she withdrew her hands from the water. She studied them, not quite understanding what she was seeing.

"We—we—" she began again, before the words caught in her throat.

The water was red.

Blood red.

She turned back to the circle. "The water is red!" she cried and held her hands out for them to see the stain against her skin. "There are dark forces at play—go home to your families and make sure they're safe!"

Galvanised, the small gathering scattered through the clearing until only she remained.

Then, she turned and reached inside the skirts of her long dress to retrieve a pouch filled with pound coins, which she threw into the well, one by one.

"Blessed Samhain," she said.

Available to buy now!

LOVE READING?

JOIN THE CLUB...

Join the LJ Ross Book Club to connect with a thriving community of fellow book lovers! To receive a free monthly newsletter with exclusive author interviews and giveaways, sign up at www.ljrossauthor.com or follow the LJ Ross Book Club on social media:

　　　　@LJRossAuthor
　　　　@ljross_author

ABOUT THE AUTHOR

LJ Ross is an international bestselling author known for her atmospheric mystery and thriller novels, including the DCI Ryan series which has sold over 12 million copies worldwide. Her debut novel *Holy Island* published in 2015 and reached number one in the Amazon UK and Australian digital charts. Louise has since released over thirty novels, most of which have been UK number one digital bestsellers. She is also the creator of the bestselling Dr Alexander Gregory series and the Summer Suspense series. Louise is a keen philanthropist and proud to support numerous non-profit programmes in addition to founding the Lindisfarne Prize for Crime Fiction, the Northern Photography Prize and the Northern Film Prize.

Born in Northumberland, England, she studied Law at King's College, University of London, then abroad in Florence and Paris, and worked as a lawyer before pursuing her dream to write. She lives with her family in Northumberland.

If you would like to get in touch with LJ Ross on social media, please scan the QR code below – she would love to hear from you!

Discover the international bestselling DCI Ryan series from LJ Ross

Atmospheric mysteries set amidst the spectacular landscape of the north east of England.

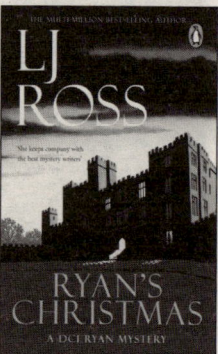

Discover the 24th novel in the DCI Ryan series...

New for 2026

If you enjoyed this book, why not try the bestselling Alexander Gregory Thrillers by LJ Ross?

Atmospheric thrillers featuring forensic psychiatrist and criminal profiler Dr Alexander Gregory. Loved by readers for the fast-moving and page-turning plots, international locations and shocking twists, with psychology adding fascinating depth to the stories.

Discover now the bestselling Summer Suspense series from LJ Ross

Suspense and mystery are peppered with romance and humour in these fast-paced thrillers set amidst the beautiful landscapes of Cornwall.